the beginning  of after

the beginning of after

JENNIFER CASTLE

HARPER TEEN
An Imprint of HarperCollinsPublishers

HarperTeen is an imprint of HarperCollins Publishers.

The Beginning of After
Copyright © 2011 by Jennifer Castle
All rights reserved. Printed in the United States of America.
No part of this book may be used or reproduced in any manner
whatsoever without written permission except in the case of
brief quotations embodied in critical articles and reviews.
For information address HarperCollins Children's Books,
a division of HarperCollins Publishers, 10 East 53rd Street,
New York, NY 10022.
www.epicreads.com

Library of Congress Cataloging-in-Publication Data is available.
ISBN 978-0-06-198579-9

Typography by Erin Fitzsimmons
11 12 13 14 15   CG/RRDB   10 9 8 7 6 5 4 3 2 1
❖
First Edition

For Sadie and Clea

ONE

nyone who's had something truly crappy happen to them will tell you: It's all about Before and After. What I'm talking about here is the ka-*pow*, shake-you-to-your-core-and-turn-your-bones-to-plastic kind of crappy. One part of your life unyokes from the other.

I use this word, *unyoke*, because I spent my last few hours of Before studying the *U*s on an SAT vocabulary list. It was April of my junior year in high school. I was sixteen, and I had the test date, less than two weeks away, marked with three purple exclamation points on my wall calendar.

Unyoke: to separate. Mr. Lee from my SAT prep course taught us to create a mental image that would help us remember what a word meant. I pictured myself making cake frosting in our chipped blue china bowl, pulling the snot of an egg away from its yolk. I moved on to *upbraid*.

My mom yelled down the hallway from her bedroom. "Laurel, tell your brother to get dressed! We have to leave in twenty minutes!"

Otherwise known as twenty minutes until my Chinese water torture. I would have been happy hanging with the *U*s all night, but instead I just drew an arrow next to *upbraid* to mark where I'd left off, and headed toward the sweet, slightly indecent smell of my mother's pot roast to do what I was told.

Thanks to all my Mr. Lee–inspired visualizing, I remember my family that night, as they got ready to leave our house and never come back, in moving snapshots. My mother fluttering between her laptop and closet, answering emails while trying on her blue dress, then her green dress, then the blue one again. My dad trudging up the driveway, fresh from the neighborhood carpool out of Manhattan, sliding his tie free of his collar. My brother, Toby, playing Xbox in the den, sunk so low into his tricked-out gaming chair it was hard to remember that he actually had a spine and could walk erect.

"Mom says you have to put on your khaki pants and the brown shoes," I said to him from the doorway.

"You mean my geek clothes? Uh, no way." He didn't look up.

"It's Passover. She's making me wear a dress."

"I don't get why we have to do this."

"Mrs. Kaufman was worried we'd be lonely because Nana isn't coming down for seder this year." We were in the New York suburbs, just an hour north of the city, but Nana lived upstate. The Kaufmans were our neighbors three houses away.

"I was hoping we could just order pizza."

"Tell me about it," I said.

"What, you don't want to hang with your best buddy over there?" Toby actually lifted his eyes from the TV to toss me a little-brother sneer.

"Shut up," I said lamely, heat surging to a spot on the back of my neck.

"Guys!" my dad said, suddenly in the room. "None of that tonight, okay? Especially you, Mr. Attitude." He playfully poked Toby's shoulder. "Be a grown-up. You did just get bar mitzvahed, after all."

"And he's got thirteen hundred dollars in checks from the relatives to prove it," I said. At that, my father smiled at me, one of those dad-smiles that make you feel like the only daughter in the world.

Soon we were all changed and heading out the door, my parents each carrying a foil-covered dish. Toby tugged quickly at the crotch of his good pants, thinking nobody saw.

Mrs. Kaufman was tiny. So tiny, people were always asking her if she was okay. Dad said he worried about her on windy days. The sharp jut of her collarbone made me wonder if it would hurt to touch it.

Now she sat at the head of her big oak dining table, drumming two manicured fingers on her good china. My parents and Toby and I shifted in our chairs, while Mr. Kaufman stood in the corner of the room with a glass of scotch, saying "You betcha, you betcha" again and again to someone on the other end of his cell phone.

"I'm sorry," Mrs. Kaufman said to us. "David said he'd be right down."

We waited another few minutes. I was nervous and hated it, trying to ignore Toby kicking my ankle under the table. Finally, Mr. Kaufman hung up the phone, stomped to the stairway, and pounded his fist on the banister. "David!" he bellowed in a voice that shook the Kaufmans' crystal water glasses.

A pause. I heard footsteps, a door closing, stairs thumping. The sound of David Kaufman joining us for seder.

Then there he was, all stoopy and scruffy-looking in the doorway. His wavy black hair hung in uneven chops around his face—it was the kind of haircut he could have either done himself or gotten at a pricey salon, you could never tell. Everything about David was so familiar to me but so unsettling, like spotting someone in person after

4

you've seen his picture a million times.

When he got to the table, he swept a chunk of that hair behind one ear and glanced at me, at Toby, then at my parents, with big, bright eyes that never matched the rest of him. Especially now. He seemed confused, like he'd forgotten why our family was here, in his house, interrupting his nightly listening-to-my-iPod-and-surfing-online-porn session.

"Hey," he said, looking not at me but at a point two feet to my left.

"Hi," I said, and this time, when Toby kicked me, I kicked back hard.

David was a year older than me and once, so long ago it could have been a dream, we were little-kid friends. Now he was a member of what everyone in our town called the Railroad Crowd, which meant he spent most of his time hanging out in the train station parking lot, smoking and drinking and carving words into the wooden benches that were supposed to be for normal people to sit on. We hadn't spoken to each other in years except for the rare, painfully unavoidable "hi" at neighborhood parties or when we passed each other at school. But I knew what I was to him: a girl whose name was always in our local paper's High Honors listings, the one member of the drama club who never actually appeared onstage. Despite our past as children playing together, despite our families' friendship, David and I were in different orbits.

I survived dinner by forgetting he was there, which was surprisingly easy to do because he just ate quietly, staring blankly at his bitter herb. When it was his turn to read, David shook his head no and passed the Haggadah to my brother. If he looked at me at all, it was when I was glancing the other way.

After dinner, I was helping my mother do dishes as Mrs. Kaufman put away the leftovers, and I saw a window of escape.

"Hey, Mom?" I asked. "After we're done, can I skip dessert and just go home? I was working on my SAT words and haven't even gotten to my homework yet."

She just paused. "I think Mrs. Kaufman has spent a lot of time making a flourless apple tart."

"Me?" squeaked Mrs. Kaufman, surprised. "Deborah, I thought you were making it!"

They looked at each other for a very tense moment, and I actually thought some kind of fistfight might break out. But then they were laughing.

Mrs. Kaufman led us back into the dining room, clearing her throat to interrupt the men, who were deep in discussion about money-market funds. Toby was standing by the window, fogging it with his breath and drawing shapes. David stood nearby and watched him with a slight, begrudging amusement.

"Hey, guys?" said Mrs. Kaufman. "We had a little

dessert mix-up and, well, there isn't any. I do think we have some Easter chocolate from Gabe's office, but that doesn't seem right."

Mr. Kaufman stood up. "I'd say that's a perfect excuse to go get ice cream. How about it?"

"Freezy's?" Toby asked, his finger paused in the middle of making a big *O* on the window.

"Heck, yeah," said Mr. Kaufman. "We've done our job here. Let's go out and have some milk shakes."

I tugged at the back of Mom's dress, and she took the cue. "Oh, Laurel's going to head home. She's got some homework to finish up."

"We'll bring you something back," said my dad, winking.

Now David, who was still by the window, sprang to life.

"I can't go either. I have to go down to Kevin's. . . ." He was thinking quickly. "He promised to help me with calculus."

Mrs. Kaufman looked at her son, and I got the sense that she had never even heard him say the word *calculus* before.

"Fine," she said defeatedly. "But I want you back here as soon as we come home. I'll call if I have to."

"Yeah, yeah, whatever," David was saying, already on his way to the hall closet.

"It's drizzling. Take an umbrella," said Mrs. Kaufman.

He looked at her, rolled his eyes, and grabbed his

leather jacket. He waved at us, murmured something that passed for good-bye, and was out the door.

The dads were talking about transportation now. Mr. Kaufman had a new hybrid SUV and was anxious to show how roomy it was. I walked with everyone down to the garage, where the car sat all shiny and eager to please.

Mrs. Kaufman handed me an umbrella out of nowhere. "Here. I know you don't have far to go, but why get wet?" she said. Her look seemed to say, *I wish I had a daughter just like you, who preferred homework over that bad egg Kevin McNaughton.*

Toby climbed into the backseat of the car, humming something. My mom opened the other back door and leaned to kiss me on the cheek. "You have your key, right?"

I nodded, patting my purse. As the garage door opened and Mr. Kaufman started the engine, I walked toward the driveway and waved at my dad in the front passenger seat.

Then I opened the umbrella as they drove past me, so Mrs. Kaufman could see, but once they turned the corner, away from the house and down the hill, I closed it again. The rain was light and dainty, and I loved the feel of it on my skin as I headed toward home.

TWO

y cell phone rang an hour later, just as I was finishing my French homework at the kitchen table.

"Can you talk?" whispered my best friend, Megan Dill, who lived one street over.

"Yeah, I came back early and nobody's here. Sweet freedom."

"How was it?" she asked.

"Awkward but survivable. David barely talked to anyone during the whole dinner."

"He's such a freak."

I heard meowing and turned around to see our cats,

Elliot and Selina, sitting anxiously at the back door, waiting to go outside.

"I know," I said, getting up. "It's like, once he decided to be friends with the Railroads, they gave him an instruction manual. Rule one, be grumpy and brooding at all times."

I opened the door and the cats scrambled past my legs, apparently late for some appointment in the woods across the street. Elliot paused for a second to look back at me with half-closed "Don't wait up" eyes, and then they were gone.

"Rule two," continued Meg, "you may only smoke Marlboro Reds, wear high-top sneakers, and carry all combs in your right back pocket. They're such a joke. They want to be rebels, but they're obsessed with fitting in with each other just like anyone else."

"You're the one who had a crush him," I said, noticing a pot roast glob on the kitchen counter. I wiped it with my thumb and sucked the sauce off, knowing how completely gross that was.

"Like a hundred years ago, when he was still partially human." *He's alterna-hot,* Meg used to say. I preferred not to go there at all with David; I'd known him for too long, and it was weird to think some girls considered him good-looking.

"Speaking of guys, how is Will these days?" I asked, ready to change the subject.

"I think it's safe to say he's not going to ask me to the prom."

"Why not?"

10

"Apparently he started going out with Georgia Marinese last week."

"Oh, Meg, I'm sorry."

"Eh, it's kind of a relief that he doesn't like me anymore. I would have gone to the prom with him just to go, you know."

"You can do better."

"We'll both do better."

The prom was more than a month away but the frenzy was already building, and I wasn't sure I wanted any part of it. As juniors we were eligible to go, but there was nobody I liked enough. There had never been anybody I liked enough. Meg was the one who clicked with every boy she ever met, with her easy wit and striking black Irish beauty. I was the runner-up version of her; the quieter brunette with straight, thin hair that could only sometimes inspire a ponytail or braid.

As a pair, we were not popular but not outcasts. Not gorgeous but not ugly, not fat but not thin. I was best known for getting As, starting the Tutoring Club, and painting scenery for the drama productions. Meg was in the show choir, and while she never got the lead in plays and musicals, she usually nabbed a juicy supporting role. Mostly people just didn't think about us, which Mom always said was a good thing, but I never got why.

"If we don't do better," Meg added, "we won't go at all."

Good, I thought. *That would make my life easier.*

Suddenly, I heard something near the front of the house.

"Meg, hang on," I said. "I think someone's at the door."

We sat silent for a few seconds, and I could hear my breathing sync up with Meg's on the other end of the line.

There it was again, two short knocks. Insistent. But I wasn't supposed to answer the door if I was the only one home.

"I'm walking you into the living room," I said to Meg, shifting the phone to my other ear. "If it's an ax murderer, you'll be able to hear the whole thing."

There was a big window adjacent to our front door, and I slowly drew aside the curtain, just a few inches, to see who it was.

A police officer, holding his hat in his hands, looking down at his feet.

That was it. The end of Before, and the beginning of After.

Now I had a new mental image for *unyoke*.

There weren't many details about the accident for Lieutenant Roy Davis to explain to me. Things were said and things were asked, and suddenly I was sitting cross-legged on the living room floor, pushed down there by the weight of new information.

My mother, father, and someone they assumed was my brother had been pronounced dead on arrival at Phillips Memorial Hospital.

So had Mrs. Kaufman.

Mr. Kaufman was in the emergency room. Not dead on

12

arrival. More like pretty seriously messed up on arrival.

Somehow, the new SUV had gone off the road, tumbled into a steep ditch, and caught fire. They didn't know how, and they didn't know why.

These were simply facts with nowhere to go. Leaves fallen on the water, floating in clumps, too light to break the surface.

And now, things just stopped, hard. Like the air; I couldn't feel it moving around me anymore. Or my ability to swallow; I was sure that if I tried it, my throat would freeze up and get stuck like that forever. It was as if I was suddenly sealed up in a bubble where everything was completely and totally wrong, wrong, wrong and I had to get out.

How do I get out? Can I take one big step and be on the other side of it? Maybe if I say something, anything, the whole thing will just POP.

So I blurted the first thing that came to mind: "What should I do now?"

Lieutenant Davis started to answer but stopped himself, biting his lip. Then I realized the scale of my question.

"I mean, do I need to go to a morgue or someplace?" I said. "Do I need to sign something?"

His face softened into a real sadness. "We do need someone to identify the . . . them . . . but it doesn't have to be you. Is there a relative you'd like us to contact?"

Nana. I thought of her getting home from dinner at her friend Sylvia's house. Combing the hairspray out of her hair, wiping the Clinique off her lips. There was no way I was making that phone call.

I gave Lieutenant Davis my grandmother's number and handed him the phone.

An hour later, I lay on the white couch in the living room, the one we used only when guests came over, with my head in Meg's lap. Mrs. Dill, Meg's mom, sat on the floor holding one of my hands. Theirs was the second number I had given Lieutenant Davis. Mr. Dill and Megan's sister, Mary, were on their way north, a three-hour drive, to get my grandmother.

"Just close your eyes and breathe," said Mrs. Dill. "Just breathe."

All I could think was, *Mrs. Dill smells a little like cranberry bread.*

Suzie Sirico showed up shortly after midnight. I hadn't asked for her. I didn't even know who she was. Lieutenant Davis said she was a grief counselor who sometimes worked with the police department. I tilted my head in Meg's lap and looked at the woman sideways. She was short, with large features.

"Hi, Laurel," she said slowly. "I'm Suzie."

Mrs. Dill got up from the floor. "Can I get you some coffee?" she offered.

"That would be wonderful, thanks."

They passed each other right then, switching positions

14

like some careful team maneuver. Suzie squatted on the floor so we were at eye level.

"I know we've never met," said Suzie, pressing her lips together with seriousness, "but I'm hoping you'll let me help you with whatever you need right now."

"There is something you can help me with right now," I told her. "The cats are probably at the back door. Can you let them in?"

Suzie Sirico cocked her head to one side and raised an eyebrow. Probably making a note on a mental pad. I didn't care.

"I'll do it," said Meg, and a second later she was gone into the kitchen.

If this woman touches me, I thought, *I will barf right here on the white couch.*

"Laurel, you're clearly in shock, and that's normal," said Suzie, reaching for my hand but trying to balance in that squat position at the same time. "We don't need to talk. I'm really just here to meet you and let you know that I'll be available to you, for any reason, over the next days and weeks as you deal with what has happened to your family."

My family.

The word hit me in the chest, a real punch that knocked the wind out of my lungs. I looked at Suzie Sirico the way, in a movie, someone looks at the person who just stabbed them, that moment of surprise before the pain kicks in and the blood starts gushing.

I heard the back door open, then close. Elliot and Selina came running into the room, their tails pointing straight up into the air, ready to get warm and dry and curled up for the night.

I made a noise like a whimper, but loud. It felt like it came not from me but something half-human, crouched at the base of my spine.

I was in bed when Nana got there, sometime before dawn. Mrs. Dill had given me two of the pills she always had on hand for her panic attacks. The medication was having fun with me, making me believe one thing was real, then another. In my mind, I was talking to someone at the Athens Theater ticket counter, begging them to let me in even though the movie had already started. "But everyone I know is in there!" I was yelling.

I felt my grandmother put her hand on my head, smoothing my eyebrow with her thumb. "I'm here, Laurel," she was saying.

Now the popcorn machine behind the ticket counter smelled like Chanel No. 5.

The hallway outside my bedroom door was buzzing slightly with echoed voices from the living room. Somebody blew their nose.

Back inside my head, I wasn't trying to get into the movie anymore. I'd given up and moved on, wandering down the street toward a supermarket, suddenly starving.

THREE

Pretty much everyone came to the funeral, which was held on a day so beautiful, normally everyone would be walking around saying cliché stuff like, "Spring has sprung!" The air smelled fresh and sweet, and the slight breeze was the kind that tickles a little.

Our whole neighborhood showed up. Relatives I hadn't seen in years, and my parents' friends from college, and people from my dad's office. Toby's friends and his whole soccer team came with their parents, and all his teachers. Two of them had been my teachers too, just a few years back. Some kids from school who I was friendly with and their families, plus dozens of people I either didn't know or couldn't remember the names of. It was standing room only in the funeral home.

Nana and I sat up front, where almost nobody could see us, and she held my hand tight while people spoke. I knew I was supposed to listen and nod and cry like everyone else, but I was busy composing a letter in my head:

Dear Mom and Dad and Toby,

There are a lot of people here. That's good, right? Doesn't everyone always wonder who would show up to their funeral? So now you know. If you're watching. I'd like to think you're watching, but just in case you're not, here are the highlights:

Dad's college friends Tom and Lena reading a poem they wrote together.

Toby's music teacher, Ms. McAndrew, singing "Amazing Grace." Did somebody not tell her this was a Jewish funeral? But it did sound pretty.

Mom, your friend Tanya reading an Emily Dickinson poem. Was that really your favorite one like she said?

It was cool of the rabbi to do the service, since we never bothered to join the synagogue—I guess when there's only one rabbi in town, that's how it goes. He talked about community kindness and mitzvahs. I wish I could be more specific, because apparently what he said made a lot of people cry, but when he was speaking I was watching two squirrels in a tree outside the window.

Nana cried out loud twice. I had to give her some Kleenex because she used up her handkerchief. I didn't have anything black, so I borrowed one of your dresses, Mom. It was a little big in the bust, but otherwise I think it looked nice.
Love,
Laurel

At the burial, Nana sprinkled dirt into the graves with her hands shaking, walking gingerly around them like a garden she'd just planted. The rabbi offered me the shovel, but I shook my head no.

That was when I saw David.

He was hanging back, hovering near some stranger's headstone, wearing a black blazer over a black T-shirt and black jeans. People kept turning around to look at him and whisper. Almost gawking, like some rock star had made an appearance at my family's funeral. But he didn't look back at them. He just watched the three caskets intently and ignored anyone who was alive.

Earlier, I'd heard someone say that they were leaving the tent up and just moving it down the hill a bit, because Mrs. Kaufman's funeral was the next day.

When it was time for us to stand up and leave, I glanced back to where I'd seen David, but he was gone.

Mr. Kaufman was in a coma. He was in ICU, and the hospital was making a very special exception by letting David stay there in an empty room.

That's what I heard at the reception back at the house. I was planted in a chair in the den, a great spot for hearing snippets of conversation as they floated by me. Megan sat next to me, eating a sesame bagel, not talking but occasionally rubbing my back.

Some people came to me. They'd lean in to talk closer to my ear or squat down so they were looking up at my face. At times I felt like a queen on her throne, and at others like a four-year-old kid. I knew they were just trying to be nice, the neighbors and friends and classmates and all the rest. They were just doing what they thought they were supposed to, which was exactly what I was doing too.

I was in the bathroom when I heard Mrs. Dill and the Dills' next-door neighbor, Mrs. Franco, talking in low tones on the other side of the door.

"Do they know anything more about what happened?" asked Mrs. Franco.

"I don't think so," said Mrs. Dill. "They might be putting out a call for witnesses, to see if other drivers may have seen something."

"What do *you* think it was?"

A pause. I sat still on the toilet, leaning in.

"Probably Gabe," whispered Mrs. Dill. "I bet he had a little too much to drink at dinner. Don't you remember the Christmas party last year?"

"I remember," said Mrs. Franco sadly. "Betsy had to force him to let her drive them home."

I thought of Mr. Kaufman on his cell phone that night, with his drink in his hands. And then I thought of wrapping my fingers around his throat and squeezing hard, which was not something I wanted to be thinking in the bathroom at my family's funeral with a house full of people on the other side of the door. I wiped the image away, out of my head with a mental eraser.

I waited three minutes and then peeked my head out of the bathroom. Mrs. Franco and Mrs. Dill were gone, and the coast was clear.

My grandmother, June Meisner, had class. Everyone said so. She wore crisp linen skirt-suits and well-made pumps and never left the house without makeup. She got her hair done twice a week at Marcella's Salon and kept it dyed dark brown. Nana volunteered at a local nursing home filled with what she called her "old ladies," even though many of them were younger than she was.

I guess it was because she had so much class that she made me get back into my mother's black dress and go to Mrs. Kaufman's funeral the next day.

Nana looked so small in the big, boxy driver's seat of our Volvo station wagon, her hands correctly positioned at ten o'clock and two o'clock on the steering wheel, her nails perfectly manicured. As we drove to the cemetery she turned to look at me, her eyes still red from the crying she did at night when she thought I couldn't hear her.

"I thank God every hour that you weren't in that car."

I pressed my nose to the window, not able to look back. "Nana, don't."

"You know me. I like to count the blessings I have."

"If you need to thank something, thank all the French homework Mrs. Messing gave us." I looked at my grandmother now, to let her know I wasn't just being a smart-ass.

"What if you'd gone with them and I'd lost all of you?"

"I'm not having this conversation."

She and my mom were experts at this tactic: Bring up serious stuff when driving in the car, so the child you are mortifying with your particular conversation has nowhere to go, no bedroom to retreat into; they were stuck.

I didn't want to tell her the truth, something that sat red-hot in the pit of my stomach and weighed me down, heavier each day. If I'd gone with them, if I had maybe finished my homework earlier or just blown it off to do in the morning, it would have been one more person to try to squeeze into the Kaufmans' SUV. Maybe my dad would have insisted on taking separate cars. Maybe I'd be driving with my parents and Toby right now, to bury Mrs.

Kaufman. One funeral, one person, the way everyone's used to doing it.

I couldn't talk about it, I couldn't think about it. If I did, I felt that fireball again, dragging me that much farther into the ground. It seemed like the only way to keep breathing was to focus on the here and now, moment by moment, keeping my mind frozen cold to anything else.

Mrs. Kaufman didn't have quite the same turnout my family had, and those who went both days were looking a little more haggard at having to do the whole thing over again. I found myself glad that they'd done my family first, while people were still fresh to their grief. Even the rabbi seemed weary. It made me happy, for a second, and not ashamed about it. *Our funeral was better.*

David wore the emo-goth outfit I'd seen the day before, and this time I noticed his black army boots. He was surrounded by relatives. His grandparents were staying at the house, I heard from one whisper. They were encouraging him to come back from the hospital and sleep in his own bed, but David wouldn't do it.

I watched him as the rabbi gave the cue, and David stood up to throw the first bit of dirt on his mother's grave. As he did this, someone in the crowd burst out with a sharp sob. David looked up for a moment, the shovel in his hands, to see where it had come from. It was the first time that day I'd seen his face full-on, unshrouded by his

23

shaggy hair now combed back, his bright eyes moving. He kept scanning the guests as the rabbi started talking again and an uncle put an arm around his shoulders.

Those eyes landed on me, flickering with some kind of new energy and purpose. David raised his head a little more now, really registering me with an acknowledgment. I looked back, held his gaze for a few moments, but that was all.

It felt like enough.

FOUR

ana was letting me sleep in the mornings, but not too late. She'd wake me by sitting on the edge of the bed.

"Laurel, sweetie, it's already ten o'clock," she said on the Monday after the accident. It had not yet been a week.

Nana and I didn't talk about how long she'd be staying; we both knew it was for good. I'd listened to her on the phone with lawyers and bank people, dealing with the wills and becoming my legal guardian and other things that had to matter now. She did it without complaining. After all, she was the only one left who could. Her husband, my grandfather, had had a heart attack when I was still a baby, and my mother's parents died before I was five. Both my mom and dad were only children, so there were no aunts, uncles, or first cousins. But Nana had always been there for as long as I could remember, and now, of course, she was here in our guest room.

If it was ten, that meant third period at school, which meant Meg was in journalism class. I would have been in history. They were giving me an indefinite amount of time off, and nobody had even said anything about bringing me homework assignments.

That was the expected thing, the thing the school automatically had to do. I knew that. But the thought of my classmates having a normal day without me just made me feel deeply, despairingly lonely.

"What do you want me to do?" I asked Nana, who was now flicking cat hair off my comforter. I needed her to tell me what came next, because staying in bed wasn't cutting it. All I could do in bed, when I wasn't struggling to get back to sleep after some screwed-up dream, was watch Toby's movie collection on his portable DVD player. He liked action and martial arts movies from all eras, and most of them were awful, but they were great at helping me not to cry.

I was sure that once I started to cry, I would never stop. I mean, how could I ever stop?

"I'd like you to come in and eat some breakfast. I don't

think you've had a decent meal all week."

It was true. Seder had been the last time I'd eaten a solid, balanced amount of food at a normal time. I always thought it was totally soap-opera for people to lose their appetite after something huge, but now I understood why. It wasn't just that I couldn't even imagine wanting to eat. It was that the emptiness combined with the little nag of hunger seemed like a duty.

"What about you?" I asked Nana. "Will you eat with me?"

"My stomach's still a little upset, but I'll have some matzoh and ginger ale."

In the kitchen, I sat down at the table, and she served me up a plate of pancakes, turkey bacon, and eggs.

"What about Passover?" I asked, eyeing the pancakes.

"I think we get excused this year," she said wryly.

I picked up one of the pancakes, slightly warm in my hands, and started to eat it like a big, limp cookie. It was something Toby and I loved to do, and it drove Nana crazy. But this time she just smiled and pushed the newspaper toward me. "Here," she said. "I know how you like to keep up with the headlines."

It was the *New York Times*, not our local paper, the *Herald Gazette*. Because every day the *Herald Gazette* was publishing a new article about the accident and how the police were looking for someone, anyone, who might have seen what happened. Nana had stopped the *Gazette*

27

delivery service two days earlier.

Now she sat down across from me with her ginger ale and matzoh, but didn't eat. "Laurel," she said. "Suzie Sirico called this morning. She's the grief counselor you met the other night, remember? She wanted to know how we were."

I looked up from the paper. "How did she get our number?"

"I gave it to her."

"You told her I was fine, right? That we were both fine?"

Nana broke off a piece of matzoh and nibbled. "She thinks the two of you should talk."

"You met her. She's creepy."

"She's a professional who can help you."

"Do I look like I need help?"

Nana actually did look at me, up and down my face, across and back. She knew better than to answer.

"Next time she calls," I said, "please just tell her not to."

Nana stood up, put what was left of her matzoh back in the box, and quietly left the room.

I turned back to the paper and started reading an article about trouble in Latin America, and there it was in the first paragraph: *demagogue.* It was one of my SAT words. It meant "rabble-rousing leader," and my study trick image popped into my head. On the steps of our school, a straggly bearded guy wearing a T-shirt that said DEM on it was speaking to a crowd of students, working them into a frenzy.

It had been more than a month since I was in the *D*s, but there was *demagogue*, crystal clear. The tests were in five days. I walked to my room and found my SAT vocabulary book on the desk where I'd left it, bookmarked, untouched since the night of the seder. I picked it up carefully; I'd had only two more pages to go on the list of a thousand words my dad had challenged me to memorize. He wanted me to go to an Ivy League school, preferably Yale, like he did. I wanted it too, because I'd visited Yale during one of his reunions and thought it was cool, but I didn't tell him that. I needed him to think he was convincing me.

"I'll pay you a dollar for every point you score over seven hundred on Critical Reading," he'd said. "It's not a bribe; it's motivation. Just a little something, because I know you can do it."

I put the book back down and went to find the phone.

"Are you absolutely sure you want to do that?"

Mr. Churchwell, my school guidance counselor, sounded happy to hear from me.

"Yes, I'm sure. I'm ready. I don't want you to take me off the list."

"I have no doubt that you're ready, Laurel. But your frame of mind . . . well, we just want you to be able to perform at your ability. There's another test date in June."

"I need to take it at the same time my friends are."

I tried to keep my voice from shaking. *I need to take it because if it weren't for all that time studying for this test, my parents and Toby might be alive right now. I would have gone with them that night and we would have taken our own car.*

That thought grabbed hold of me and held on tight.

Mr. Churchwell paused, then said, "Okay, Laurel. I'll see you on Saturday. If you have anything else you want to talk about, don't hesitate to call."

"Thank you," I squeaked out, then hung up.

Wiggle out of it. Focus.

I grabbed my SAT prep book and stared at it again, and it was like a hole I could climb through to escape this tight little box of guilt. I headed to my favorite study spot: the three-foot alley behind the white couch and a wall of windows in the living room. I was just getting settled in when I looked out the window and saw our neighbor Mr. Mita out on the street, walking Masher, the Kaufmans' dog. Masher was straining at his leash, desperate for a little speed and freedom, but Mr. Mita was having trouble keeping up. Masher was a good dog, a black-and-white Border collie with a T-shaped blaze down his forehead. He was always getting out of his yard and roaming the neighborhood, checking up on our houses like they were his flock of sheep.

I thought of Masher in the Kaufmans' house, not understanding why everyone was gone but sensing something big had happened. Whining at the windows. Scratching at the front door. Confused and devastated, sort of like me.

Fifteen minutes later, I found myself on the Mitas' porch, knocking.

"What?" said Nana when I told her.

"I feel it's the right thing to do," I offered in my defense.

"Can I at least think about it overnight?"

"Mr. Mita's bringing him over in half an hour. He's just getting the bowls and food and stuff from the Kaufmans'."

"Laurel . . . ," Nana said, dropping her head so she could rub her forehead with two fingers. "You know how I feel about dogs."

But then she looked up at me and I met her eyes, and I could see her giving in.

Wow, I thought. *She can't say no to me.*

I'd always wanted a dog, for as long as I could remember. "We travel too much," my dad would say when I mentioned it. "I'm not a dog person," my mother would whine.

So I chose to picture only Toby's reaction—laughing, rolling on the floor with glee—when Masher burst into our living room that night, all hyper and poking his nose everywhere he could fit it. He smelled musty and his coat was dusty, and he kept shaking it out like he was trying to brush off the lonely, dark, sad place his home had become, and I vowed to give him a bath in the morning. In minutes he was curled on top of me, panting and licking my elbows, and getting dirty looks from the cats.

I started studying like crazy. It seemed my fingertips were always on the edge of the SAT book, feeling the frayed softness or running across the glossy surface of its cover. When Meg came over so we could quiz each other, we didn't ever talk about school, but one night she said casually, "Julia La Paz came over today and talked to me. She asked me how you were."

"Ew."

Julia was David's girlfriend and had neon-pink hair down past her shoulders. Sometimes people called her "My Little Pony" to be mean.

"No, she was like, kinda nice. Depressed, actually. She hasn't heard from David in a week."

I tried to picture Meg and Julia chatting together by a locker, their heads close, but couldn't do it. It was like trying to imagine the earth flat.

"Did she go to the hospital? She knows he's there, right?"

Meg nodded. "She knows. She's just scared."

And then I shut up, because yeah, I would be scared too.

On SAT Saturday I awoke from the deepest sleep I'd had since the accident. I didn't have any dreams, and my sheets weren't even soaked with sweat. Right away, words started marching through my head. *Assiduous:* "hard-working." *Ostentatious:* "displaying wealth." *Vindicate:* "to clear from blame." *Rancorous:* "hateful." They came in an order that made no sense to me but seemed prearranged by something.

Dad? Is it you, doing that?

Then I shook the notion loose, out of my head. There was no room for that today.

An hour later, the Dills' minivan pulled up the driveway where I was pacing back and forth, and I was surprised to see Mrs. Dill behind the wheel with that wide, rigid smile she'd always had for me, even before the accident. Meg was slumped in the backseat. As I climbed in next to her, she rolled her eyes.

"Mom insisted on driving us. She says she wants me to relax."

"Are you nervous?" I asked.

"I stopped studying at eight o'clock and watched TV all night. I figure, if I don't know it by now, I never will."

We rode in silence toward the high school, and it hit me. I was going to see people. They were going to see me.

As we stepped inside the lobby of the main entrance, I locked my eyes onto a spot on the floor, not knowing where to look. But within seconds I felt a hand on my shoulder and turned around to see Mr. Churchwell.

"Laurel!" he said with a plastered-on grin. "It's so good

to see you." Then, his voice got lower and the grin vanished. "You're okay? You still want to do this?"

I nodded, and then he pulled me aside.

"Well, we've arranged something a little special for you. The College Board gave us permission to let you take the test in a room by yourself. I will be there too, of course, but no other students. Would you like that?"

I looked at his bright eyes, that earnest wrinkle in the middle of his forehead, and wondered if anyone in the adult world thought he was cute.

"Thank you," I said. "That would be great."

"I'll take you to the classroom we've set up for you." He started to lead me away, and I turned back to Meg, who had been watching us and was now shooting me a puzzled glance. I just shrugged at her before turning to follow Mr. Churchwell away from the crowd.

I hadn't even gotten the chance to wish my best friend good luck.

It was a long morning taking the critical reading and then the writing parts of the test at a desk in the middle of the faculty lounge, Mr. Churchwell sitting at a nearby table with a copy of *Rolling Stone*, but the tests didn't surprise me at all. I felt prepared—thank you, SAT prep course! During the breaks I got at the end of each hour, I used the teachers' private bathroom and listened to the buzz of voices in the hallway.

I finished the math section early and signaled Mr. Churchwell.

"I'm done. What should I do?"

"You want to check your answers?"

"I did. I'm done."

He glanced at his watch and came over to me. "Then I guess I'll just take that," he said, holding out his hand for the test, "and you can go early." I handed him the answer sheet and he took it gently, like it was something precious. "How do you think you did?" he whispered.

The way he said that, as if he was begging for me to share a secret, sounded almost exactly like my mother.

Do you think Mrs. Dixon liked your project? Did everyone laugh at the right times during your mock newscast?

She never wanted to sound like a pushy, overbearing parent. She wanted to be like the encouraging friend, confident that I'd do well in whatever I tried. So she'd ask me with her voice at half volume to sound like she only half cared, which totally bugged me. Because she fully cared, and I knew it.

The sensation of missing Mom came at me fast and hard, right into my chest. I might have even stumbled backward from the impact.

Not here! Not now! And definitely not in front of Mr. Churchwell.

I quickly imagined that I could reach my hand into my chest, yank out that awful feeling, place it on an invisible cloud of air right in front of me, then push it away. *Push it away.*

And it worked. I could almost see it float past Mr. Churchwell's head and out the door.

"I think I did okay," I finally said, trying to pick up his question even though several long, terribly quiet moments had passed.

"You have a ride home?" he asked. If he sensed how close I'd just come to losing it, he didn't let on.

"Megan's mom."

"And so I'll see you again . . ."

"On Monday." That just came out. I hadn't really decided when I was going back to school. But now that I was there, it seemed so totally possible. I could come back. I could pick right up where I'd left off and still finish the school year on time.

"Are you sure?" Mr. Churchwell asked.

"Absolutely," I said, and stood up, moving toward the door. "Have a great weekend."

I opened the door slowly and peeked my head into the hallway. It was empty, so I slid out, knowing exactly where I needed to go to wait for Meg. I made it outside quickly and flew down the steps of the school's entrance, following a concrete path around the side of the building and to the oak tree. It was our oak tree, the only one on school grounds with a trunk wide enough for two people to disappear behind, now fully green with shade. This was where Meg and I liked to hang out at lunchtime.

Most kids coming out of the school would be headed straight for their cars in the opposite direction; they'd never think to come this way. I pulled out my cell phone and sent a text message to Meg that just said:

@ d tree

Then my thumb reached toward the 2 button that would speed-dial the house.

And I froze. I'd been about to call home. *Holy crap, is it that easy to forget they're not there?*

No. You were just going to call Nana. Nana, who IS there.

It was simpler at that moment not to call at all.

I heard the front doors open and some voices, loud for a moment or two, then fading slowly. The front doors again, then fading voices. A third time I heard the doors open, and the voices, but they didn't fade; they were getting stronger, along with footsteps.

I looked up, hoping to see Meg, but it was Andie Stokes and Hannah Lindstrom. Pretty and popular, not mean but unapproachable. Generally superhuman. And they were walking toward me.

"Hi, Laurel," said Hannah.

"Megan Dill said you might be here," said Andie.

I had to shield my eyes from the sun to look up at them, but didn't stand. I was really just too nervous to move, and then I felt like an idiot for that. These were girls from my school who I'd known forever. Once, when we were little, I'd taken a bath with one of them, but I couldn't remember which.

Now they came and sat down with me, on the ground made bumpy by the oak tree's roots.

"We just wanted to say hi and let you know how sad we are for you," said Andie, sweeping her famous chestnut brown hair away from her face. "You must be going through hell."

"It's so brave of you to do this today," added Hannah, blond, touching my shoulder.

"Thank you."

"We're starting up a memorial fund, from our class to your family," said Andie. She was known for her obsession with charities, always coordinating some kind of clean-up day, food drive, or group donation. Some kids did sports, Andie did Good.

"We'd like to do something, you know, permanent. Maybe plant a tree at the rec center park," chimed in Hannah, who was wearing one of the craveable dresses she designed and sewed herself.

"Okay," I said, still feeling like a moron. Why couldn't I say something funny or smart? I was always looking for a chance to talk to these girls, and now here I was, mute.

The rec center park. That was a nice spot, near the town pool and tennis courts, where they had Family Fun Night every summer. The year before, Toby and I had almost won the egg toss, but he'd dropped it when there were just three pairs left. I was pissed, that evening in late August. I'd never won anything at Family Fun Night and was sick of Mom always packing a picnic from the Taco Bell drive-through instead of preparing sandwiches and salad and cookies like all the other moms did, and making us go home before the fireworks because they gave her a headache.

It wasn't a great memory, but the thought of it still made my throat close up. Fortunately, just then Meg appeared around the corner with a mortified look on her face. She came toward us and said hi to Hannah and Andie, then reached down and helped me up without asking if I needed the hand.

"My mom's here," said Megan, and we said quick good-byes before stumbling away.

"What the hell was that?" I asked her once we were out of earshot.

"I am so sorry. They cornered me after the test and asked if I knew where you were, and for some reason I told them because I'd just gotten your message, and before I could follow them out, stupid Mrs. Cox came over to talk to me about my English paper."

"It's okay," I said. "They were just being nice."

At least, I think that's what it was. If Andie Stokes and Hannah Lindstrom being nice felt like being run over by a steamroller and thinking you should be grateful, then yeah, that was it for sure.

When Mrs. Dill dropped me home, Nana was on the phone with someone. She waved at me as I closed the front door, then turned away. Masher ran in from another room, and I knelt down to bury my fingers in the fur on his back.

"Yes, I understand," she said in what I knew was her "I was raised to be pleasant to everyone" tone. "Well, we appreciate the update, Lieutenant. If there's anything we can do to help, just let us know." She hung up the phone quickly, then turned back around. "Oh! I was hoping to be able to give you a big congratulations hug the second you walked in!"

"Who was that?" I asked. I stood up, and Masher darted from the room, like he knew his job for now was done.

"It was Lieutenant Davis, just filling us in."

"On what?"

"Can we talk about it later? I want to hear about the tests."

"After you tell me what he said."

Nana sighed and looked at the ceiling. "They're trying to determine an official cause of the accident. They need to do that, you know, for their records."

"I know about records."

"Well, they said Mr. Kaufman may have had too much to drink; they tested his blood alcohol level in the hospital that night. It was right on the borderline. But Lieutenant Davis personally thinks there was another car involved. So they're still hoping someone will step forward."

I sat down, remembering what I'd overheard at the funeral, and felt almost glad that the blame on Mr. Kaufman was becoming more official. If I could blame him, I couldn't blame myself. I could hate him, even, and nobody would fault me for it.

Not my dad. I knew he always disliked Mr. Kaufman a little, along with the two or three other dads in our neighborhood who made lots of money and bought lots of big, obvious things with it. My parents didn't think I knew but they struggled to support us, and sometimes they didn't quite make it and needed help from Nana.

"But I don't want you to concern yourself with all this accident stuff," said Nana now. "It doesn't affect us."

"Of course it affects us. How can it not affect us?" I asked, not ready to drop it yet.

Now Nana turned from sad to a little fierce, her eyes narrowing.

"We have our own job with grieving and getting on with our lives. I won't let them keep you from being able to do that."

I saw that she had tears in her eyes, and all I wanted was to take them out.

"I'm sorry, Nana," I said. "You're right."

She nodded, then went into the kitchen and came out with a plate of brownies. "I made these to celebrate the SATs."

And just like that, the conversation was over.

FIVE

It rained hard the next day. "Pissing," as my dad liked to say. It was pissing out, drumming a steady, angry rhythm onto the roof of the Volvo and the slate stones of our front terrace. Nana let me stay in bed, watching TV, eating my special SAT brownies. Masher lay on my left, stretched out alongside my body with one front leg across my arm. Elliot and Selina took turns at the foot of the bed.

Once, toward late afternoon, I heard Nana approach my bedroom door. I quickly dropped my head to the side, closed my eyes, and opened my mouth a bit in expert pretended *zzz*'s. I knew this made her happy; one more thing to check off on her mental daily list. *Make sure Laurel gets enough sleep.*

But then someone knocked on the front door.

I heard Nana open it, and a voice I couldn't place. After a few minutes, curiosity got the better of me, and I wandered out of my room.

David Kaufman was sitting on the bench in our foyer, taking off his boots. He was drenched, and Nana was already in the kitchen making him coffee.

"Hi," I said, and he looked up.

"Hi, Laurel," he said, and it occurred to me that he probably hadn't said my name out loud, to anybody, in years.

He looked bad. Dark circles pressed themselves against the skin under his eyes, which didn't seem as round as they used to be, and he'd broken out. I couldn't help staring at this one really big zit on his nose.

David took off his jacket and reached up to hang it on one of the wall hooks, then noticed that Toby's jean jacket was already there. He paused; when I didn't react, he carefully put his jacket on top of Toby's.

I didn't know what else to say to him. It seemed crazy yet perfectly sensible that he should be in my house at this moment. I could continue with "How are you?" but knew I hated the question myself.

Then I thought of Mr. Kaufman, and the anger rose in me. Keeping my voice steady, trying to make it sound more curious than vengeful, I asked, "What's going on with your dad?"

"They've moved him out of ICU, but there's still no change," he said, rubbing one of his feet where the sock had soaked through. I had a quick flashback of David and me sitting on that bench when we were kids, pulling snow-encrusted mittens and hats away from our limbs and onto the floor.

"He could wake up any day, they say," continued David. "They say my being there might help that happen, so that's why I'm not coming home." This came out all practiced and mechanical, like it was a line he'd been using a lot. He said it like there was no reason why I wouldn't want his dad to be okay.

Nana came out of the kitchen and beckoned us over to the table.

"Is Masher here?" said David. "I came home for some clothes, and my grandfather said you'd taken him."

"Yeah. Mr. Mita wasn't—"

"Thank you," David said, cutting me off. Hearing David's voice in the house must have woken Masher up, because, on cue, he came bursting down the stairs.

David fell to his knees to hug his dog, his face in the thick ring of fur around his neck, and they stayed that way for what seemed like minutes. I put two very large spoonfuls of sugar in my coffee, slowly.

When he finally let go of Masher, he was fighting

45

back tears. Nana handed him a box of Kleenex—she had installed one in every room—and he turned his back to us, cleaning himself up.

"He seems happy. Thank you," said David when he swiveled back around. "Do you mind watching him for a little while longer?"

Something about David's face right then, so fragile and temporary, felt familiar. Had I seen it before on him? Or maybe, on myself? My guard fell, and a voice inside me nudged, *David is not his father. You don't have to hate him, too.*

"No, I don't mind," I said. "He hogs the covers, but I can deal with that."

David burst out with a little laugh, just a snort really, and smiled a bit. He crawled back into the chair and took his first sip of coffee.

"You've been home all this week? Out of school?" said David.

"Yeah. I'm going back tomorrow." Just saying it made me feel that much more like I would actually do it. "What about you?"

"Nah, I'm failing two of my classes anyway. I'm done."

The nerd in me felt alarmed, and I couldn't help saying, "Done? Like, dropping out?"

David just shrugged and looked at me, like he was daring me to ask more, challenging me to try to talk him out of it.

"Well, you're lucky then," was all I said, picking at a thumbnail. "Because you'll miss that whole stupid senior talent show thing."

David snorted again and nodded, and then we went silent. But the air felt a little thinner, a little warmer now. After a few more moments, he slid back down to the floor, and Masher, who'd had his head resting in David's lap, stretched out in front of him.

"I've got some stuff to do, to get ready for tomorrow," I said, getting up and taking two steps toward the stairs. He didn't look up to say good-bye.

"Stay as long as you want, David," said Nana from the kitchen doorway. "Do you want a sandwich?"

I didn't wait to hear his answer, because suddenly being back in my room, without having to make conversation with David Kaufman, was all I wanted in life.

There was a picture of the two of us, David and me, in a family photo album somewhere. We're on my front lawn. It's my first day of third grade and his first day of fourth grade. I'm grinning wide while holding a Snoopy lunch box, and he's standing with his hands on his hips, so over the whole thing. I remember us walking to the bus stop and then him moving away from me to talk to Lydia Franco, who was ten and unimaginably streetwise. But on some weekends we went for walks in the woods, and he'd show me the old stone homestead walls that ran through the back of our neighborhood.

We did this until the year David started middle school. Although we waited at the same stop, he took a different bus now, and he had simply stopped talking to me. I think I asked him a question once and he just looked at me, smiled, and turned away. That was it, like someone finally switching off a TV that's been left on too long. If I felt hurt, I never admitted it. Soon, Meg moved to the neighborhood and I had someone, and that was all that mattered.

When I got to my room, Elliot and Selina were both on the bed, giving me these looks.

"Sorry, guys, the dog's not leaving yet," I said, and crawled under the covers.

SIX

Mr. Churchwell got up from behind his desk to join me on the small, beat-up leather couch in his office, forcing me to inch a little farther toward my end. The cushion made a *poosh* sound as he settled in, smiling at me. It felt like being on a date with someone's tragically dorky uncle.

"So, you feel okay? Anything you want to talk to me about?" he said.

I had made it here, to school, just like I said I would. Mr. Churchwell had asked me to come in a bit early, before homeroom if I could, to "check in" and "touch base." It hadn't even been two weeks since the accident, but it didn't seem possible that I could be anywhere else.

"I'm glad to be out of the house, actually," I offered. It was true. I had been able to look at people's faces when I walked into the school and down the main hallway toward my locker. Some had smiled at me, and I had smiled back.

"Mmmm, yes. I don't blame you. It's important to resume your usual routine."

"Plus, I was starting to get a little too good at *The Price Is Right*. Do you believe what a good washer-dryer combo costs these days?"

He donated a short, humoring chuckle. "Well, take it easy today. If you need some time out of the classroom, a break or anything, just let your teachers know. They're ready to help."

"You talked to them about me?" I asked.

"Just to tell them you were coming back. And I spoke with Emily Heinz about the Tutoring Club. She says she can take charge of things until you feel like getting involved again."

I'd started the Tutoring Club my freshman year because of Toby. He'd struggled all through elementary school until they figured out he had dyslexia, when he was eight and I was eleven. Somewhere along the line I'd started helping him read and do his homework. He wouldn't let my parents do it; he'd get annoyed with them and they'd fight. But me, he liked working with me. Somehow I found ways to make things click for him, like using his plastic soldiers to form letters on the floor.

Eventually my mom started paying me five bucks an hour to help him, although I would have done it for free. It was the only time we got along.

In ninth grade I wrote a paper about this, and my English teacher asked if I was interested in helping her put together a group of students to tutor other students. It seemed like a golden opportunity to get involved in something I already knew how to do, and Toby would need the Tutoring Club when he got to high school. My dad fought hard to keep him in regular classes, even though Mom would have let him go into special ed. "He won't get bullied so much in special ed," she'd say, but my father wanted so badly for him to have the most normal experience possible.

A clear vision of Toby, slowly sounding out words on a page with his brow furrowed in concentration, started to push me off a little cliff in my mind. What was the point of the Tutoring Club now if Toby would never be able to take advantage of it?

"Laurel, are you okay?" said Mr. Churchwell. "Do you want to talk or stay here for a little while?"

No, no, no, you don't, I thought. We were not going to do this now, eight minutes before homeroom.

"I should get going," I said, standing up and slinging my backpack over my shoulder. Mr. Churchwell nodded but stayed where he was.

"Have a great day, Laurel," he said, and with that I was out the door toward homeroom.

Somehow, I made it until the final bell. As I entered each classroom, the teacher took me aside and told me a version of the same thing: *Don't worry about taking notes, don't worry about needing to excuse yourself for a break. Everybody wants to help. Everybody cares about you.*

Then I looked around at the other students filing in, glancing quickly at me and then away, almost embarrassed, like I was standing there naked, and I had a real hard time buying the "Everybody cares about you and wants to help" part. But I accepted the no-note-taking part, no problem. I'd always wondered what it would be like to be one of those kids who blatantly ignored the teacher and did their own thing in class. Now I could listen but doodle, knowing I'd get sent home with a copy of the teacher's own notes for my binder.

It was one period, then another, then another, then eating three bites of my turkey sandwich in the far corner of the cafeteria with Meg, then more periods just like the first ones. I listened, and I avoided people's eyes, and I drew trees and flowers and hillside scenes across the straight lines of my notebook.

I found French to be the toughest class. Looking at the textbook, I thought of my French homework that night

and how I'd been reading through it in the kitchen, clueless about the accident. I couldn't help wondering which
page I was on at the moment of impact. Wondering what
would have happened if Mrs. Messing hadn't given us
so much homework and if I'd decided to go to Freezy's
instead.

Deep, deep breaths pushed the panic back down. I was
not going to cry at school. It was not an option. I imagined
my tear ducts filled with dry desert sand.

Finally, at the end of it all, Meg found me at my locker.

"Are you going to drama?" she asked, knowing I'd forgotten all about it. The spring production of *The Crucible*
was only a week away. Meg had a small part as Mercy Lewis,
one of the teenage girls who pretend to be possessed by
witchcraft. I was not in the cast. I was a backstage scenery
person, no matter how much Meg had begged me to try
out this time.

Mom was a painter too. She made money at it. Deborah
Meisner Portraits had its own website and regular ads in
the *PennySaver*. Two or three days a week, my mother
spent the day at a studio she shared with another artist, and covered canvases with happy families, smiling
kids, cuddly dogs, kissing couples in their wedding wear.
Clients would give her photos and she'd take it from there,
and now her work hung in houses all over town.

She painted her own things when she had time, which
wasn't often. Sometimes I'd visit her studio and there

would be an easel in the corner, tucked away like she was ashamed of it. A half-finished image of an old man on a park bench, or an abstract splatter of shapes that only suggested a face. Mom often talked about entering art shows or trying to arrange a gallery collection, but it never happened. The work that earned her a living took priority.

In our own house, there were just two of her paintings. One of my dad that she painted shortly after they first met, when he was still writing for a newspaper in the city. He's sitting in front of an open window with skyscrapers and looks so young, most people who saw it thought it was Toby. I always used to look at that painting and think about him giving up the newspaper job for one in advertising right after they got married and Mom got pregnant, because it offered a higher salary.

They had each made their sacrifices, for our family.

The other painting, hanging in our dining room, was one of my brother and me as little kids, leaning against a tree in our backyard. We have the same face, an eerie medley of our mother's and father's features; I'm just taller and have longer straight brown hair than he does. I'm holding a cat that I don't remember us ever owning.

"You have so much talent," Mom had said to me the last time she saw one of my scenery flats. "But you never draw people."

"I can't. I've tried. They come out looking really

disturbing." We'd had this conversation at least a dozen times by then.

"Take a life drawing class. There's a good one at the community arts center."

"I just don't have time," I'd said to her, but to myself: *She's so embarrassed. It must suck to be a portrait painter and have a daughter who can only draw scenery!*

She used to take me to the Metropolitan Museum of Art once a month. I loved those trips, even though she often borrowed my drawing pad to go sit on a bench somewhere, sketching other visitors, while I wandered the rooms alone.

The sadness came into my chest again, so I pushed away the image of my mother sketching and thought of how much I loved taking a tall canvas and turning it into something with dimension and depth; a street that curves on forever or deep rows of green hills. Maybe the truth was, I just didn't like painting people.

"How are they doing with the flats?" I asked Meg.

"They still need some work. That's why it would be great for you to come and help. Even Sam said so."

"That's just because of what's happened. Do you remember how obnoxious he was a few weeks ago when I tried to start a house without him?" Samuel Ching was the stage manager in charge of the sets and generally a control freak. I was a better artist than he was, every-one knew it, but he never let me do anything without his approval. Once he painted over an Alp I did for *The Sound of Music*, which made me cry a little.

"I remember," said Meg, "but they really do need you."

I followed her into the auditorium, where most of the cast was goofing off in the seats and some of the finished scenery flats—a stone wall, a front door—were already onstage. She nodded me a little silent good-bye, and I headed for the backstage door. Inside, I found Samuel cleaning paintbrushes in front of a blank scenery flat.

"Hi, Sam," I said.

He looked up at me and seemed surprised at first, but then his mouth settled into something practiced.

"Laurel, I'm so glad to see you!"

"Need help?" Now I felt we were reciting lines in a little play of our own.

"Do we ever. Here," he said, handing me a brush and nodding toward the tall canvas. "This is the town square wall you sketched out before"— he tripped up for a moment—"last time. Do you think you could tackle it?"

Sam usually liked to be the one to paint on my sketches. It always felt like he was grabbing credit for the things I drew, but I couldn't do anything about it because he was a senior and in charge and I didn't want to be a whiny tattletale.

Now I smiled and said, "Just leave it to me."

The next day, at my locker, taking too long to switch out my books because I knew I could be late for class and it wouldn't matter, I overheard two seniors talking around the corner.

"I can't believe Laurel Meisner's back already," said one, whose voice I couldn't identify. I froze when I heard my name.

"Yeah, if it were me, I'd pull a David Kaufman and vanish," said the other. "But she looks pretty good."

Flattering.

"I heard the police found out there was another car involved, some kid from Rose Hills who was driving too fast."

"Really? That's weird, because my mom said that Mr. Kaufman tested way over the limit for DWI and they're going to arrest him."

"Jamie, he's in a coma. How are they going to arrest him?"

The voices moved away and I started to breathe again. I didn't know which to feel weirder about, the fact that people were talking about me or that there were rumors like this floating around. At least, I hoped they were rumors.

I called Nana, who said, "Laurel, do you really think the police would keep information like that from us? People like to gossip. It gets them attention."

At lunch I asked Meg, who rolled her eyes. "Those aren't even the most creative ones I've heard," she said. "My favorite is the one about someone leaving an anonymous note at the scene of the accident saying sorry. I mean, people should get creative writing course credit for some of these whoppers."

Meg looked at me, and it must have shown that I didn't find these as funny as she did.

"You make it sound like there are a lot," I said.

"Not really." She shrugged, then looked at me again. Something shadowy flickered across her face. "Okay, yeah," she continued, her voice serious now. "There are a lot. This is a boring town. Rumors are, like, a specialty here."

"But you tell people when they're not true, right?"

"With some of them, of course."

"Like what?"

Meg frowned. "Do you really want to know?"

Did I? I wasn't sure, but I said yes anyway, as firmly as I could.

Meg sighed, like she was prepping herself. "Well, I've heard a few people say that the reason you and David weren't in the car that night was because you guys were, you know. Together somewhere."

I jerked my head back. The thought of David and me and the words *together somewhere* being linked in any way made me instantly nauseous.

"Gross," was all I could say. I tried to make it sound funny, but Meg knew better.

"I always set them straight on that one," she said, putting her hand on my back. "Always, Laurel. As soon as anyone brings it up."

So maybe that's what some of those looks were. They thought I'd been fooling around with the Railroad Crowd's biggest pothead while my family was burning to death.

I felt the tears hot and sharp in the corners of my eyes, and the urge to bolt to the nearest bathroom to throw up. But that meant everyone in the cafeteria seeing me run out, and maybe someone in the bathroom hearing me puke. And that meant more gossip that I didn't want to give them.

So I swallowed hard and took a sip of water, and blinked until I could see again, then shrugged Meg's hand off my back.

On my third day back, our school principal, Mr. Duffy, called me into his office. He had a huge potbelly and a bright red face. Some students liked to mess with their little siblings and tell them he was really Santa.

"Laurel, I didn't get a chance to attend the funeral, so I wanted to tell you in person, privately, how very sorry I am. How are you holding up?"

"I'm taking it day by day." I liked saying this. It was honest, short, and seemed to satisfy people.

"That's all you can do. Are you . . . Do you have professional support?"

For a second I thought he was talking about my bra.

"You know," he continued, "a doctor or counselor . . ."

"There's someone the police hooked me up with," I said. "A crisis person."

"And what about David Kaufman? Have you seen him or talked to him?"

"I saw him a few days ago."

"How's his father? We haven't been able to get in touch."

"I think he's about the same."

It felt very strange to be providing this direct line to David's state of affairs. Mr. Duffy nodded and pushed a piece of paper toward me.

"I'm giving you off-campus privileges. In case you want to go home or just need a break, or to see someone. I thought it might help make things easier."

I looked at the paper, which was an official-looking form he'd filled out and signed. Wow. This was a really, really nice thing to do, and it would actually make things easier.

"Thank you," was all I said, my voice shaky.

He put his hand lightly on my shoulder as I stood up. "You're welcome. Anything else you need, don't hesitate to ask."

I looked at the paper in my hand and had a brainstorm.

"Actually," I offered, "the one problem with this is that I'm sort of not driving these days, if you know what I mean. Could we extend these privileges to Megan Dill?

She's been chauffeuring me around."

Without even a second's pause, Mr. Duffy took the paper and laid it on his desk again, scribbled something on the side, and gave it back to me.

"All set," he said with a grin.

The next day when fourth period ended, Meg and I rendezvoused by my locker. We were going to McDonald's. Not just because we could, but because lunchtime had become my toughest period. People were trying so hard not to get caught staring at me. I still felt like they were watching me out of the corners of their eyes, every bite and every chew, and I was having a hard enough time wanting to eat as it was.

Meg and I strolled through the north lobby, through the crowd, and out the door toward the parking lot. We walked slowly, making it obvious that we were doing nothing wrong. Flaunting it.

At McDonald's, we sat in the corner by the window. I scanned the room and realized with relief that I didn't recognize a single face. Meg took the first, eye-crossing drag on her milk-shake straw and leaned back, looking amused.

"What?" I asked.

"I heard something, but I'm not sure if I should tell you."

My heart sank. "It's not something else about me and David Kaufman, is it?"

"No, this is a good one. I think you should be prepared, in case it's true." She took another short sip of milk shake and shot a glance around the restaurant. "Okay," she said, looking me square in the eye. "It's very possible that Joe Lasky is going to ask you to the prom."

"Who?"

"Lasky!"

It seemed like all noise in McDonald's, the hum of voices and ringing of cash registers and even the sizzling grill sounds, stopped suddenly. Because the key words here, *Joe Lasky* and *ask* and *prom*, had plugged up my ears, making them pop a bit.

"Shut *up*," was all I could say.

I hadn't really thought about the prom since the night of the accident. There was a photo in the family room of my mother in her baby-blue prom dress, all taffeta and ruffles, standing at the base of her parents' staircase with some nerdy, pizza-face date. She used to tell me that when I went to prom, she'd snap a photo just like that of me, and then we'd put the two pictures in a nice double frame. And I'd nod and think, *Not even a pizza-face nerd would take me to the prom, but you believe what you want to.*

When I felt my throat start to close up again, I pushed the thought of Mom's photo away. *It doesn't exist, it never existed. Concentrate on something else.*

What I thought of was a word from my SAT list. *Aghast:* "struck with terror and amazement."

Joe Lasky. Even though we hadn't spoken since eighth grade, he was on my personal list of Ten Cutest Guys at school. Meg and I had made one up back in September; while Meg kept revising hers, mine held fast. Even though he was not unhandsome, he was crazy tall, with such bony legs and arms that most people called him Joe Skellington. But I loved the way he bounced a little when he walked, and how he'd worn his brown hair in the same Beatles cut for years, and the way he sketched made-up superheroes on his notebooks.

"Mary heard it from his sister's friend, or something," said Meg. "I think that's a decently reliable source."

"Why? Out of pity?"

"Laurel, don't—"

"He's asking me out of pity."

"What makes you think that?" Meg grabbed a couple of french fries, looking down, away from me.

"Why else?" I watched Meg shove her fries into her mouth, and remembered that she and Joe were on Debate Team together. The question came out before I could think it through. "Did you put him up to it?"

"No!" she said, through the french fries, her eyes wide with hurt. "No way!"

Now I felt guilty. "Sorry. It's just . . . he's never acted like he likes me."

"So what? You've never acted like you cared about any of the guys you've liked. I don't think I've ever seen you

63

as cruel as when you were crushing on Mike Shore. You totally ignored him."

It was true. I wasn't good with liking someone. My instinct was total self-preservation; show no sign of weakness. This was my pathetic way of being shy.

"Isn't he worried about David Kaufman and me?" I said sarcastically. "I mean, hasn't he heard the buzz?"

Meg looked down and her shoulders sagged. "Laurel, you need to get over that. Anyone with half a brain or who knows you at all knows it's BS."

"This is great," I said. "Now I'm going to be walking around every day, wondering when it's coming . . . if it's coming."

Meg raised her head hopefully. "If it is, what will you say?"

From Meg's face, I could tell that this was very important to her. It made sense. Me saying yes to the prom meant it was okay for her to say yes to it too.

"I don't know what I would say. Joe Lasky, huh?" I drew out the moment, taking a bite of my burger. Something about this piece of news made me feel strangely hopeful. Just like the SATs, here was something that would carry me through the next few weeks.

Looming up ahead and blocking everything that came after it, there it was: PROM.

SEVEN

ike an idiot, I waited all night for the phone to ring, not even sure I wanted it to. I was thinking that if asked, I would go to the prom. I would do it to show how resilient I was.

But the next day, Joe Lasky managed to surprise me. I was in the north stairway en route from history class to French on the second floor, thinking about the assignment I'd barely finished, when someone called my name. It echoed against the brick and metal and was followed by the *clank clank* of steps being taken too fast.

Joe. Bouncing that lanky body up the stairs. He was wearing a vintage Who T-shirt and baggy jeans, his books hooked under one arm.

"Hey," he said, arriving on the landing where I had frozen.

"Hi, Joe," I said. When I talked to guys, my big-sister-ness tended to come out. Too much sarcasm, that urge to prove how much smarter I was than they were. I totally sucked at flirting.

"Listen, I haven't really seen you this week, but I wanted a chance to say how sorry I am. How has it been so far, back at school?"

He stooped a bit as he talked, but his eyes were wide, deep, sincere. I'd heard this type of line so much recently, and noticed how different people delivered it. What Joe Lasky seemed to be forgetting—or hoped I was forgetting—was the fact that he hadn't said a word to me in almost three years.

"It's been okay. The cliché is true. One day at a time." I paused, reminding myself to *be nice, just be nice!* So I added, "Thanks for asking. That's sweet."

Joe shrugged and reached into his pocket, pulled out a CD. "Listen, Laurel, when my grandfather died last year—and I know that it's not in the same ballpark—this album helped me. It's this really obscure band nobody's ever heard of, but they totally rock, and I think you'll like it. I burned a copy for you."

He held out the CD and I looked at it, tears suddenly welling up in my eyes. *No, no, no, Laurel. It's one thing to be less sarcastic, but do not cry in front of Joe Lasky on the north stairway.*

"Thank you," I choked out, taking the CD. We both stared at it for another moment, not wanting to look at each other, and suddenly the class bell sounded.

"Gotta go, Laurel," he said, glancing over my shoulder now. "Let me know what you think of the band."

Then he was gone, and I started walking toward French, fingering the plastic corners of the CD case as I went.

"Did he write anything on the inside?" asked Meg when I showed it to her at McDonald's after school.

"No," I said. It was one of the first things I checked.

"So if he asks you, will you go?" prodded Meg. "Pity or no pity, he's a cool guy, and it's the prom."

I knew I owed her an answer. I wasn't sure of it myself until the words came out of my mouth.

"Yeah, I think I would. If he asks."

"I was thinking of asking Gavin," said Meg. Gavin was Meg's chemistry lab partner, and they had this weird secret hand gesture they did to each other when they passed in the hallway.

"Gavin would be a good one," I said.

"We could double-date. Gavin and Joe are kind of friends, I've seen them hang out together."

I looked at Meg, who was trying so hard to stay casual.

"You have all this figured out, don't you?" I said.

She just shrugged. "I've thought about it for a few minutes."

"A few *hundred* minutes, you mean."

Meg tossed a McNugget at me and stuck out her tongue.

This had all been her idea, I was sure of it now. But why? For me, or for her? So she could go to the prom and not feel guilty about it, because I was there too?

Maybe a little of both. And maybe the truth didn't have to matter.

At home that weekend, our lives seemed to be about always having something to do. There was homework, of course, even though there was a silent understanding that I could be as late with it as I wanted to. Nana started giving me some chores. Vacuum here, Windex there. Nothing heavy, but enough to count as a first baby step toward something. In between, I'd scour Toby's DVD shelf in the den and find new movies to watch.

David Kaufman called on Saturday morning to ask if he could come over and see Masher; it had gotten busy with other visitors at the hospital and he needed a break. I heard Nana telling him that he didn't have to call, that he was welcome whenever he wanted to stop by, and I winced.

I was out in the back, sweeping the terrace and listening to my iPod, when he showed up. Joe's obscure band had turned out to be just what I needed. Sorrowful moaning set to music, sad yet sweet and blindly optimistic. I had been listening to it pretty much nonstop since the previous afternoon.

Nana knocked gently on her side of the big dining room window, and I looked up. She was standing there with David, Masher already at his side. She waved, and he sort-of waved—it was more like a hand flutter—and they retreated away from the glass. I wasn't sure if I was supposed to come in and keep him company. I just kept sweeping.

Five minutes later she was at the window again. When she finally got my attention, she pointed energetically toward the den, her eyebrows raised. I shook my head no. She nodded yes. I shook my head again and then there she came, out the back door to pull the headphones out of my ears.

"You go in and say hi to him," she said, annoyed.

"You're the one who said he could come over! You talk to him."

"Don't be silly."

"Nana, you don't understand. We're not friends. I barely know him anymore."

She looked at me and softened, then handed me back my headphones. "I was thinking," she said, "that maybe you'd need someone to talk to."

I paused, turning to glance toward the open back door.

"Well, I don't. At least, not someone who's basically a stranger. If I wanted to blab to a stranger, I'd go call that Suzie person."

For a second, Nana looked like she might force this. It reminded me of when I was younger and she was always trying to nudge me out of my shyness. *Go sit with your Great-Aunt Ruth, she hasn't seen you in so long. Go ask the saleslady if there's a ladies' room you can use.* But she just smiled, patted me on the shoulder, and went into the house.

A minute later, David came outside.

"Hey, Laurel," he said, looking around the terrace. Masher followed him out and made a beeline toward me, sticking his nose into my crotch.

I jumped back. David shouted, "Mash! No!" then turned to me. "Sorry. We've been trying to get him not to do that since he was a puppy."

He didn't have to know that Masher did it to me all the time and I thought it was hilarious.

"If it's any consolation," said David, "he only does it to people he really likes."

"Well . . . who doesn't?"

David snorted a laugh, then we fell silent. Big awkward pause. I examined a spot on the ground near his feet.

Finally, he said: "I'd ask how you were doing, but you probably hate that question even more than I do."

I looked up at him. He wasn't smiling, but the corners of his mouth seemed relaxed and happy.

"Yes," was all I said, but I hammered down on the s and he nodded.

"You should see what it's like at the hospital. They all want to *cure* me of something."

"It's pretty ridiculous at school, too," I added.

"Ugh! I can only imagine," he said. A shadow moved across his face and he frowned, seemingly at a spot on the ground near *my* feet now. "I'm guessing the police told you about my dad."

I felt an adrenaline shot of anger rush through me, but swallowed it down.

"They told my grandmother, so, yeah."

"He wasn't drunk, you know."

"Okay," was all I said. Swallowing again. My heart thudding in my ears.

"Officially they say he was borderline, but I'll tell you, I've seen him drink a lot more than he did that night and be totally fine. Driving, I mean."

"I'm sure," I said. It felt like no matter what kind of stupid agreeing grunts I came out with, David would still sound like he was correcting me.

"They promised they're looking for another driver, but I think they're too lazy. It's so much easier for them to blame it all on my dad."

I blame it all on your dad! I felt like saying. But I

swallowed that down too, tougher and more bitter than anything else. Then I looked at David and realized he was losing it a little as well.

I just wanted to be out of this conversation but felt completely pinned.

Then Masher jumped up on David and broke the tension. I loved that dog.

"Listen, do you happen to have a Frisbee?" said David casually, like the previous horrible moment had never happened. "I was going to go out in front and toss it around with him for a while. He's desperate."

"I think Toby has at least one," I said. I started walking around the house toward the side door to the garage, and they both followed me.

Toby, pretending to aim a Frisbee at my head. Spinning one on his finger like a top. Being pissed off that the glow-in-the-dark one didn't glow at all, and taking it back to the store.

On my way into the garage, I averted my eyes from the spot on the front lawn where my brother liked to play with all his guy stuff.

Toby kept his Frisbees stashed in a box with soccer shin guards, a badminton birdie, and a single mateless cleat, which still had dirt caked on its sole from some long-ago soccer game.

If I smell this, I thought, *will it smell like him, or just be disgusting?*

Stop. Stop it. Push it away.

I swallowed hard, took one of the Frisbees, and tossed it to David, who caught it with both hands.

"Thanks," he said, and headed out to the front yard. I stood on my tiptoes to watch him through one of the garage door windows. David crouched down low and shot the Frisbee diagonally toward the trees, where Masher caught it in his mouth, a good four feet off the ground.

That night over dinner, Nana said, "I hate seeing you get so upset about some boy." For a second I thought she was talking about David, and then realized she meant Joe. Someone had filled her in. Mrs. Dill, I bet.

"*Guy*, Nana. Nobody says *boy* anymore."

"I can't imagine why anyone would play with your emotions at a time like this," she said now, spreading butter on a roll. "Should I call his parents and let them know what he's doing?"

"For the love of God, no!" I nearly shouted.

After a pause, she said, "Even if this boy Joe doesn't ask you, I think you should go to the prom anyway."

"Go stag? Right. Like that's what I want, people having one more reason to look at me like I'm a freak."

An expression of horror flashed across her face. "Do people look at you like that?"

I shrugged, trying to downplay. I had planned to keep this whole area of information from her.

"Laurel, I understand that people might treat you differently, at least for a while, but you can't let them get to you. You have to show you're strong."

"I am," I said, then clarified: "I am showing I'm strong."

"But you'll tell me if this boy causes problems for you? You'll tell me if anyone does something to hurt you?"

I looked at her, so small and dainty in her brown cashmere cardigan. What was she going to do, show up at someone's doorstep with a bat?

"I can stick up for myself," I said, "but I'll tell you if I need any help."

I had two classes with Joe Lasky: History during second period, then later, after lunch, English. The thought of seeing him had kept me up half the night.

When I walked into the history classroom on Monday, he looked up from his desk in the front row and nodded. I smiled quickly and headed to the back of the room, one aisle over. It allowed me a clean line of sight to the whole left side of his head. His hair on that side flopped forward over his eyes when he bent down to take notes; he was left-handed, so he kept reaching across his face with his right hand, pushing the hair back.

I also noticed his feet. Scanning the line of legs below desk level, I saw that most people tapped their toes or had their ankles crossed, swinging slightly. But Joe's feet were still, placed neatly together directly under the desk, his long legs forming a perfect L as they bent.

These things were enough to make me like Joe Lasky, right there in a windowless classroom while Dr. Garrett was lecturing us about the Hundred Years' War. I found myself wanting the period to be over quickly, then not wanting it, then wanting it again. Several times, Dr. Garrett paused to glance back at me and saw me doodling in my notebook. I saw this out of the corner of my eye, along with several people turning around to see me, and knew he wouldn't say a word.

When the bell rang, I instinctively shot up, but then saw Joe taking his time and hung back a bit. It took everything I had to walk slowly down the aisle and stop parallel to Joe's desk instead of zooming out of the room like everyone else.

"Hi, Joe," I said. He was actually finishing up something he was writing, a final scribble at the bottom of his notebook page. He snapped it shut and looked up at me, a little distracted.

"Hey. What's going on?" He looked like I'd shaken him out of some fabulous dream.

On Friday he had said my name at conspicuous places. *Gotta go, Laurel.* Now I just get a "hey"?

I took his CD out of my pocket and held it up. This was premeditated; I thought it would be a good way to fill a pause.

"So, you liked it?" Joe asked, taking my cue.

"Yes. You were right about the comfort part. There's something about hearing someone else moan and wail that makes you feel a little better. Like—"

"They have it worse," he said.

I just nodded, looking at the CD instead of him. I was glad we had this prop between us.

"That's the whole thing about grieving," Joe continued. "It's part of the deal: You get to be alive and to love, but in exchange you also have to put in some serious hurt time."

I couldn't believe he was saying these things to me. Nobody had been so direct about my situation. Not Mr. Churchwell, not Suzie Sirico that night on the white couch, not Nana driving our Volvo. Meg had the strong, stoic thing wired into her blood and would never dream of being so simple and ridiculously true.

"I'm sorry," he said. "I have no right to talk to you like that."

"No," I said, snapping out of it. "You can talk to me like that. I appreciate it." It sounded too bland and polite. In my mind I was throwing myself across the desk corner that separated us, wrapping my arms around his neck, adoring him.

Joe finally stood up. "So, Laurel," he began, "I know that you know that I want to ask you to the prom." He was smiling as he said this, showing that he appreciated the weirdness of what was coming out of his mouth. His eyes said, *Go ahead. Play along.*

"Okay. And I guess now I know that you know that I know."

We both laughed a little nervously.

"You wanna know how I know? I'm the one who started the rumor. I told my sister and her friend, and told them to make sure they told Megan Dill's sister. I guess that's not really enough people to be a rumor. Maybe just a buzz."

"A buzz," I echoed, nodding, feeling stupid.

"To give you a heads-up. I didn't want to take you by surprise."

"That's considerate," I said, cringing at another word from the Bland and Polite collection.

"I'm glad you think so," said Joe. "I was worried that maybe it was kind of chicken. Like it was the easy way to do it."

"There's nothing wrong with the easy way. I'm a big fan of it myself."

He looked at me and smiled again, those eyes, those eyes. It was the second or third instant with him that I thought, perhaps pity has nothing to do with this.

"So. Will you? Go to the prom? With me?"

"Yes. Of course," I said. It came out sounding vague, like I wasn't sure what I was agreeing to. "It'll be fun."

"That it will."

We paused. Suddenly, brilliantly, there was Meg standing in the doorway. She looked back and forth between us, as if she'd been flipping through channels and landed on something strange but fascinating.

"Hi, guys," she said, then looked sideways at me. "Do you still want to go eat?"

"Yeah. We're going into town," I told Joe. The whole school knew about our off-campus privileges.

He looked at Meg with a "You can trust me" face, then turned to me. "I'll call you. We'll talk."

I looked straight into his eyes again and forced myself to hold them there, counting one, two, three, before it became unbearable and I had to glance away.

EIGHT

I went with Meg, Nana, and Mrs. Dill to Bettina's Boutique to shop for our dresses. It was the one store almost everyone went to for the prom, since decades ago. They actually kept track of who bought what so you wouldn't get caught wearing the same thing as someone else—unless you wanted to, of course. Meg had desperately wanted to try Macy's or even go down to the city, but her mother insisted.

"It's a tradition," she said. "I bought *my* prom dress here."

"Further evidence as to why I should skip it," snorted Meg as we walked up the store's brick steps.

The boutique was now owned by Bettina's daughter, whose name we could never remember, so we called her Bettina 2.0. She greeted us as we walked in and smiled wide at me and Meg.

"Hello, girls!" she chirped. "All the prom stuff is over there; I call it the 'Prom Parade of Prettiness.' See the banner?"

She doesn't know who I am, I thought, and felt disappointed, and then felt bad about feeling disappointed.

Nana hurried toward the prom racks, which were organized by color, and in seconds was holding up something pink and fluffy.

"Oh, I like this," she said, as if she were going to wear it herself to the next Hospital Auxiliary luncheon. I shook my head and frowned, then followed Meg toward the dark dresses at the far end of the racks.

"Black all the way," Meg said. "Don't you think?"

"Not for me," I said. "Too obvious."

Meg froze for a second and looked at me sadly. "Right."

As she plunged her arms into the rows, I scanned the whole rainbow of the Prom Parade of Prettiness, not sure what I was even looking for. Bettina 2.0 had put up extra banners that said FUN & FLIRTY! and FOREVER YOUNG! but nothing jumped out at me. I let my eyes wander past the prom racks, into the rest of the store. There was a mannequin near the front, and all I could see was that she had her arms up in a sort of "Oh, to hell with it" pose. I went

80

over to get a closer look.

The dress did not make the mannequin look Fun & Flirty or Forever Young. It made this mannequin look like she was at the Oscars and owned the red carpet, even though she was made of plastic and had no face. It was a color blue I'd never seen before, and a material I didn't even know what to call. It caught the light in dazzling ways and begged me to touch it.

Somewhere in the corner of my gaze, I saw Bettina 2.0 and Mrs. Dill talking in low voices. I made out the words *remarkably well*.

Now I felt their eyes on me as I found the dress in my size on the rack next to the mannequin. I paused, then took a moment to notice the feeling of my jeans loose around my waist, saggy in the butt. It was a feeling I'd been ignoring, because it felt so unfamiliar. I let my fingers find the dress in the next size smaller, and headed to the fitting room. Meg noticed my beeline and motioned for the others to follow.

Minutes later I stepped out, toward the scary three-way mirror where everyone was waiting.

The dress wasn't perfect; at least, not the "It's so me!" kind of perfect. Instead, it looked like it was worn by someone else. This not-Laurel person's skin glowed pale against the blue fabric, and the overhead fluorescent light deepened the shadows under her eyes. She was older, and came from somewhere foreign like Europe or Vermont.

And it hung on her just right, with a long flared skirt, beaded bodice, and gauzy sleeves.

"This is it," I said to Meg. She nodded. I raised my head to look at Nana's reflection over my shoulder. I said it again: "This is it."

"It's not really a prom dress, and the color . . . ," Nana said weakly, but I just twirled, letting the fabric caress my legs. Finally, she just said, "You've lost weight." In the past, coming from her this would have been praise. Now she said it with worry, like she wasn't doing her job of getting me to eat.

I shrugged as casually as I could. I'd been trying half-heartedly for a year to drop a size, and now it had just happened and all I could feel was sad about it. I mean, could I afford to lose anything else?

Not the time or place to be sad, I told myself. *These were pounds you didn't want. Push it, push it, push it away.*

"Nana," I said as solidly as I could. "I love this dress. Don't you love it?" And Nana had no choice but to nod.

At the register, Bettina 2.0 looked wide-eyed at me as I handed her the dress, as if I were a celebrity she'd just now recognized.

"This is one of my favorites," she said. She fumbled for the tag and looked at the price. I'd already checked it and knew it was more expensive than any of the prom dresses. It was probably more expensive than anything else in the store.

"Oh . . . this is wrong," said Bettina 2.0, frowning. "This dress is actually on sale."

"Isn't that lucky!" exclaimed Nana.

I looked around the store. "There aren't any signs," I said.

"That doesn't matter," Bettina said, touching my arm across the counter. Now she looked at Nana. "I'm the owner, and I can put things on sale whenever I want."

I felt heat rise from the middle of my back. But Nana winked at Bettina 2.0 as she pulled out her MasterCard, and the someone-else dress was thirty seconds away from being mine.

The next day, Meg and I were walking through the senior parking lot on our way out of school when we heard a car driving slowly alongside us. I looked up to see that it was Andie Stokes's canary yellow VW Beetle.

"Hey!" yelled Andie from the driver's seat. She was alone in the car. I didn't think I'd ever seen her without Hannah or one of her other friends. "Laurel! How are you?"

I'd talked to Andie almost every day since I'd come back to school. She was always seeking me out after class or by my locker, touching one finger to my arm as she asked how I was and gave me an update on the memorial fund plans.

Meg and I approached her car. Other students walked

by extra slowly to check us out. *I am talking to Andie Stokes*, I thought, *and people are seeing me talk to Andie Stokes.*

"Hi Andie," I said.

"I'm glad I ran into you guys," she said, letting her eyes bounce between Meg and me. "I was in Mr. Churchwell's office today, looking at the prom seating chart, and noticed you weren't assigned to a table yet."

"We were going to let the guys figure it out," said Meg, which was sort of a lie. We hadn't even talked about tables.

"Well, I'll tell you that we have four empty seats at ours, and we'd love for you to join us."

Ours. We. Andie moved through life in a collective. I wondered what that would feel like, to always be part of a whole.

"I— Thanks— Cool—" was all I could say. I was still working on the not-a-moron thing with her.

"That's totally sweet of you," said Meg, stepping in. "We'll talk to Gavin and Joe and see if that works." Suddenly Meg and Andie were entering each other's cell numbers into their phones. While they did this, other students were forced to squeeze their cars around the Beetle on their way out of the lot.

Business done, Andie waved good-bye and drove off. Meg turned to me.

"What do you think?" she asked.

"What do I think about going to the prom and sitting with the cool crowd?"

"Other than the fact that it reminds you of *Carrie* and you might end the evening covered in pig's blood."

"Could be fun, could be so bizarre our heads will explode."

"I agree. But I'm going to bank on the fun part."

We stood there, popping our eyes at each other. The exciting reality of all this was beginning to sink in. The prom! The someone-else dress! Joe Lasky! Andie Stokes!

"Let's go to my place and put on our dresses again," said Meg, and I followed her through the parking lot.

In the mornings, right when I woke up, I usually had about two seconds of feeling like nothing had changed. I was in my bed in my room, and the light coming in from my blinds was the same light as always.

Then I'd remember.

And then I'd have to think of something to get me out of bed. Usually it was as simple as walking Masher or a test in English. Today, it was the SAT scores.

They had been available online as of five a.m., which was when I knew Meg had logged on. I checked the clock. Six thirty. Earlier than I usually woke up. My body must have known.

I walked slowly downstairs and wondered if I was nervous, how much I cared. Clearly a lot, since my hands shook a bit as I found the paperwork where I'd written my log-in information. They still shook as I entered it, and clicked the mouse where I was supposed to.

710 on the math. 790 on critical reading, 760 on writing.

790 on critical reading! A near-perfect score. I turned around to tell someone, but realized Nana was still sleeping. I picked up the phone to call Meg.

"How'd you do?" she answered.

I gave her the numbers.

"Rock on!"

"I didn't think I did that well. I wonder if they thought I cheated, since I took the test by myself."

"I doubt that."

We had another one of our awkward pauses.

"Laurel?" Meg asked softly.

"Yeah?"

"Aren't you going to ask me how I did?" Her voice got high.

"God, I'm sorry. How did you do?"

"I kicked butt too." Another pause. "I've got to go. We'll celebrate after school today."

We hung up, and almost instantly my speeding, soaring sensation—*festal*: meaning "joyous"!—hit a brick wall.

Dad.

He would have been standing here. Maybe he would have been the one to jiggle me awake just past dawn. He would have given me a high five and a hug, his customary

"I'm so proud of you, kiddo" combo, proclaiming that all my studying, the prep course, him quizzing me—it had all been worth it.

The image filled me with instant agony. *Make him go away. Don't ruin this, don't ruin this, don't ruin this.*

And with that, my father was gone.

When I walked into the house after school that day, I expected to find Nana making dinner. But it was quiet, and I followed that quiet upstairs to find the door to the guest room closed. I stepped closer to knock, but heard something soft and muffled on the other side. It sounded like one of the animals we sometimes heard in the woods at night.

It wasn't an animal. It was my grandmother, crying.

I jumped back, ran down to the kitchen. How long had she been doing that, while I was at Meg's, trying on our dresses and experimenting with hairstyles, snacking on Oreos and diet soda? I wondered how often she did that while I was at school, and then I stopped that wondering as quickly as I could.

There was no room in my head for the thought of Nana losing it. I needed her strong and wise and stoic. I needed her to remind me that my life could work, because her life seemed to be working.

I needed her to not need anything from me, because I had nothing to give.

Still, I found myself turning to go back upstairs, prepared to knock and see if she was okay, when the phone rang. I dove to get it so that Nana wouldn't be disturbed. "Hello?"

"Hello . . . Is this Laurel?"

"Yes?"

"Laurel, it's Suzie Sirico." She said it like we'd been chatting every day, the best of friends. Way too bubbly.

"Oh. Hi."

"I just thought I'd call and see how you and your grandmother were doing."

"We're okay," I said. "Busy." *I really am busy*, I added to myself. *I have new friends and I'm going to the prom with Joe Lasky in an awesome dress!*

I glanced up at the stairs, where I now heard the door to the guest room creaking slowly open. I pictured Nana on the landing, listening to try to figure out who I was talking to.

"I want to make sure you have my number if you need it." Suzie's voice, so steady and sure of itself, was possibly the most annoying thing I'd ever heard.

Was this how people in her line of work were supposed to drum up new business? God, she was no better than a telemarketer.

"We have your number," I said, not sure if that was true. "Thanks for calling."

I hung up as Nana came into the room. Her face was

freshly washed but her eyes tired, unfocused.

"Was that Suzie Sirico?" she asked.

"Yes," I said. "I have to get started on some homework." With that I brushed past her, knowing I should stay and chat or help her cook dinner, but unable to make myself turn back.

NINE

he limo driver's name was Manny, and he did crossword puzzles while waiting for people to be done with their weddings or finally arrive on late flights at the airport. He had a wife and a baby, and his sweet '78 Mustang was just back from the shop.

We learned these things about him during the ten-minute drive from Meg's house to the Hilton. It was easier to talk to Manny, through the open smoked-glass window dividing the front seat from the rest of the car, than make conversation with one another. I sat with Meg in the way-back, Joe and Gavin facing us. Gavin had a line of perspiration beading across his upper lip. He'd wipe it away, then two minutes later it was back.

"The Sweat Mustache," whispered Meg, her breath minty against the side of my face.

Joe playfully kicked my foot, which was dressed in one of Nana's black satin pumps and looked unattached to my body. I kicked back and smiled. Other than a light arm around my shoulder when we were posing for pictures, it was the first time we'd touched all evening.

At three, Meg and I had had our hair done at the Cosmos Salon. Hers: an updo with lots of curls. Mine: all down and straight. I got it trimmed a bit, to shoulder length, and even a few inches' weight off my head felt like a huge relief. We had spent the time since then getting dressed in Meg's room while Nana and Mrs. Dill drank tea downstairs. Meg showed me her new bra and announced her plans to fool around with Gavin at one of the after-prom parties. Later, I threw up in the Dills' hallway bathroom sink.

We'd done photos on the front steps, then, after the guys arrived, more in the driveway and over near the big pine tree at the edge of the lawn. Nana went inside twice to get Kleenex, and each time she took too long.

I thought of the photo of my mother in her prom dress. It would have been easy to suggest we take one picture inside, of Joe and me in front of the stairs, and even though it wasn't our house, it would have counted enough to make it into the double frame. But I didn't want to. Not then, at that moment, when things were moving along so smoothly.

At the Hilton, there was a long line of limos dropping kids off. Quick swishes of colors and fabrics. Gel on the boys' hair that glistened in the fading sun, and on the girls, corsages of every flower imaginable. If they put all their hands together, they'd make a field of bright, non-matching blooms.

We watched everyone from the right-side window, quiet. When it was our turn, Manny got out and opened the back door. The guys exited first and moved away, cluelessly leaving Manny to help us step from the car.

"Thank you, sir," said Meg, winking at him.

I just looked at the ground as he took my hand and pulled me onto the concrete, feeling everyone's eyes on me. When I raised my head to see where I was going, there was Joe, holding out his hand now like he was offering me a lifeline.

And then there was Andie Stokes and Hannah Lindstrom, with their dates, Ryan and Lucas. I wasn't sure who was with whom, but I couldn't imagine it mattered. Andie hugged me, tight, and then dropped back to check out the dress.

"Oh my God," she said. "You look amazing."

"Thanks."

"We have the best table. Come see." She beckoned, and we all followed her into the ballroom. As we passed under the orange and blue balloon arch, I turned to see where Joe was. But he wasn't behind me. I scanned the lobby until I spotted him talking with Mr. Churchwell, who shook his hand and clapped him on the back before letting him run to catch up. I turned back quickly so he wouldn't know that I saw.

Mr. Churchwell. It hadn't occurred to me before, but maybe he had something to do with all of this. With Joe, and with Andie and Hannah. But things were moving too fast for me to think more about it.

We did have the best table. It was farthest from the stage, centered along one side of the dance floor, next to French doors that opened onto the ballroom's balcony. Most of Andie's friends were already seated at the next table over—the second-best table—and we all waited for Andie to choose her seat. She did, and then everyone else fell into place, Meg and I next to each other.

I did a quick sweep of the rest of the room and the large circle of other tables. It was clear how the clique system of our school dropped invisible boundaries into this space. The popular seniors were on our other side, and I wondered how it was that a bunch of juniors got the prime real estate. Fanning out before us were the in-between kids, the ones who were jocks or geeks or a little bit of everything. On the opposite side of the circle, across from where I stood, was one table of Railroad Crowd kids. Not even a full table; just two pairs of couples sharing with members of the only decent rock band at school.

One half of one of those couples was Julia La Paz, David's girlfriend. Or former girlfriend, judging from how enthusiastically she leaned into her date, another Railroad guy. I tried to picture David there with her, at the prom, but couldn't. I would have bet money that proms weren't David's thing. Maybe Julia had been relieved that they'd broken up and she could go.

Dinner was loud and awkward. Joe and I and Meg and Gavin tried to talk over the din, while Andie and Hannah kept shouting to their friends at the next table. After everyone was done eating, the DJ started up his party music, but nobody made the first move to dance yet. I took the opportunity to go back to the bathroom and stand for three minutes in front of the full-length mirror.

This is me, I thought, nodding to the girl I saw in my reflection. With mirrors I was always looking for something wrong, something that could be thinner or brighter or higher. But unbelievably, I liked everything I saw in this girl.

This is me at the prom, and I look a little bit pretty.

The girl in the glass nodded too, as if to say, *Your secret's safe.*

For a second, I imagined my parents standing behind me. Mom on my left, Dad on my right. Nodding and proud. Now stepping into the frame was Toby with his video camera, shooting me a thumbs-up.

I whirled around fast to make them go away.

When I came back from the bathroom, everyone at our table was on the dance floor. I stood by the doorway alone for a moment, watching. It felt odd to be the one staring at everybody, instead of the other way around. Within seconds, Mr. Churchwell was next to me with his hand on my elbow.

"You okay?" he yelled.

"I'm just looking for my date," I yelled back, and jerked my elbow away from him.

Suddenly, Joe had wriggled out of the dance cluster, taking my hand, his palm warm and too tight, leading me to where Meg and Gavin were.

Then somehow I was moving, and Joe was looking at me like I was interesting, and the blue dress tickled as it swished around my ankles. Andie and Hannah smiled at me when I caught their eye. Some petals broke off from my corsage as I moved, and I watched them drop, then disappear under Meg's feet.

TEN

In the limo on our way to Adam LaGrange's after-prom party—new golf team captain, just got contact lenses, trying to build a rep—the configuration had changed. Gavin and Meg sat together on one seat, leaving Joe and me to share the other. My ears were still ringing and my feet were hurting, so I took off my shoes. Now they looked like part of my anatomy again, naked and familiar. I put them up on Meg's knees, and she started to rub.

"Do I get to be next?" said Gavin, nudging Meg with his elbow.

Meg smiled but didn't look up. "Sure."

She was going to do it, I could tell. She was going to fool around with Gavin, and I was pretty sure it was going to happen before we'd even left the party. I looked at Joe, who was trying to get something decent on the radio, the hair at his neckline fringed with dance-floor sweat. I felt an overpowering sense of dread.

When we got to Adam LaGrange's house, it was already packed. Meg and Gavin went into the yard to look for Adam, while Joe took my hand and led me downstairs to the den, where a folding card table had been converted into a fully stocked bar.

"What're you having?" he asked in mock James Bond.

I thought of the time Meg and I took samples from her mother's liquor cabinet, one capful at a time, taking notes on a Hello Kitty pad.

"Vodka tonic?" It was my dad's drink, every Friday night before dinner.

Joe mixed one for me, then one for himself, totally guessing on how much Smirnoff to put in. It hissed at me as I put it to my lips, bubbles hopping. It tasted sweet and dangerous. I started to go back upstairs, but Joe grabbed my hand again, pulled me toward a couch. There were maybe five other people in the room, and I saw them track us with their peripheral vision.

"So, did you have fun? It seemed like you did." I was getting used to this directness from Joe.

"Yes, of course. Couldn't you tell?"

"You're a great dancer."

"You too."

A pause. Drink sips, in unison.

"But you're feeling good, so far? You're feeling okay?" Joe said this with what looked like practiced concern on his face. I remembered the way Mr. Churchwell put his hand on Joe's shoulder, the nodding of their heads.

"You've been talking too much to school counselors," I said, pulling together all my courage to put my hand, lightly, on his knee. "Don't worry about it. I'm fine."

Joe drank again, then put his hand over mine. My heart skipped, *nervous, panic*, but then I glanced back up at the other people in the room, now two or three more. They were a horizon to focus on when I started to feel queasy.

So you might get your first kiss. Chill!

But I had waited so long for the right opportunity. When I'd come close in the past I always blew it. I got nervous and too jokey. The more I anticipated it, the more terrifying it became.

Where was Meg? I needed to grab her and drag her into a bathroom or closet, clutch her arm and say, "Is this it?" Meg had already had her first, second, and third kiss, all with guys who worked at her family's yacht club.

Now Joe was finishing his vodka tonic and going back to the bar, and I was gulping mine to keep up, something warming in my stomach. Then Meg was fluttering down the stairs, two at a time, holding her shoes in one hand

and the edge of her dress in the other. She ran up to me, laughing.

"There you are." She eyed my drink, then glanced at Joe behind the bar, getting a lesson in vodka-to-tonic ratios from a senior. "I see you're all taken care of."

"Want one?"

"No. I just wanted you to know where I'll be."

I gave her a dumb look.

"Manny told Gavin that the limo will be parked on the street," Meg said, "a couple houses up. Adam's folks set up a little party area for the limo drivers behind the pool house, so he won't be there."

"So?" Still dumb.

"So Gavin and I are going to hang out in the limo for a while."

I let my mouth fall open wide. It was meant to look like mock horror, but it wasn't all that mock.

She just smiled, kissed me on the cheek, and shot back up the stairs.

Suddenly Joe was at my side. "What was that?"

"They're going to hang out in the limo for a while."

Joe grinned, as if remembering something. "Let's go up to the backyard," he said. He grabbed my hand again, and I was getting used to that feeling of sudden heat, *zing*, shooting up my arm when he did that.

Upstairs, the party had gotten crowded, and getting to the backyard took several minutes. We wound our way through people, saying hi where appropriate, careful not to spill our drinks. Finally, stepping through the sliding glass doors onto Adam LaGrange's brick patio, a blast of fresh air. There were Christmas lights strung all around, reflected in the pool water. A cluster of people around the buffet table provided a low murmur against the music coming from inside and the soft shriek of cicadas.

I found myself looking around for Julia La Paz, but didn't see her, and felt relieved.

Joe's friend Derek came up to us with two beers, handed one to me, then the other to Joe, and walked away. I just stared at it, amber slightly glowing from the lights.

"Isn't there a saying about liquor before beer, or something like that?" I asked.

Joe just shrugged. "I've never been able to tell the difference." And then he finished his vodka tonic, placed the beer cup inside the empty one, and took a big long sip. Before he was finished, I did the same thing.

"If I get you drunk, your grandmother will never forgive me," he said, watching me gulp.

I swallowed and looked down at the beer again, churned up and foamy, an ocean after a quick summer storm. Already, I was feeling muscles relax that had been so tense for so long, I'd forgotten they even existed. My neck felt soft and my toes started to blend into one another so that I couldn't wiggle just one at a time.

Another beer and a half, and we found two lounge

chairs by the pool. They leaned us back too far to watch the rest of the party, so instead we stared at the sky. It was only halfway clear, with the stars muted, trying to make themselves seen through a layer of clouds.

"Wow," I said. "I can see Orion's Belt, but not the rest of him."

"Where?" asked Joe. "Oh, yeah. You're right. Where's the rest of him?"

"Maybe he left his belt behind and is off doing something else."

"Borrowing the Big Dipper to make some soup."

"Or hitting on Cassiopeia. I heard he does that."

Joe snorted and some beer came out his nose, which made me laugh too. Before I even realized I was doing it, I reached up and wiped the front of his shirt, now dotted with beer spray.

"I don't want you to get charged extra by the tux rental place," I said, avoiding his eyes as I did this.

"You know what I want?" he said. I still didn't look at him. "Actually, it's what I wish." He paused, and it seemed I had no choice anymore but to meet his gaze.

"What do you wish, Joe?"

"I wish Gavin and Meg weren't in the limo right now."

For a second, I didn't get it. Did he want them here with us? But then it dawned on me. He wanted *us* to be in the limo. Alone. Without people's eyes wandering toward us, always scanning to see where we were and what we were doing.

First, panic again. But I looked at him, him looking back at me as if we'd known each other forever, and I wasn't afraid anymore.

"Well, we still have most of the night, right?" It wasn't me who said that. Blame it on the girl in the not-Laurel dress.

"We have most of the night," Joe echoed, and then he was standing up. "I've gotta go find a bathroom. You all right here?"

I had my arms resting lightly on the lounge chair's edges, my ankles crossed, my heels popped out of my shoes. I was slightly drunk, and the thought of people seeing me sitting alone by a pool had no effect on me. I was definitely all right.

Joe was gone about a minute, maybe five. I'm not sure. I closed my eyes and listened to the murmurs, the music, rubbing my fingers lightly over my skirt.

"Hi," someone said from above me. I opened my eyes.

It was David.

This took a few seconds to register, the outline of his head frayed with Christmas lights. He had a bottle of something, too big to be a beer, in his hand, and there it was again, that pot smell. He was wearing a black jacket, but I could see the markings of a T-shirt decal underneath.

"Hey," I said, slowly sitting up. None of my usual David reactions were firing. No wanting to hide around a corner.

No urge to pretend we'd never played Batman and Robin or collected rocks in the woods or even known each other at all.

He walked around me and sat on the edge of the other chair, his elbows on his knees, the bottle—it was a two-liter soda bottle with no label, a flat, amber liquid inside—dangling between them.

"What are you doing here?" he asked.

"I was at the prom."

"You're drunk." David's bottom lip curled down a bit, and he sniffed.

"I don't think so." This conversation wasn't going in the right direction. "What are you doing here? Aren't you supposed to be with your dad?"

The thought of Mr. Kaufman made my vision tilt a little.

"Haven't been to the hospital in a few days," said David casually.

"Where have you been staying?"

"This guy I know. His folks are out of town." He looked at my dress, from the hem up. His eyes traveled quickly but steadily along the seam of the skirt, landed on my shoulder. "Nice outfit." David took a swig from his bottle and shook his head slowly.

"What?" I asked, taking the bait.

"I just can't believe you're here. All dressed up, doing the prom thing. A freaking corsage."

I fingered the miniature roses on my wrist, unable to

move beyond that, not knowing how to answer his non-questions. David took another swig from his bottle, and it occurred to me that he hadn't yet looked me in the eye. My hair, my shoes, anywhere safe and only distantly related to the person he was saying these things to.

"Leave me alone," I finally said, swallowing hard. It came out lame, weak, a little kid being bullied on the playground. My mother had taught Toby what to say when I teased him: *Sticks and stones may break my bones, but words will never hurt me.* It only made me laugh and tease him harder.

"You're living it up over here with Joe Lasky. Aren't you even the slightest bit broken up by what happened to you?" David said.

Something dark inside me knocked twice. *He's right, you know. Why are you in this place, when they can't be? Just like you were home that night when you should have been with them.*

"That's none of your business," I said, trying to make it sound forceful. But then suddenly I popped out with: "What about you? If you're here, why can't I be here?"

"Because we're just crashing this party. Do you see me wearing a goddamn tux? My buddies and I came here to pour some kamikaze in the punch, then leave."

He held up his bottle as proof, but the kamikaze—if that's what it was—was almost gone. Where was Joe? Joe would make David go away.

David saw me looking toward the house. "Laurel, you can go to as many proms as you want, but it's not going to change things."

"I know that."

"You're an orphan. That's what I heard someone say inside. 'She's an orphan now.'"

The word made me think of Dickens, of Pip and David Copperfield and even *Oliver!* It wasn't me. Clinically, officially, yes, but I'd never connected to it.

I must have looked shocked, because David regarded me now with more regret than anger.

"That came out sounding way harsher than I thought it would," he said, then looked down at his kamikaze accusingly. I noticed his hands were shaking. "I wasn't prepared to see you here," he added, his voice a little deflated now.

But if he was deflating, I was doing the opposite. Something in me was filling with air.

"You're an orphan too," I said, as matter-of-factly as I could. This made David stand up, his confusion giving way to defensiveness.

"No, my dad is still alive. He'll be fine."

"If that's what you want to believe. Personally, I think he's going to be a veg forever."

I blamed that one on the alcohol, making me brave for one or two seconds at a time.

"Shut up," he snapped.

So I'd struck a nerve.

"Which is what he deserves," I said, "considering he killed four people."

David paused, his hand squeezing the plastic bottle so tight I heard it pop a bit. "My dad wasn't drunk."

"He didn't have to be drunk," I said. "He just had to be careless. Either way, he's a murderer."

David wanted to hit me. I could tell. He wanted to hit me so bad that his heels came up out of his shoes. I had put my beer cup on the ground, and now he kicked it into the pool, where it landed without making noise.

Even though he was standing and I was sitting, I could feel things shift. I had found a box of ammunition somewhere, tucked into the back of my mind. What else was in it?

"What about Masher?" I asked, as if we were a married couple breaking up, figuring out custody of our joint life.

"What about him?"

"I don't have to take care of him. I can give him back to your grandparents."

David shook his head, looked away. "You can't do that. They don't want him."

"Then you want me to take care of him?"

David's face had caved in a bit, the shadows carving deeper across his cheeks and chin. He didn't seem that different from Toby after one of our arguments, after I'd beaten him on every front. This was when Toby would have jumped on me for the wrestling portion of the program, but I was pretty sure David wasn't about to do that.

"Yes," he said, and placed his kamikaze bottle carefully on the ground.

"Yes, what?" That's what this ammunition box was. Big-sister power. The only power I had in the world, at least when Toby was still in it.

"Take care of my dog, please," whispered David. He turned around and walked back toward the house, then around it in the direction of the driveway. I watched him cross paths with Joe, who looked at David, registered where he was coming from, and searched me out in the half-light. In seconds he was running over to me.

"What was David Kaufman doing here?" asked Joe, breathless. "Did he talk to you?"

"Yeah."

"What did he say?"

I opened my mouth to recap it, to report it to Joe in order to make it all real, but instead a noise came out like a sob. Loud, a short barking burst.

"Oh my God," said Joe, and he scrambled onto the lounge chair with me, his hand on my back. "What happened? What's the matter?"

I turned my head to answer him and wow, his face was so much closer than I thought. There wasn't enough room between us for words.

So I kissed him. I had practiced on my pillow dozens of

times, and I was so used to that pillow that I didn't even expect Joe to kiss back. But he did, his lips warm and larger than I imagined they'd be. Hesitant at first, a little confused, but then confident and well-trained. He put his hand on the side of my head, his palm moist against my ear, his fingers crunching against hairspray. I stepped out of us for a second, in my head, to get a wide-angle shot of how it looked from a few feet away, wondering if it matched what I'd seen in movies and on TV.

Joe pulled back after a little while, glancing around to see who might be watching.

"Why are you stopping?" I asked, also looking around.

Joe turned back to me and smiled. "I have no idea." Now he put both hands on my face, one on either side, and drew me closer. His turn at kiss initiation was softer than mine, gentle, as if we had all the time in the world.

Fooling around with Joe lasted minutes, but I couldn't tell you how many. I had crawled into a place inside myself, hearing only my own thoughts and what Meg called "mixing tuna" noises. *Do I open my eyes? What if I open them and his are open too? I should open my eyes.*

Happy, nervous, angry, excited. Neurons exploding in fireworks.

I was laughing and then, I was crying. It started when I was still lip-locked with Joe, and it took him a few moments to pull away and see why my shoulders were heaving up and down.

"Laurel?" he asked.

I wanted to look up and smile, wipe away my tears, then wink at him for some damage control. But I couldn't. I was just staring at his hand on my knee, and I was wailing.

"Oh my God . . . ," said Joe, standing up. Backing away.

I put my face in my hands and let the top half of me fall toward the lounge chair, a violent crumple. Noises were coming out of me that I didn't think I was capable of. Noises like I was being physically attacked, afraid for my life, a girl in an alley at midnight.

The pressure of my hands against my eyelids was making me see starbursts, yellow and red, but I was seeing David's face too.

A freaking corsage. You're an orphan.

I heard Joe's feet move away, scuffling against the patio. "Hang on, I'm going to get Meg," he said.

I looked up to watch him go, running. Running from me, because I'd totally freaked him out. Three minutes ago we were playing Tongue Twister, and now he was fleeing for his life. I should have been wearing a label on the back of my dress that said CONTENTS UNDER PRESSURE. OPEN WITH CARE.

"No!" I yelled, an answer to nothing. *"No!"*

I stood up, grabbed the lounge chair, and flung it across the patio. It was lighter than I thought it would be.

Now I had an audience. Whoever had been standing around, sneaking peeks at Joe and me, was signed on for

110

the full performance.

I picked up the other lounge chair and threw it into the pool. It landed with a big splash and slowly started to sink. Things got very quiet, and I think someone even turned off the music inside the house. With no place to sit anymore, I moved to the lawn and lay down on my side, my right arm over my face, my left hand pulling chunks of grass out of the ground. The wailing came back, rushing out of my body.

Before too long, Meg was kneeling in front of me. "Laurel? It's me. I'm here."

I couldn't even pull my arm away from my face. Didn't want to look at her. "I'm sorry. God! I'm so sorry."

"Laurel, please just get up. Sit up. . . . Gavin, can you go get some Kleenex or something?"

I heard Gavin rush away, his feet on the patio like Joe's a few minutes earlier.

For Meg I sat up, even as another wave overtook me and I sobbed again. She held me and I felt her wrist corsage poke the back of my neck. We began to rock.

"Shhhh . . . shhhh . . . it's okay," she said.

"I—"

She cut me off. "Don't talk. Just breathe."

Gavin was back. Joe was with him. They stood there, their legs forming a sparse, silent forest around me and Meg. Joe held out the box of tissues, letting it hover over our heads, but neither of us took it from him.

ELEVEN

I woke up to the sound of thunder and heavy rain pinging against my window.

It wasn't really "waking up," exactly. It was more like opening my eyes away from the half sleep that had been pulling my mind along a string of strange thoughts and images.

At one point I was thinking about what my brother looked like when they buried him, whether they'd combed his hair back with gel or left a careful forelock to frame his face. Which made me think of the six months in middle school when I used styling mousse because I thought it made me look more like a character on my favorite TV show. That led me to my seventh-grade art teacher, Ms. Weber, who married our English teacher Mr. Weber and everyone thought it was so incredible that they already had the same name. Then this got me thinking about whether or not I would keep Meisner when I got married or become a Mrs. Somebody.

I jumped back to that first thought of Toby in his casket, feeling horrified and ashamed. How could this have landed me in the "fantasize about your future husband" place?

It had been three days since the prom. Three days since Manny drove Meg and me and Joe and Gavin to my house in total silence, me hugging Meg tight with my eyes closed, and Nana giving me a pill and putting me to bed for the night. In those three days I had not gotten out of bed, and since the moment that pill wore off I hadn't gotten any real sleep, either. I wouldn't let Nana dose me again. It felt like cheating.

Meg called the day after.

"I don't know what to say, Laurel. I really just don't have a clue." She sounded nervous, unsure of herself.

"It's okay," I said. "I'll be okay." I tried to sound like I believed it.

"Call me if you need anything," said Meg, more casually now, as if a quick trip to the drugstore for shampoo and Tylenol would solve all my problems.

Joe had called too. Twice. I'd had Nana tell him I was

sleeping. It was nice to know he was concerned—*Tell Laurel I hope she's feeling better* was the message—but I couldn't bring myself to talk to him. Even though I could still feel his lips on my lips, his hand on my neck, when I tried to picture his face all I could see was how he'd looked at me when I started to sob. It was just too mortifying.

Then there was the thought of David, smirking and frowning and collapsing, and retreating. David cruel and bullying, then David quivery and scared like the little boy I still remembered despite my best efforts not to. All that morphing left me baffled and intrigued and ultimately filled with sorrow; then I reminded myself of what he'd taken from me—a lovely night, a sweet first kiss, a memory to hold on to—and that brought back a swell of fury. If the swell started to go down, I added in the image of Mr. Kaufman driving his SUV, squinting and slurring and swerving, and it grew again.

Sometimes I imagined what I'd do if I had a time machine and could go back to a single minute, any minute, of my life. In this time machine I'd travel to the minute of the accident night where, instead of asking permission to go home and work, I'd decide to go to Freezy's with everyone else. My parents and Toby and I would walk back to our house and get into our own car, planning to meet the Kaufmans there. Mr. Kaufman would even be kind of bummed that we won't get to check out his sweet new car, and my dad would be glad about it. We'd have dessert, and it would be totally boring, and then we'd come home to more boringness. But my parents would be downstairs now, arguing with Toby about leaving his socks on the couch.

The no-sleep thing made it all worse, of course, but I didn't seem to have any say in the matter. I'd gotten used to the headache and the pain behind my eyes, the sensation of pressure on my every muscle. This kind of exhaustion made me feel somehow more awake.

And my family's bodies kept me company.

I couldn't stop thinking about what they looked like. Nana had insisted on closed caskets. It was Jewish tradition, she said, but I knew it was also because of the burns and because of my mother. She'd been an organ donor, and somewhere out there, there were people alive with parts of her in them. I knew I'd be able to get that information someday. I might even want it, someday. But for now, all I could do was think of Mom as Sally from *The Nightmare Before Christmas*, with stitchwork seams holding her together.

What did their skin look like? How bad were the burns? Did their faces look peaceful, or anguished?

I wished I'd had the presence of mind at the funeral to really look at those three caskets, one shorter than the other two. To tell myself that this was the last time my parents and Toby would physically be in the world together, and hold that moment close enough to feel like a good-bye.

Now the rain tapped harder against the glass, as if trying to shake those images loose. I had to get my family out of those caskets and talking, breathing. Doing stuff.

What a shame not to be outside today, Mom said in my head. My mother hated any day that didn't involve sunshine. She'd seek it out wherever she went, moving her plastic lounge chair around the backyard as the bright spot traveled. She sucked up sunlight like a plant in photosynthesis, and never saw the beauty in bad weather.

Dad did, though. His voice now: *Whoa, look at how the wind blows the rain sideways. Watch the sky. We might just see some lightning. Hey Laurel, there's a word on your SAT list that fits here. Can you guess it?*

Yes, Dad. *Fulminate*: "to cause to explode."

Toby. What was Toby saying?

I'm going outside anyway! I pictured him by the door, putting on his rubber boots, grabbing an empty jelly jar in case he found something worth keeping. He liked to bring back slugs and pour salt on them to watch them shrivel up, and I'd yell at him for being so cruel.

My body shook down into sobs again, and I grabbed the towel Nana had left folded on my nightstand. We'd given up on Kleenex that first post-prom day.

Now Nana must have heard I was officially awake and knocked on the door once before coming in. She didn't creep into the room slowly anymore but rather stepped briskly all the way inside.

"Will you get out of bed today, sweetie?"

"Probably not."

Nana's mouth fell into a flat line, and I turned to gaze at the ceiling.

"I think you should. I talked to Suzie Sirico. She can make time to see you today."

"Please stop with the Suzie stuff. It's not going to happen."

Nana sighed and left with the same forced-fast movement she'd arrived with. I got the feeling that to her, my bedridden, grief-soaked, deep-black funk had a forty-eight-hour time limit and had just expired.

But time didn't seem to matter anymore. It was something that could be stretched or twisted or thrown down to the floor as I saw fit. In the back of my fuzzy, buzzing mind, I knew it was now Tuesday. I imagined the rhythm of the school week, the air still electric with tales of Laurel's Freak-Out. The people who'd actually witnessed it suddenly in demand and more important. And Joe, who'd actually been *kissing* me at the time. I couldn't even think about it.

I rolled toward the wall and covered my head with a pillow, then heard Masher come in, the slight jingle of his collar. Nana must have left the bedroom door ajar. *Sniff, sniff, sniff,* very businesslike at my shoulders and back.

Thud as he planted his butt on the floor, *thump, thump* went his tail. Usually it took Masher just a few seconds of my not responding to leave, the jingling slower and fainter on the way out. But now the *thump, thump* kept thumping. I took the pillow off my face and turned to face him.

"Sorry, buddy, not today. Ask Nana to let you out in the yard."

Masher was doing the big-eyed head tilt that dogs do when they're trying to work you, but to me, right now, he belonged to the person who had caused the most embarrassing moment of my life. I rolled back and waited for the sound of him leaving, which took a few seconds. Then the sound down the hall of Masher whining, and Nana muttering something, and the back door opening and closing.

It was the last thing I heard before drifting into a real, complete, dreamless sleep.

"Laurel? You sound weird."

"I just woke up from a nap."

I'd been sleeping for eight hours when Meg called, and Nana brought the phone in and made me sit up. The light had traveled to the late-afternoon spot in my room, and although my body was still only half-awake, it felt full, like it had been starving and just stolen a huge meal.

"How are you feeling today?" Meg asked, her voice insecure again. I hated to hear her like that, with me.

"I slept. That's good, I guess." I wanted to ask her about

school, about Gavin. I had a vague memory of Meg holding me the other night, her hair fallen out of its updo, the straps of her dress crooked on her shoulders from the interrupted make-out session in the limo. But the words didn't come.

"That's definitely good," she said, then drew in a quick breath and added, "I know it's probably the last thing you want to think about right now, but I have to ask you a question."

"Okay."

"About PAP."

Ugh.

PAP meant Performing Arts Program. It was a nearby day camp run by the county. A few months ago, Meg and I had both landed sought-after summer jobs as assistant counselors.

"You forgot about it," she teased gently.

"No," I lied, my throat suddenly dry.

"Well, our paperwork is due this week."

"You said you had a question."

"Are you still going to do it? With me?"

When I'd interviewed for the job, the director asked me why I wanted it, and I'd answered, "Because I love theater, especially everything that goes on behind the scenes, and I want to share that love with young kids. I think I have a lot to give your campers."

But now it seemed like years ago that I'd had anything

120

to give anyone, especially a bunch of overdramatic middle schoolers.

"I don't think I can," I said to Meg, struggling to keep my voice from collapsing.

"That's what I figured, but . . . I had to ask." She paused. "Is it okay with you if I still do it?"

We'd gone to interview together, and when we heard we'd been hired, our texts to each other contained a thousand exclamation points. A summer together! Working at this fun camp! With cute older college guys as counselors!

"You should do it," I said, then, brighter: "I want you to do it."

"Okay." Meg paused. "I miss you."

"Talk later," was all I could say back, before I hung up and crawled back under the covers to cry.

The stairs in our house usually creaked, but I knew where to step on each one to avoid that. On some steps the creak was on the left, on others it was the right, and with one it was exactly in the middle.

I put my foot on this step and gently moved my weight over it, remembering how long it had taken me to find the sweet spot. Years, really.

Getting up in the middle of the night for a drink of milk was a thing I'd done forever. When I was a toddler, I took a sippy cup to bed. My parents let me, probably because it helped keep me asleep all night, but my first cavity at age five put an end to all that. They offered me a cup of water as a compromise, but I refused. Then I'd wake up and reach for something that wasn't there anymore, and start to thrash when I realized I couldn't suck milk through my teeth and wash away the bad dreams. I started sneaking into the kitchen to take a swig from the gallon jug in the fridge, swish it around my mouth, and then go upstairs and back to sleep.

Even during these days after the prom, it was the one time besides going to the bathroom that I ventured out of my room. I didn't want Nana to know. I was aware of her keeping track of my bathroom visits, could feel her listening to my movement across the hall and back. She and Masher were alike that way; if Nana's ears could have pricked up like a dog's whenever the door of my room opened, I'm sure they would have.

But Masher was the only one who knew about my milk trips. I'd just make it into the kitchen and reach for the refrigerator door when I'd hear the *click, click, jingle, jingle* of his toenails and collar on the hardwood floor behind me. Before the prom, I welcomed the company, taking a few moments to pet him before heading back upstairs.

Now he stared at me as I opened the milk carton and raised it to my lips, a needy intrusion. I ignored him.

When I was done, I looked at the carton. In the past, it was always a gallon jug; we needed that much milk in the house, between Toby and me drinking it and Dad's coffee and Mom's tea, and cereal and scrambled eggs and the occasional cookbook recipe.

I hadn't seen this difference until now; Nana was buying less milk. I looked around the half darkness of the kitchen, illuminated only by the stove light. What else had changed?

In the pantry, the shelves were full but familiar things were missing. Like the Flamin' Hot Cheetos that Toby loved so much. My mom would buy them for him and then yell about the neon orange dust on everything he touched.

The counters were clean. That was unusual. My mom and dad played a game of Wiping Chicken when it came to the counters. Each one thought it was the other's job and would only give in with sighing resentment. Which didn't happen all that often; crumbs and spill stains were things I'd stopped noticing a long time ago.

Then I noticed the knife block. Nobody in our house could agree on which knife went in which slot. We each had our own way of doing it. Dad always put them in so the blades were facing left because he was left-handed; Mom and I did it randomly. Toby always put the small knives in the big slots out of sheer laziness. But now they were organized perfectly; each one in its place, each blade facing to the right. I pulled one out and it looked shinier, sharper than ever.

Holding the knife with the blade against my palm, it

became so clear how my life would only contain shadows now. Shadows of things gone; not just the people themselves but everything connected to them. Was this my future? Every moment, every tiny thing I saw and did and touched, weighted by loss. Every space in this house and my town and the world in general, empty in a way that could never be filled.

I can't do this.

The thought doubled me over and I sank to the floor, the knife still in my hand.

And besides, why should I?

Seeing the silver of the knife in contrast to the textured skin on my wrist, I couldn't push the dangerous question out of my head.

What do I have to live for that's worth this much pain?

I'd seen the movies in health class and gone to the school assemblies. I had considered myself depressed a few times, in middle school and for a good solid month in ninth grade. I'd wondered about the different ways you could off yourself, and which one I might choose if it came to that. Didn't everyone think about that stuff?

But the word *suicide* had always seemed rather cliché.

Yeah, yeah. Don't make that "final decision." We get it!

But now I got it in a totally different way.

"You know how Hemingway killed himself?" my dad once asked me when he saw I was reading *A Farewell to Arms* for English class. "He put a gun in his mouth and pulled the trigger. I have a lot of respect for that. Messy, but quick. Who wants to bleed to death in a bathtub or free-fall for several seconds off a building?"

"I like the car-running-in-the-garage approach," I'd said. My father and I had a way of turning these types of conversations—horrifying, really—into an easy joke.

"Too wimpy," he said. "So you go to sleep and it's not messy or painful. I mean, if you're going to do it, do it!"

If you're going to do it, do it.

There was nothing at this moment to stop me. I looked at the knife again for what could have been two seconds or two minutes. Everything around me and inside of me froze.

"Laurel?"

Nana's voice like a phone ringing, that high, clear startle. The kitchen flooded with light.

I looked up at her, as she looked down at me and then at the oversized utensil in my hand.

Her expression made me drop it to the floor with a clang.

TWELVE

Suzie Sirico's office was really just a small converted den in her very large house. It was on the first floor and had its own entrance around the back, and I felt a little like hired help as I made my way along the stepping-stones across the grass to a white wooden door.

Inside were a couch and two chairs, with a coffee table between them. Everything was overstuffed and brightly patterned, like one of those rooms you see in a home catalogue that you can't imagine real people ever actually using.

"Oh, look," my mom would say when these things came

in the mail. "One-stop shopping for people who don't have any style but want to pretend they do." She could be a snob about who was born with an artistic eye and who was not.

Suzie sat in one of these carefully designed chairs with a legal pad and pen on her lap, resting her hand in her chin as she gazed at me with curiosity.

I sat on one end of the couch—the end farther from Suzie—with both hands tucked between my knees.

I was here. Bathed, dressed, out of the house.

"Laurel, you will do this. For me. Yes?" Nana had half asked as she put me to bed the night before.

Yes, I would do this. For her.

Now Suzie smiled a bit, still curious, like I was a package she'd found on her doorstep but didn't want to open yet. We had been sitting in silence for a full minute.

"I'm glad you're here," she said finally.

It wasn't a question, so I didn't answer.

"I heard that Gabriel Kaufman was moved to a long-term care facility in New Jersey, and that David's staying with relatives nearby."

"Oh." Even just hearing Mr. Kaufman's name was like a slap in my face, but I didn't let on.

"I thought maybe you'd heard from him, since you still have his dog." She made it sound like I'd borrowed one of David's CDs and kept forgetting to give it back.

"No, I haven't." I stared at my thumbs lined up next

to each other and noticed how the two sets of knuckle creases didn't quite match.

"I bring up David because I understand you recently had an upsetting experience with him."

Yeah, thanks for reminding me.

"Do you want to talk about it?"

I looked at her now and just shook my head. Suzie regarded me for a second, then wrote something on her pad. I watched the tip of her pen wiggle as it made a smooth scratching noise, as if whispering something back to her.

"Okay," she said abruptly, plopping the pad down on the end table next to her. "Then I have something fun I'd like to show you."

Suzie got up and went to her bookcase, found a wooden box next to a figurine of a fairy sitting on a rock, and sat back down. She opened the box and pulled out what looked like an oversized deck of cards.

"We call these Feeling Flash Cards," she said, smiling as she glanced at one. "I think of them as a game. I show you a card with the beginning of a sentence, and you say the first thing that comes to mind to complete the sentence. Shall we try it?"

This sounded stupid, but I didn't even have the energy to say that. It was easier just to shrug and nod.

Suzie pulled out a card, eyed it with another grin, and flipped it toward me.

Below a picture of a red wilting flower were the words: I BELIEVE WHEN SOMEONE DIES, THEY . . .

Are watching me.

That's what popped into my head, taking me by surprise. But I couldn't echo it with spoken words. I hated to think of what that would lead to.

Instead, I said, "Gone."

Suzie raised an eyebrow. "Gone, how?"

"Just gone."

I looked back at the card expectantly, like *Hit me again.* Suzie frowned but flipped over the next one.

I AM ANGRY BECAUSE . . .

Nothing will go as planned.

Huh? No.

"I have to be here today."

Suzie gazed at me, again with the curiosity, and then gingerly laid the card back on the deck. She took great care to slowly replace the first card, put the top on the box, and place it on the end table next to her pad. Her movements seemed calm, yet hostile.

"Laurel," she said, looking at me now with commitment, her face clear of questions. Right in the eyes. "Do you believe your relationship with your parents and your brother is over?"

The force of this made me unfurl. My shoulders hit the back of the couch and my hands came out from between my knees. I didn't know what to do with them, so I folded them protectively over my stomach.

"Of course it's over. They're dead."

"So they will never be part of your life again?"

"Well, yeah. They're *dead*." Why did I have to repeat that? Had she gotten me mixed up with someone else?

"They won't have any more influence on you? They won't contribute to who you are or the decisions you make?"

Now it was my turn to look at Suzie with curiosity.

"Laurel, you have suffered a terrible, horrible loss. Greater than most people can imagine. But you can survive this trauma, and one of the many ways that will help you do that is to think of your relationship with your mom, your relationship with your dad, and your relationship with your brother as things you can work on and develop, even though these people you love are not living."

I felt something latch open inside me, and the first heat of tears in my eyes. It was an unfamiliar heat, of relief.

Suzie did not smile or nod or seem at all victorious at breaking through like this. She looked at me with even more determination.

"This will be hard, Laurel. But it will be worth it."

I slept that night, but woke up early to the sound of someone gagging and coughing. When I opened my eyes, the first thing I saw was Selina on the pillow next to me, staring with disgust at the source of the sound.

Which was Masher, in the middle of my room, spitting something onto the purple rug. There was a foamy pink stain next to a pile of my clothes.

Gross, I thought. What had he eaten that was pink?

But my color-mixing skills as a painter snapped on and reminded me, *Red and purple make pink.*

He was puking up blood.

I jumped out of bed and grabbed Masher gently by the ears, forcing him to look at me. His eyes were bloodshot, and although this was the first time I'd touched him in days, he didn't seem to react. He just pulled his head away and dropped it to the floor, where I noticed an older pink stain a few feet away.

"Nana!" I yelled.

I heard frantic footsteps getting louder, and then Nana burst into my room, looking panicked. "What? What happened?"

"Masher's sick."

She closed her eyes and put her hand on her chest. "For goodness' sake, Laurel!" She steadied her breathing. "The dog?"

"Did you notice anything last night?"

Nana looked at Masher distastefully at first, then softened.

"No. He wanted to go out, so I let him. He came back a little later than usual, maybe."

"I think we need to call the vet. The number's on that

emergency list by the phone downstairs."

Nana looked at me, then back at Masher. I don't know which of us looked more pathetic.

"Do you want me to get it?"

"If you could," I said.

Dr. Fischer had been our vet for years. Her daughter was in Toby's class. Then I thought of her and her staff, seeing me. Knowing what had happened on prom night. Knowing, period.

Nana was almost out the door when I said, "I don't think I can take him. Can you do it?"

She turned slowly and made a little *ha!* noise. "No, Laurel. You took this dog in. You are responsible for him."

I turned to Masher, his eyes not even pleading any-more, and pushed David's face out of my mind so it was no longer connected to the dog.

"Then bring me the Yellow Pages," I said. "I'll find another vet."

Ashland Animal Hospital was on Ashland Road in the town just east of ours, but lucky for them they were listed first in the phone book. Nana pulled into a parking space and glanced at me in the rearview mirror. I was sitting in the backseat with Masher in my arms.

"Do you want me to call David's grandmother? I'm sure she can get in touch with him."

"No!" I said.

"Laurel, he should know."

"It's my fault he got sick. I'll deal with it."

"You'll have to tell him eventually."

"Not if I can help it. . . ." My voice was on the verge of anger. I could only see Nana's eyes and eyebrows framed in the little rectangle of the mirror, but from her silence I knew she got it.

"Do you want me to come in?" she asked, sighing a little. Giving in.

"Only if you want to."

"I brought a book," she said, pointing to a paperback lying on the front seat next to her, which I took to mean that Nana would be reading in the comfort of the car and not a smelly animal hospital waiting room.

"Okay. I'll come out and keep you posted."

I hooked Masher onto his leash and lifted him out of the car, then guided him slowly into the building. The second we walked in, a tiny dog wearing a red sweater started barking at us. Masher could have nibbled that thing like a snack, but he cowered from it, and that told me just how serious this was.

We made it to the front desk by walking the perimeter of the room, away from the yapping mini-whatever.

Just five minutes later, we were in an exam room with Masher lying on the table, staring at the wall. I followed his gaze to a poster of two fluffy kittens wearing sunglasses and berets, with the caption "A Couple of Cool Cats!"

"Yeah," I said to him. "That's just wrong."

There was a quick knock on the door before the doctor came in.

"Hi, I'm Dr. Benavente," he said in a voice that sounded much younger than he looked. He had salt-and-pepper hair and big glasses, and looked more like a mad scientist in his white coat than a vet, but also like someone you could trust.

"I'm Laurel, and this is Masher."

He smiled sadly at Masher. "Hi, buddy," he said. Then, almost as an afterthought, he glanced at me and added, "Nice to meet you. So what's going on with this guy? They tell me he's coughing up blood?"

"Yes. And he seems pretty out of it."

"It just started this morning?"

"Yes." I thought so. Truth was, he could have been doing this for a day or two and I wouldn't have noticed.

I watched as Dr. Benavente examined Masher's eyes, ears, and mouth, and felt around his belly. His face was like a stone, and I couldn't read it.

"Has he had diarrhea? Anything with blood in it?" the doctor asked.

"I—I don't know." How could I tell him nobody had been walking Masher lately? Then I remembered something from the day before: Nana yelling at him downstairs, saying things like "disgusting" and "shouldn't be doing this" loud enough for me to hear.

Dr. Benavente looked at me a little differently now, like I'd just slid into a new category for him. Someone who did not take good care of her pet.

"We'll run some tests, but my gut feeling is that this guy has ingested rat poison. It's unfortunately very common; to dogs, rat poison looks just like kibble. But it's also potentially lethal to them. I think we may have caught this early enough, but he's going to need some emergency treatment."

I put my hand over my mouth and then struggled to say something intelligent. "So why is there blood?"

"Some rat poisons kill by interfering with an animal's blood clotting, so Masher's bleeding internally. I think he ingested it at least twenty-four hours ago, so it's too late to induce vomiting, but we can give him vitamin K injections that will help his blood clot and stop the hemorrhaging. I'd like to keep him here for a couple of days for treatment and observation. Does that sound okay?"

He'd had me at "bleeding internally." The tears were streaming down my face now, and I couldn't even look at Masher; I had to focus on the ridiculous beret kittens to keep some control.

"Please do whatever you have to do," I said.

"Go out front and give this to Eve," he said, handing me a yellow paper with illegible scrawl on it. "We'll get started, and I'll give you an update as soon as I have one."

I just nodded, and while Dr. Benavente picked up

Masher, I locked eyes with the dog once and said, "I'm so sorry . . ." before running out.

At the front desk, a girl a few years older than me, maybe college age, was punching at fax machine buttons and cursing under her breath.

"I'm supposed to give this to Eve," I said, waving the yellow paper.

"That's me," she said, reaching out to take it. She glanced at the notes and her lower lip jutted out, turned down. "Poisoning is rough. But you're in good hands."

"Thanks."

"Do you want me to run up an estimate of the costs?"

The costs.

Before I knew it I was crying again.

"Oh God, please don't cry . . . ," said the girl. "It's going to be okay. There are ways we can help if it's a financial burden."

I sniffled and shook my head. "No, it's not that. I mean, it is a little. But mostly I just feel so awful. This isn't even my dog, but it's my fault he got sick, so of course I should—"

"This isn't your dog?" Eve asked, a new concern drawn on her face. She had long blond bangs that half-covered her eyes.

"Not officially. I . . . He lives with me, but he's not . . ." I looked at Eve, who was listening, confused and interested. She did not know me or David or what had happened.

This was why I'd come here. I realized it was the first time since losing my family that I was with people who didn't know about the accident, which felt frustrating and freeing all at once.

"His owner can't take care of him at the moment . . . ," I finally continued, steadying myself. "So I took him in for a while."

Eve's wariness turned into a big smile, like now I was speaking her language. "Good for you," she said approvingly. She stared at me for another few seconds and then said, "Hey, I don't know if you're looking for a job or anything, but we need someone to help out in the office for the summer. We have a current student, but she's leaving next week."

I stood frozen for a moment. A job?

"Or maybe you know someone. I was going to post something at the high school today. It's just a few hours a week. I'm not sure how much time you have."

I thought of Nana in the car and Meg at school and the wide, unstructured expanse of my bed. Then I asked, "Can you tell me more about what it involves?"

i want to c u! can i come dwn?

I texted Meg as soon as Nana and I got home. The sky had gone white and the air was hanging heavy in preparation for something. But after my morning, the punch of seeing Masher suffering and having to leave him at the vet's, and then arranging to come in on Monday to start training as a summer office assistant, I didn't feel like staying in the house.

r u kidding? get here asap! came the text back from Meg.

"Is it okay if I go over to Meg's?" I asked Nana. Her eyes brightened. They had already sparkled a little when I'd asked her permission to start working at the vet's. Anything that got me out into the world again, doing stuff, apparently caused some kind of power surge inside her.

"Of course. Just call me if you think you'll be awhile."

I nodded and headed down the hill to her house.

It was the first time since the accident that I'd walked the distance between our house and the Dills', instead of driving, and it hit me: *It's summer.* It had still been spring when my family died, the trees just starting to swell again, the grass patchy. Now, just seven weeks later, a thick fabric of green draped the houses in my neighborhood and fell in clumps along both sides of the road I'd walked so many times in my life. The wind blew everything this way and that, the buzz of cicadas rising and falling with the same rhythm. I was used to noticing scenery and landscapes because of my Drama Club painting. This time, it was like the landscape was noticing *me.*

I thought of Masher. Part of me wondered if he had done it on purpose, eaten the rat poison—probably at a neighbor's house on one of his late-night outings—just to spite me into snapping out of it. It was as if he was say-ing, *Therapy's great and all that, but at some point you're going to have to start paying attention to stuff.*

Like my best friend.

When I got to Meg's, I opened the back door and called for her, then walked in through the kitchen and past the cozy breakfast nook under which loopy embroidered letters spelled out "Bless This House" inside a frame. Although our homes were built the same year by the same company, and had almost the same layout except for a few small differences—in Meg's house, the L of the kitchen swung left, while at mine it swung right—inside they were worlds apart. Mrs. Dill decorated her rooms with complete furniture and fabric sets from Pottery Barn so everything matched. They weren't littered with fifteen different things from eight different trips abroad, the way ours were. Meg's house always looked so much more like the houses we saw on sitcoms and in movies, and some-times I envied her for that.

"Hello?" I called from the stairs.

I heard the door to Meg's room open, then close, and Meg came bounding down the hall.

"Hi, you," I said.

She didn't stop but instead, hugged me tight and fast. "I can't tell you how glad I am that you called. Come," she said, grabbing my elbow and tugging me back toward the door. "Let's go for a walk."

Just before I swiveled to follow her, I heard voices coming from Meg's parents' room and loud music from Mary's.

Outside, Meg jerked her head toward the woods behind her house and I went along, still unable to get a look at her face. But something in the way her shoulders squared off at right angles told me all was not well. Once we stepped through the wall of trees that lined the Dills' yard, I tugged at the back of her tank top.

"What's up?" I asked softly.

She turned to me, looking a bit guilty. "I needed someone to talk to, but I was afraid to call," she said, like an apology.

"Well, I'm here."

Meg looked down at the dirt and rocks surrounding our feet, then back up at me. "My dad was out all night last night. He came home this morning and . . ." She stopped, and her eyes swept across my face. "You seem different. Are you okay?"

"Something happened today. But I'll tell you later. Your dad was out all night and he came home and . . ."

Meg paused, then shook her head. "No, it'll be fine. It's no big deal. He and my mom just had a wicked fight, and it kind of freaked me out. I want to hear about the thing that happened to you."

"Are you sure?" I asked. It was strange to be the one putting a hand on my friend's elbow and sounding concerned.

"Positive," Meg said, and she motioned for me to keep

walking. So we shuffled our usual way through the woods, past the neighbors' houses, up the hill to a flat rock that was always just big enough for the two of us. I told Meg about Masher and the vet and Eve and the job.

"That *is* awful but good about the job," said Meg. "So I'm guessing you're not coming back to school this year?" She said this with a forced casualness, especially the "back to school" part, throwing her glance at the treetops.

"I'm not ready. There's only two weeks left, anyway, right?"

Meg nodded but kept staring up. I wasn't sure if my not being at school made things harder or easier for her.

"You should email Joe," she said finally.

"That ship has sailed," I replied flatly. "Gone."

"Oh, I think that ship might just be circling the harbor. He asked about you a couple times."

"If he wanted to know how I was, he could have emailed me."

Meg shrugged. "He's a guy. What do you expect?"

I had no answer to that. We were silent for a few moments.

"Hey, do you want to see my pictures from Six Flags?" she said suddenly. "Some of them are hilarious."

"Maybe some other time." Or never. I had no desire to see the rest of my classmates having a totally fun, normal, end-of-school trip to the amusement park.

We paused again. This time, I was the one who felt the need to fill the void.

"So do they still talk about me? About prom night?"

Meg paused. "No, I think they stopped. Lucky for you, someone smashed up four of the front windows in the science wing, and that's the hot topic right now."

"When they find out who did it," I said, "remind me to thank them."

Meg smiled and then turned serious. She reached out and touched me on the shoulder.

"It's going to be a good summer, Laurel. We'll make it a good summer."

She was right, and I hugged her, and while we had our arms around each other I made a mental note to find out, someday soon, the full story of her dad not coming home and why she had so desperately needed to talk. Someday soon, for sure.

THIRTEEN

Masher was going to be okay. After two days in the hospital, he was ready to be released, and Eve called me from Ashland to share the good news.

Nana had received some more of her stuff from home via UPS that morning, sent by one of her friends. I stood in the doorway of the guest room, watching her unpack clothes into the old garage-sale dresser my mom and I had once covered with painted flowers.

Mom had said to me, "Honey, look, your roses have dimension!" and I wasn't even sure how I'd done it. It was one of the first times we both realized that maybe I had some talent in this area. Over the course of a few months, we found and decorated a dozen more pieces of furniture: a rocking chair with vines traveling up the spokes, a toy chest with wooden alphabet blocks.

When we ran out of room for new pieces in the house, Mom wanted us to paint a mural down the hallway wall, but my father nixed the idea, saying, "It'll look like graffiti, and the neighbors will freak when they come over."

Now I watched Nana hold up a silk paisley scarf and gaze at it affectionately before laying it into one of the rose-covered drawers. She looked up and startled when she saw me.

"Oh! I didn't see you there."

"Masher can come home."

She looked at me like, *Oh, joy.*

"I'm going to go get him."

"Do you want me to take you?"

"Thanks, but . . . no. I can do it myself. I have to get used to driving back and forth to work, right?"

"Start with little things," Suzie had said during our second session the day before. "Just jump into them and see how it feels to you." I was going to be seeing her twice a week for a while.

So I turned and walked downstairs, jingling the car keys to show that yeah, I was really going to do this.

The Volvo's driver's seat always used to smell like my mom, a strange combination of berries and coffee. Now

146

that was gone and Nana's essence of perfume-lipstick-hairspray had taken over. I rested my hands on the steering wheel and it felt okay. I glanced over to my dad's car, the green, sporty Volkswagen he'd been so excited to get because it reminded him of the Rabbit he'd had in high school.

Hi, Dad's car, I thought. *I'd take you for a spin, but he never taught me to drive stick.*

Five minutes later I was steering the Volvo to the animal hospital, going slowly at first and then eventually hitting the speed limit.

I wasn't scared or nervous, and that surprised me a little.

By the time I was heading back home, with Masher in the passenger seat next to me, driving felt downright good. He was hanging his head out the window, letting his tongue flap in the breeze with that "Is he really smiling?" dog look on his face, and I thought, *Here's a moment when everything's okay.*

Masher didn't have the same zip when I let him out of the car, but he went gladly into the house, with commitment. It was that commitment that pulled at my heart and reminded me that regardless of who he belonged to or what other things I did or did not feel capable of doing, I was his guardian now.

Inside, Nana was vacuuming the living room.

"Are we expecting someone?" I kidded.

Nana turned off the vacuum cleaner and regarded Masher.

"He looks good," she said, then after a pause: "David's coming to see him. He'll be here in an hour."

She pulled her glance quickly from me and turned the vacuum back on.

Heat flushed through my body, starting with my face and speeding downward. Making me feel suddenly ill.

"Why . . . did you do that?"

Nana kept her eyes on the carpet although I knew she heard me, which was so unlike her. It was clear how guilty she must have felt about it.

"I know you're mad at him," she called over the sound of the vacuum. She said it so casually, it set something off in me.

"Aren't you mad at him too?"

Now Nana turned off the vacuum and looked at me, unsurprised by my question. "I'm a little mad. He shouldn't have said whatever he said to make you so upset. But we should try not to judge people based on one instance."

"I don't think I can do that, with him."

"It *is* difficult. But I've been around a lot longer, and I've learned things the tough way." She looked wistful, her face full of stories I had yet to hear.

Instead of asking her to elaborate, I blurted out, "Aren't you mad at Mr. Kaufman, at least?"

Nana pursed her lips reflectively for a second, like it had never occurred to her that I would be thinking about these things. She took a deep breath and held it, which I knew was her way of preparing something important to say.

"Yes. I break my own rule on that." She paused. "But if I can't change something, I don't waste energy on it. Your grandfather went to an early grave because he spent most of his energy on things he had no control over."

These stories I had heard. My grandfather was a classic type A and when he had his heart attack at age sixty-five, he was just two weeks from retiring as a family lawyer.

"I had to tell David about his dog. That was the right thing to do and you know it," added Nana. "You can be here or not. It's your choice."

My choice. I wasn't sure I believed that, but I knew I should run while I had the chance.

I still had the car keys in my hand, and tracing my finger over the grooves in the ignition key flashed me onto that one okay-moment.

Without saying good-bye, I did a U-turn back out the door, closing it before Masher could follow me out.

I drove for more than an hour, taking a random route up and down the roads of our town. Some were familiar to the point of knowing who lived in each house. Some I knew only from a memory. *This is the way we used to go to the Birchwood Shopping Center. This is the good trick-or-treating street.* I'd get to an intersection not knowing whether to go left or right, then turn the wheel at the last second in whichever direction popped into my mind.

Eventually I went past the junior high and then down the long road that dead-ended into my old elementary school. It was a square, sprawling building, all brick and glass, and I spotted the windows of what had been my third-grade classroom.

I sat parked for a while in the parent pickup lot, watching a bunch of little kids run relays up and down the field. To be nine years old. To have life be simply about family and friends and who was mad at who and which games you wanted to play at recess, and getting gold stars on spelling tests, and feeling that first crush.

Laurel, you had everything back then, and you didn't even know it.

Rather than risk someone calling the cops on this weird girl crying in her car, I eventually started driving again.

According to the clock in the car, I'd been gone an hour and a half. I decided to do a stealth drive-by past the house and see if David was gone yet. Eventually I would have to see him, but not today. I'd just started feeling like my days were worth getting out of bed for.

But when I turned onto Meg's street, there they were.

David and Masher, ambling along the side of the road. I had to slow down to avoid them, and there was no way he wouldn't see me. I could have kept driving. We could have ignored each other.

But then he waved, and like an idiot I instinctively waved back. So I really had no choice but to stop the car.

"Hi, Laurel," he said into the open window, tossing a cigarette to the ground and stepping on it.

He looked even more tired, more haggard than he had just a week earlier at the prom. Dark circles visible under the edge of his sunglasses, his hair like he hadn't combed it in days. His jeans, covered in patches, sagged on his hips, and I realized that he must have lost weight too.

I was stuck for words so I glanced at Masher, who was beaming with an incongruous but understandable look of pure joy.

"He's doing okay," I said finally, not looking at David.

"Yeah. Thanks to you." His voice was light and almost pleasant.

"Uh . . . he almost died, thanks to me." I was staring at a tree now. Really examining it like there was a reason to.

"Hey, Laurel, don't do that to yourself."

Now I turned to David, a little surprised by the kindness in his tone. I turned off the car but didn't get out. I liked having this barrier of the door between us.

David touched the frame of his sunglasses, and for a moment I thought he'd take them off, but he didn't. I guess he liked his barrier too.

"I can't really give you a hard time about caring for

151

him, can I?" said David. "I'm the one who bailed on him in the first place."

Now he did take his sunglasses off. His eyes, usually so large and bright, looked thin and dull.

"Plus, I heard you had kind of a freak-out after I left that after-prom party. That was thanks to *me*, right?"

I didn't answer or even move.

"I'm sure I ruined things with your boyfriend," he said.

"He wasn't my boyfriend," I countered quickly, then added, "but yes, things got kind of ruined."

"Not to offer excuses or anything, but I was wasted and totally sleep-deprived."

The word *excuses* sounded trivial and stupid, hanging in the air between us. It didn't seem to fit in either of our lives anymore.

Now I got out of the car, leaning against the side for support. I didn't think I expected or even wanted a full apology from David about the prom. But as long as he was offering, it did make a difference.

If I can't change something, I don't waste energy on it, Nana had said.

Being angry at David for the prom, for what his father might or might not have done, took more energy than I had in the first place.

"So we're both sorry," I said. "Can we leave it at that?"

"Absolutely. I'm excellent at leaving things." His mouth turned up a bit with the pun, then he looked at Masher again. "So what's the deal? Your grandmother said he needs medication?"

"Vitamin K supplements. Twice a day for at least a month."

David was quiet, processing that.

"I'd like to take him back with me. My cousins said it was all right."

Then he looked at me, as if now I needed to say it was all right too. Maybe forgetting that this was actually *his* dog and not mine.

I thought of not having Masher around anymore, and it instantly made me ache. Another absence. I'd gotten used to the noises and the following and the watching. But I was going to be busy with my new job, and Nana would love not having "the dog" around, and I couldn't risk another accident.

Plus, the way David watched his dog sniffing at the weeds along the road, his body hunched and needy, I knew Masher might be required somewhere else.

"He'd love it," I finally said. "One thing, though. He has a follow-up appointment at Ashland Animal Hospital in two weeks."

"Oh yeah, I heard you're going to be working there?"

"It'll get me out of the house." I shrugged.

"Getting out of the house is good. I recommend it," said David, and he shot an ironic glance up the hill toward his home. "I'll bring him back for his appointment, no problem. Just send me the info. Let me give you my email."

While David dug some kind of receipt out of his pocket, I reached into the Volvo toward the compartment between the two front seats, where my mom always kept pens and small change. I pulled out a blue pen and gave it to David. He wrote something on the paper, then handed both back to me.

He didn't ask for my email address in return.

"You're going home—," he said flatly, not committing to it as a question.

We had done this. Seeing him again would somehow make it less clean. Plus, I couldn't stand a long good-bye with Masher.

"I'm running errands, so I have to get going. Just tell Nana you need the medication. It's all written on the label."

"Okay," he just said, then put his sunglasses back on and wrapped Masher's leash in a loop around his wrist. "Mash, say good-bye to Laurel."

Masher looked at me with surprise, and I squatted down with my arms out until he scrambled over to me. I hugged him, he licked my face. I didn't need to say anything. Not with David there, watching.

Finally I got up and Masher went back to David.

"Come on, buddy, let's go find that cat you love to hate," he said.

They walked away and I got back in the car. After I was sure David couldn't see me, I unfolded the receipt to stare at his email address, then flipped it over.

WELCOME TO ARI'S FUNZONE ARCADE, it said. THANK YOU FOR PLAYING.

The first thing Eve gave me when I showed up for my new job on Monday was a stack of folders a foot high.

"Filing," she said. "It's the backbone of our whole operation." There was not an ounce of kidding in her voice.

"That's what I'm here for," I said, trying to sound enthusiastic. My only other job had been as an intern at my dad's advertising agency the previous summer, and that had just been for a month. I was supposed to be working as an apprentice to the art director, but all I did was make photocopies and get sandwiches and answer the phone. I didn't mind; I was making more money than Meg was earning at Old Navy, and I got to ride into Manhattan on the train with my father, and sometimes he'd take me to lunch. When he couldn't, I'd sit outside in a nearby park, sketching the skyline.

I loved seeing Dad at his job as an account executive, but sometimes it felt like he was avoiding me. When I did catch glimpses of him in the office, he'd be on the phone with someone who was angry, or he was busy trying to fix a problem someone else caused. He'd look stressed and unhappy until he saw me, and then put on an instant professional smile.

"Do you ever feel sad about not being a reporter anymore?" I asked him once at lunch when he seemed especially anxious.

My question had taken him by surprise, and he put down the hamburger he was about to bite into.

"Well, I miss the work itself. It wasn't easy, but it was challenging and fun. I don't miss the instability of it. Not knowing when I'd get an assignment, or if an editor would go for my pitch."

"Maybe you could go back to it someday," I offered. I loved looking at our old newspapers and magazines with his articles, running my finger over his byline on the page.

He snorted a bit. "With college tuition just around the corner? No, I don't think so. I made a choice to do something that better supported our family and where I wouldn't be traveling so much, and I'm good with that."

But he'd looked out the window wistfully, and I'd made a vow to myself not to stay in any job I hated.

"We'll need to get you some scrubs," said Eve now, scanning my khaki pants and V-neck top, the most office-worthy thing I could find. "Dr. B is pretty strict about that; he wants us to look professional even if we're not officially vet techs. There are a couple of hand-me-downs in the back; see what you can find for now. I'll give you the names of some websites that have cute ones."

Eve tugged on her shirt to indicate the inherent cuteness of the dog and cat fairies she was covered with, then the phone rang and she spun away from me to answer it.

Despite her age, Eve clearly ruled the front desk realm. Tamara, Dr. B's sister, was the office manager and technically our boss, but she holed up in a small room off the front desk and concentrated on billing. I peeked into her office, and she looked up from something to wave at me, and I waved back.

I set to work on filing the charts into the wall of cabinets behind the front desk, and listened as Eve handled the phones, taking mental notes because that was going to be part of my job too. I'd arranged to show up at three p.m. every day—after school, as far as they were concerned, because nobody knew that I wasn't actually going to school—and help out in the front until seven p.m., when the hospital closed. Then I'd be expected to walk the dogs, some of which were boarding, some recovering from surgery or treatment like Masher had been.

I filed for twenty minutes before Eve came over to check my progress. She didn't look happy with how big the pile still was, and watched me slide a chart into the stacks.

"No, uh-uh," she said. "After you put one back, you have to use your right hand to flip through the next few tabs to make sure it's in the right place, alphabetically. In the past, charts got filed a little wrong and nobody bothered to fix it. So now we always check."

A quick flash of Toby and me working on shelving his DVD collection, him lighting up with pride when he figured out that "McQueen" came before "Master." It was a trick I'd thought of to help him with reading.

I got the sense that Eve's manner, all businesslike and bossy, wasn't something to take personally. She acted that way with everyone in the office, except the clients, for whom she adopted a more supportive persona, and the pets, for whom she became a sweet, silly, cooing thing. Besides, Eve didn't know she was supposed to treat me any differently. Being with her, always sensing her critical eye on me, actually felt good.

I'm just like anyone else.

I finished the charts and she asked Robert, one of the techs, to cover the phones while she walked me back to the kennels.

"We have just three dogs at the moment," she said as we stepped into the room. It had a high ceiling and open skylights, and reminded me of a public restroom where instead of toilet stalls, there were cages. The barking started the instant we opened the door, as if we'd tripped a wire.

"These two guys are boarding for the week," said Eve, crouching down to eye level with a pair of cocker spaniels sharing one kennel. "They're a little hyper. When you walk them, they're capable of pulling you over. I'll show you how to keep them in line."

Eve let the dogs lick her face as she murmured, "Hi, babies . . . yes . . . yes . . . you're beautiful . . . I love your kisses . . ." and I actually had to look away.

I turned to the third dog, alone in a kennel across the aisle. It wasn't any recognizable breed, just a medium-sized mutt with short, silky brown fur.

"That's Ophelia," said Eve.

Ophelia stared sadly at the two cockers, and it seemed a little cruel that she had this view, like the lonely girl forced to share a lunch table with a pair of BFFs. Then she noticed me watching her and thumped her tail.

Eve came over and crouched down again to gently grab Ophelia's muzzle through the chain-link door. "We're hoping to find a home for her, if you know anyone."

"What do you mean?"

"About a month ago, one of our clients found her lying by the side of the road. She'd been hit by a car. No collar, no tags. Totally skinny and practically starving. She had a broken leg. Look at her, she's the biggest sweetheart."

"Dr. B just fixed her up for free?"

"Yes. He does that occasionally. There are too many animals like Ophelia out there. People just suck sometimes." She spat that last part out, as if wanting to erase the bad taste of it, then added, "Dr. B is amazing that way. He knows I do everything I can to adopt them out. We've had pretty good luck."

A wistfulness came over Eve, who was clearly crushing

pretty hard on our employer. After a moment she said, "Wanna see the kitties? I have two angels I'm trying to place."

On the bottom row of the "cat room," as it was called, was a large cage occupied by tabby twins. They weren't kittens, but they weren't quite full-grown cats. As soon as they saw our legs step into view, one reached out its paw through the bars and the other pressed itself against the metal so its fur pushed through in little squares.

"Dumped on our doorstep in a sealed box. With duct tape."

"That is horrible," I said sincerely.

"Like I said, people can suck."

"Why didn't they just take them to the shelter?" I asked as Eve opened the cage and handed a cat to me. It started purring the second we made contact.

"I'm glad they didn't. The county shelter's a hellhole," she said. "They're overcrowded this time of year and putting down animals after just a few days." Eve looked at the cat, ecstatic in my arms. "That's Denali," she said. "You sure you don't want one?"

I thought of Elliot and Selina. We'd gotten them by pure chance. Elliot was part of a litter born to one of Toby's friend's pets, and Selina came crying on our doorstep one rainy night with an open wound in the scruff of her neck. It was like how people find other people to be in love with, all random and accidental and lucky.

"I have two already who would kill me," I said. "But I'll spread the word."

"That would be great. Dr. B is very patient but he gives me limits; only one cage at a time in each room for the rescues."

She sighed, like this was something she had to work on.

"Come on, let me show you the phones."

FOURTEEN

I had arranged to work at Ashland in the afternoons until the end of June. When Eve asked me "How was school?" I'd just smile and say, "Good, thanks." I'd never said I was in school. They'd just assumed. It didn't feel like lying.

The end of the year was happening without me. Finals and yearbooks and the exhibition baseball game with our rival high school. Meg would call daily with updates, thinking that I'd want to be kept in the loop. I wasn't sure what I wanted. I didn't like being absent from all that stuff, but working at the animal hospital made me feel like I'd gone away, and I wanted to be away more.

Suzie Sirico had said during one of our morning sessions, "The hardest part about grieving is that people often have to do it in the spotlight. Everyone's watching them to see what they're going to do next, how they react to things. So I'm glad that you got out of the spotlight."

Out of the spotlight, I answered phones and filed paperwork while Eve checked clients in and out. Every minute at work was full of something and kept my mind busy. At night I was so tired that I slept, albeit with dreams so tense and vivid I woke up each morning drenched in sweat.

Walking the dogs only made me miss Masher. Which then made me wonder how David was doing, what David was doing. If having Masher was helping him.

Then I thought of David's shapeless eyes, his bony elbows poking out of a brightly colored but stained polo shirt, and the almost friendly sound of his voice the last time we spoke.

"You saw that a-hole?" asked Meg bitterly during one of our phone calls, when I finally got up the nerve to tell her that David had been here. "What did you say?"

I wasn't sure what to share. It was as if by making some peace with him, I'd handed all my anger to my best friend for safekeeping. Meg knew every thought I'd ever had about every boy we knew, but how could she understand my concern for David when it perplexed me too?

"It was very businesslike," I said. "Believe me, I was in no mood to see him."

The receipt with David's email address was still sitting in front of the computer. After a few days, I found myself drafting a message to him in my head.

> *Hi, David. How is Masher? Just wanted to see how he's doing.*
> *Hi, David! How are you and Masher? Hope you are both doing good.*
> *Hi, David and Masher. Everyone okay?*

No matter how many versions I wrote, I couldn't find the right balance between "casual/friendly/concerned" and just plain lame. But eventually, I had to get it out of my brain, so I sat down to type:

> *Dear Masher,*
>   *WOOF! I hope you and David are doing well. I just wanted to remind you about your appointment!*

The next day, I got this response:

> *WOOF back. Feeling great and planning to be there.*

I couldn't bring myself to put the date on my calendar, as if writing it down would make it seem more important than it was.

WHAT REMINDS ME MOST OF THE PERSON I LOST IS . . .

"Their stuff is everywhere."

Suzie and I usually started off each session by her showing me a Feeling Flash Card and spinning a conversation out of whatever answer I came up with. I was honest and serious with my replies now.

"Do you mean their belongings?" Suzie asked.

"Nana cleaned up most of the clutter, but some things she just left. Neither of us can touch them."

I thought of the crossword puzzle my dad had been working on the morning of the accident. It often took him all week to do them, scratching in a few words every day. Nana had left this one, two-thirds finished, tucked between the salt and pepper on the kitchen table.

"Laurel, have you been able to go into their bedrooms?"

"No," I said simply.

"I understand about not touching things. It's too soon. Eventually, you and your grandmother might consider packing up the 'stuff' and giving some of it away. It's very cathartic. But for now, one thing you might want to do is go into your parents' room and stay aware of what reactions you have."

For two days after that session, every time I walked down the upstairs hallway I eyed my parents' door. All I could feel was dread and a little fear, which was ironic

166

considering how it used to represent a special kind of haven for me.

On the third night I finally got up the courage to go in.

It was cleaner than usual, with the bed made, the dresser drawers shut tight. My mother was a chronic drawer-leaver-opener, which drove my dad crazy. The books on both nightstands were stacked neatly and the hamper was empty. At some point, Nana must have done the laundry and put away the clean clothes.

I sat on the big king-size bed with the wooden antique headboard my mom had taken from the house she'd grown up in, and I actually had to remind myself that my parents were not alive anymore. They were so *here* in this room.

Suddenly, I remembered one night when I was probably seven or eight years old. I'd had a nightmare and wandered into the room, then scrambled onto the bed, to find that spot between my parents that was always warm and safe and waiting for me if I got scared.

Not saying a word, my mother held back the covers for me to snuggle in.

"I had a scary dream about hot lava," I'd said.

"I'm sorry, baby. I hate bad dreams."

"Do you get afraid too?"

"All the time."

"What do you get afraid of?"

I'd hoped she would say monsters, or falling off a bike,

or her friends not inviting her to their birthday parties. But she was quiet for a few moments and then said, "I'm most afraid of losing you or Toby."

Arrrgh, I'd thought. "That doesn't count. What else are you afraid of?"

Mom was quiet again, a deeper, more intense quiet, then said, "You losing *me.*"

I was little, but I'd known where that came from. One of her friends from college had just died of breast cancer a month or so before, leaving behind two kids.

Now I lay facedown on the bed, sobbing for the woman who once slept here not knowing that someday one of her worst fears would come true.

At the end of June, another day came on my calendar that I knew was the last day of school. It would be a short day, with each class lasting only twenty minutes instead of forty-two. Teachers would have parties or show funny movies or, if they were clueless, actually go over what the class had covered. That live current of excitement and celebration, of ending and starting.

I tried to distract myself by opening up the journal Suzie had urged me to start. She'd suggested I buy a simple unlined notebook with something silly on it, so I would feel free to write stupid and seemingly meaningless things in it. I'd found one adorned with a kids' cartoon character I'd never heard of, its thin pages a bright, hopeful white, and cracked open the old set of colored pencils

I hadn't used since my sketches for the last Drama Club show.

"Draw what you remember," Suzie had said. "Draw what you feel. Write a word on the page, like *angry*, and then give it form."

So I tried to do that, but my drawing slowly morphed into the faces of dogs and cats I'd met at the hospital.

Finally, Meg called me at noon sharp.

"It's done! I'm free!" I heard laughter in the background. "Wanna play today?"

"I have to work, remember?" I said, then tried to make my voice a shade lighter. "Come up tonight and we'll make ice cream sundaes."

So later, Meg and I sat outside on our back patio, eating Rocky Road topped with frosted cornflakes and whipped cream. I knew the rest of the junior class was at a bowling alley for the traditional "Now We're Seniors!" party.

"There's still time to go over to Pin World," I offered after we'd slurped together for a few minutes. "I won't mind."

Meg licked her spoon and tried not to seem like she was thinking about it. "Maybe. But the person I really want to celebrate with is you, so what's the point?" She paused. "It was really weird not having you at school."

"It was weird not being there. But you know . . ."

"I know." She plunged her spoon back into the sundae for another load. "But you're going back in September, right?"

September felt so far away. Far enough that I could say, "Of course," and not think about it anymore.

"What are you going to do about the stuff you missed? Will they let you finish over the summer?"

"I think so. Mr. Churchwell talked to Nana and said I should contact him as soon as I'm ready."

Meg nodded and examined my face. "Let me know if you need help, okay?"

I always got better grades than Meg, but I saw she needed to offer something.

"I would love that," I said, and we smiled at each other.

As soon as I'm ready.

Well, what the heck. I didn't know what ready was supposed to feel like, so now seemed as good a time as any. The next day, I sent an email to Mr. Churchwell through the school website.

> *Hi, it's Laurel Meisner. I'd like to finish my schoolwork and finals for the year. Can you help me?*

He wrote back almost immediately, while I was still online, which made me sad to think he was sitting in his office alone, the school emptied of students.

> *Laurel! I was hoping you'd get in touch and that you are well. I spoke to your teachers, and since you*

have an A average in all of your classes and you only

missed about two weeks of regular course work,

they're going to excuse you from that. However, there

is the issue of the New York State Regents exams

(U.S. History, English, and Trigonometry this year),

which I highly recommend you take if you want to stay

on track. You can still do that in August. I will send

you some information, and please let me know if you

need anything; you can reach me at this address

at any time.

Ugh, the Regents. I'd forgotten about those, which I would have taken in June with everyone else if the accident hadn't happened. Dad would have quizzed me on the practice tests, and Mom would have bought me a bouquet made of one flower for every point I scored above ninety.

Mr. Churchwell had said, *Stay on track.*

I had a job and was going to therapy and generally functioning as a human being. Was that staying on track? If it was, I wanted to stay some more.

I wrote back to him to say yes, and please, and thank you.

On the day David was scheduled to come in with Masher, I found myself reluctant to put on either of the two scrub shirts we'd bought. One was black and white printed with dogs chasing one another's tails, and the other was a simple blue with a cat embroidered on the pocket. Both made me look like I was wearing a costume, which I'd liked before today. Now it seemed too obvious.

To feel more like me, I found one of my favorite necklaces: a silver chain with a small silver disk stamped with my name. Toby had given it to me for my last birthday, and I hadn't been able to admit to him how much I loved it.

I also blow-dried my hair for the first time in weeks.

Was I looking forward to this or dreading it?

You're going to show him you're doing just fine, I thought, knowing that it probably didn't even matter to him whether I was fine or not.

The appointment was for two o'clock, and the morning went slowly. I tried not to keep checking the time. Now that school was out, I was working full days, and it was taking some getting used to. Fortunately, Eve asked me to join her for lunch. It wasn't an invitation, it was more like, "Tamara said she'll watch the front desk while we go eat."

We'd been friendly, but the busy and sometimes tense hospital atmosphere didn't allow for much chitchat. Which was one of many things I loved about being there, and now I was nervous about having a real conversation with Eve.

She was nineteen, going to the community college and living at home while she "worked on the animal thing," as she called it. "There are a lot of paths I could take. I'm trying to figure out which one," she told me over burritos at Taco Bell, with a straight, serious face, and offered no additional explanation. She didn't ask me any questions about myself, and I didn't offer. I was just supposed to be some girl in high school, and not have any stories yet.

When we got back, it was one thirty, and although I settled in to do some photocopying, I glanced up every time the front door opened.

David could be early. He could show up late. I didn't know him well enough to make a call on that.

Eve noticed my anticipation. "Expecting someone?"

"Masher's coming in today. His owner . . . my friend . . . is bringing him."

My friend. That felt like another little lie.

At two exactly, the door opened and I looked up, and there they were. I pictured David sitting in his father's Jaguar in the parking lot, watching the minutes change so he could pinpoint the exact punctual moment to get out of the car.

The waiting room was empty, but Masher seemed to remember getting bullied before and sniffed the air nervously. David saw me and sort-of waved with one hand, pulled off his sunglasses with the other.

"Hi, Laurel," he said, sounding formal, his eyes sweeping the space. He was dressed in a long-sleeved thermal shirt and black corduroys, even though it was easily eighty-five degrees outside.

"Welcome," I said, giving formal back to him.

I came through the half door that separated the front

desk area from the waiting room, and as soon as Masher saw me he ran over and jumped up. I caught his front paws in my hands and let him lick my face. David seemed puzzled.

"How's he doing?" I asked after I finally got the dog off me.

"Good." He paused. I noticed now that he'd put something in his hair to slick the sides back behind his ears, which looked newborn pink and too exposed. "I think he's been a little sore or something. That's actually the first time I've seen him stand up like that."

I nodded, and now that the moment had turned awkward, I wondered how I could smoothly get back behind the safety of the front desk.

"How's the job?" asked David, and looked me in the eye.

"I love it," I replied, loud enough so Eve could hear.

I wasn't sure what to do next but fortunately, Eve piped up, "Why don't you take them into room two? Dr. B will be there in a minute."

So I led David and Masher to the exam room, David holding onto Masher's leash but Masher walking close to me. Once we were in, I wasn't sure whether to stay or go. I waited for an invitation from David, but it didn't come. He just examined the poster of two golden puppies in football jerseys and blackout under their eyes—"Wide Retrievers"—and let out a little laugh.

I had no idea what to say so I didn't say anything,

which seemed the worst choice of all, as I left the room and closed the door behind me.

Fifteen minutes passed. I spent most of it on the phone with a client who was disappointed with the grooming her Persian cat had received at a pet store, and wanted a promise from Dr. B that he could fix it.

"They were supposed to give him the lion cut, but he looks more like a poodle!" the woman said, on the verge of tears.

Eve and I had developed a hand signal for this type of call; I put a finger-gun to my head and pretended to shoot. Eve smiled, glad she'd dodged that bullet.

Finally, I heard a door creak open and Dr. B appeared. He was filling out some forms.

"We're going to do a blood panel on Masher to check his coagulation levels and overall health. Apparently it's been a while since he had a checkup or even any vaccinations. Pam Fischer has all his records, so call over there to get them faxed."

Dr. B shot me a puzzled look, and although I knew he was wondering why I hadn't brought Masher to his regular vet that day, I remained silent. If he wasn't going to ask directly, I was definitely not going to answer.

The doctor disappeared again, and then I heard footsteps through the waiting room. I looked up just in time to see David walking out the front door, then watched him through the window as he sank down onto the stone bench right outside.

When I stepped out to join him, he was sitting on his hands, staring into space. He just glanced up at me with no expression.

"The doctor says it's going to be a few minutes," he said, and I just nodded. I'd watched a lot of clients waiting on this bench for test results and good news and bad news. It was designed to look like a big rabbit, with one end shaped like the head and the other, the tail and hind legs. Most people got on their cell phones or whipped out a magazine. But David didn't seem to need anything to pass the time.

Finally, I found something to say. "How is it, staying with your cousins?"

He shrugged. "It's not fun, but they leave me alone. It'll do until I can figure out my next move."

My next move, like he had a plan.

I knew I should ask him about his father, but I couldn't bring myself to do it. It opened up too much for me that was so neatly shut tight.

Instead, I offered, "I'm sorry about not taking Masher to Dr. Fischer. I knew she was your vet."

He looked up at me and there was something about his eyes, suddenly warm and familiar. "It's okay. I know why."

The relief of that washed over me, and I felt like I could breathe for the first time all day.

Then David slid over on the bench to make room. I

wasn't supposed to be on a break, but I sat.

"My grandparents went down to their place in Florida," he said flatly.

"I noticed I hadn't seen them around."

"They want me to come stay with them, but I don't know. . . . On one hand, there's the beach. On the other hand, there's two old people who annoy the living crap out of me." He swept a glance up and down my face. "Your grandmother is much cooler than mine."

I'd never thought of Nana as "cool," but apparently everything is relative.

David let out a long sigh, the kind that takes forever to wear out and seems to contain every emotion at once. Neither of us spoke again, and we both just gazed at nothing. The silence was almost comfortable now.

Finally, the front door opened and Robert appeared with Masher.

"We'll call you with the results sometime tomorrow," he said to David, handing him the leash. Then he turned to me and said, "Eve needs you."

I bent down to Masher, who now had a small bandage on his right foreleg from getting blood drawn, and hugged him quickly.

"Bye, buddy." I forced it to sound businesslike and cold.

"Bye, Laurel," David said, as if answering for him. "It was good seeing you."

I looked up, a little surprised, and then suddenly tired

of always feeling that way about David. Some of his hair had fallen out of the slick-back and across his eyes, and I had a sudden urge to sweep it away. Those eyes were my favorite part of him, and I hated to see them covered up.

Wait—I had a favorite part of him?

"Let me know what happens, okay?" I said quickly, trying to de-focus from his face, sounding purposely vague. I wasn't sure when I'd see either of them again. He could be back next week, or never.

David nodded slowly and smiled a bit, although sadly, and this was possibly the closest thing to a farewell that we could hope for.

I went inside and didn't look back.

FIFTEEN

Masher, as it turned out, had the beginnings of arthritis; plus, he still needed vitamin K for another two weeks. The arthritis wasn't related to the poisoning, but Dr. B felt it had probably come on recently.

"Stress can trigger it," he was saying on the phone to David, down the hall but loud enough so I could hear his end of the conversation from where I sat at the front desk. I could tell that Dr. B was prodding for some more information, and I was hoping David wouldn't offer anything up.

"Well, I'll find a pharmacy near you and call in a prescription," he continued, then added a reminder to keep

Masher on the vitamin K until it ran out.

Then he was quiet for a few moments, listening to David. I wished I could hear a little of David's voice on the other end of the phone, but I was too far away.

"Let me ask around for some vet recommendations in that area," said Dr. B. "There's got to be someone good you can go to so you don't have to drive an hour every time he needs to be seen."

Something in me lurched. Did David ask for that information, or did Dr. B volunteer it? Did David not want to come back here?

I couldn't let it go. Every time I saw the bench outside, I relived those moments. David scooting over to make room for me. David and I sitting together. That comfortable silence and the strange almost-freshness of the air between us.

When Suzie asked me about work during one of our sessions, I found myself omitting the story of David's visit. She knew I'd seen David and that we'd apologized, and that he had Masher now. She stopped asking about him, which made sense. Why would he matter? On paper he was just a footnote.

A few days later I gave in once again to the email drafts in my head, and sent Masher a message.

Hi, Masher. I hear you've got arthritis now. That sucks. But I'm sure David's taking good care of you and I'm here if you need anything.

I wasn't sure what kind of response I was hoping for. I just wanted a response, period. Something to grab onto, although I didn't know what I'd do with it once I did.

The reply came the next day: *Thanks. I'll be okay.*

It wasn't exactly an answer I could grab. But I could touch it, and that was enough.

The rest of July passed quickly. It was a busy time at Ashland, with people going on vacation and boarding their pets, animals getting dehydrated from the heat or infested with fleas. Dr. B had another vet come part-time to fill in the gaps.

I'd mastered the phones and the filing, and loved walking the dogs because they reminded me of Masher and because it forced me to explore the streets around the hospital. Unfamiliar houses owned by unfamiliar people, and I didn't mind looking up to say hi when someone passed me on the sidewalk, because I knew I was a stranger to them. It still amazed me that even though I was less than ten miles from my neighborhood, I might as well have been in another state.

Eve found a nice family—blond parents, blond boy, blond girl, right out of a magazine—for the tabby cat twins Bryce and Denali. Then she placed Ophelia in a temporary "foster home," aka a friend of hers who got suckered in, because the hospital needed the kennel space.

One day, we were all so busy that we had to work through lunch and Dr. B ordered in pizza for the staff. A bunny came in that had been attacked by a dog, and a cat who had a hairball stuck in its digestive system needed emergency surgery. When these kinds of life-and-death dramas swept through, I felt almost ill on adrenaline but tried to be as useful as I could. *Please don't die*, I'd think while we waited for the outcome, watching the pet's owner in the waiting room, planning to disappear if Dr. B came out with bad news. A few times, he did. I'd go into the bathroom and spend a long time making it really, really clean.

When we were finally caught up, and Tamara said Eve and I could go home, Eve turned to me and said, "I need a little coffee after that one. How about you?"

We stepped out into the late afternoon heat, and I followed her down the street to a strip mall. There was a café where we often had lunch.

After we ordered, I instinctively scanned the room to see if I recognized anyone, expecting that relief I'd gotten used to here.

Except I did see someone I knew.

Joe Lasky, sitting at the back of the room, staring at me.

I was so surprised that there was no way I could pretend not to see him. I smiled briefly at him, and he smiled back.

Okay, maybe that was that. I turned to Eve. But she looked over my shoulder and nudged me.

"Some cutie's coming over to us," she said.

I turned again to see Joe bouncing in our direction, a

little too quickly, like he wanted to get it over with.

"Hey, Laurel," he said.

"Hi, Joe."

"I'm on my break from the movie theater," he replied to a question I hadn't asked. He pointed with his thumb to our left, and I remembered the little art house cinema at the other end of the shopping center. "What are you up to?"

"Just trying to cool off," I said, as Eve handed me my drink.

"We've had a furry day," said Eve, with no sense of how absurd that sounded.

Joe frowned. "What do you mean?"

"It's a long story," I said. We were all silent for a moment, so I added, "This is my friend Eve . . . Eve, this is Joe, from my school."

"Do you guys want to join me?" asked Joe.

Eve glanced quickly between Joe and me, picking up on something. "I should get going," she said. "But Laurel, you can stay."

I knew I didn't need Eve's permission or even encouragement, but in that moment I was glad to have it. I looked at Joe now, at those eyes that had searched me over in Adam LaGrange's backyard. He had been there for me, once. He had made me feel propped up for a few lovely hours.

So I said, "Sure."

After we said good-bye to Eve, I followed Joe to his table. It was in the back corner and the place was packed, so of course we had to scrunch in and bang our knees together to make it work. I placed my ice-blended chai next to Joe's black coffee, the wimpy chick drink alongside the grown-up guy one like they were already in a relationship, and tried to look him in the eye.

"I didn't know you worked at the movie theater," I said.

"Yeah, I take the tickets, and then when the movie's over, I get to clean up the garbage the audience leaves behind. In between, I like to pop over here."

"You don't stay and watch?"

"Well, yeah, when we first start showing something. But after twenty or thirty times, it gets old. Especially if it's, like, French."

"Too bad you take Spanish," I said, then wished I hadn't. I wasn't supposed to know which classes he took, was I? Joe laughed nervously and shifted in his chair. He had a messenger bag hanging over the back, and now I noticed a big sketch pad sticking out of it. To change the subject, I asked, pointing at the pad, "Did you get that at Walden Art Supply?"

He turned to look at it, then nodded. "You know it?"

"My mom used to buy her paint there." Joe looked instantly uncomfortable, so I added, "I've seen those pads at the store, that's all."

Now Joe reached for the pad and pulled it out. He

opened to a page and turned it toward me to show what he'd drawn: a middle-aged man in a cape and a helmet with two bugles sticking out of it like antennae, a big B inside a hot air balloon on his chest.

"I call this one BlowHard. Yesterday I was sitting here next to some dude with his girlfriend, and he was just going on and on about stuff like he knew everything there was to know, and every time she tried to correct him, he'd shoot her down."

"Do you turn everyone into some kind of superhero?"

"If they seem like they deserve it, yes." He stared at the sketch protectively, like a new parent. "I mean, isn't everyone a superhero, in their own mind?"

I smiled. "On certain days, yeah."

We were quiet again, and I tried to fill the silence by sipping loudly on my drink. Why did things have to be so weird? We had kissed. We had kissed a lot, and from what I could tell it had been pretty good, until everything imploded. Before, I'd believed that once you'd done that with someone, you'd broken a barrier, like maybe you could always kiss them again whenever you wanted and it would be completely okay. But now there was some kind of force field between Joe Lasky and me, stronger than if we'd never kissed to begin with. He felt further away than a complete stranger.

A quick flash of David and me, sitting together on the bench outside Ashland. We'd had a history between us too, but a different kind. It was confusing to think about these differences or about David at all. I pulled my focus back to Joe and suddenly felt mad.

We would have been a couple by now. But no, I didn't get to have that, just like I didn't get to have a prom memory that didn't make me want to puke from embarrassment. The wave of anger at myself came so fast and lethal, I could have slapped my own face.

Finally, Joe planted his elbows on the table and leaned in. "So. Been to any good proms lately?"

I just broke out laughing, and the rage flushed away.

"Nice," was all I could say.

"I'm sorry, I had to do it." He smiled now.

"*I'm* sorry."

"Please," he said, holding up his hand. "You have nothing to be sorry about. I should have tried harder to reach you." He took a deep breath and wrapped both hands around his coffee cup, like the heat was giving him the guts to keep talking. "I could say that I wanted you to have some space, some time alone to work through your stuff, but that would be bull. I was scared. It's not the kind of thing I know how to deal with."

I nodded. "I know. I would have done the same thing." As long as we were being honest, I wanted to ask him whether he'd been set up by someone to take me to the prom. But I didn't want this sweet, sudden normalness to end just yet.

Joe took a deep, relieved breath and then a sip of his coffee, staring at his drawing of BlowHard. Then he raised an eyebrow and said, "Hey, you paint scenery, right?"

"Yeah."

"Do you think you could give BlowHard something in the background? I suck at backgrounds, but I feel like he needs something behind him."

"For context," I said.

"Exactly!" said Joe, lighting up now.

"I have an idea."

Joe dug into his bag and pulled out a pencil, then handed it to me. As I started to draw in the beginnings of BlowHard's context, Joe said, "While you're doing that, why don't you tell me about the furry stuff?"

Meg was smug. "I told you!" she said with a grin that evening. We were sitting on our rock, feeling the air cool off. Breathing the relief of it, in and out.

Meg and Gavin had gone out nine times since prom night. He'd gotten to see that new bra eventually, and now they were a couple. At least I hadn't totally screwed that up for my best friend.

"It doesn't mean anything," I said, hoping that wasn't true.

"You deserve someone like him," said Meg, and I had nothing to counter that with.

"Do you think I should go say hi to him the next time we're at that mall?"

Meg looked at me. "We?"

"Eve and me." The way it came out, and the way Meg flinched, made me want to un-say it.

Just then, Meg's cell phone chirped with a text message, clicking us away from that awkward pause. Meg read the message, then started typing back.

"Gavin?" I asked.

"No, it's my boss from camp, reminding me to come early tomorrow. There's a big rehearsal." She looked up at me. "You should come to the performance. The kids are doing an Andrew Lloyd Webber revue."

Meg said this sincerely, but how could I go? It would only remind me of the summer I was supposed to be having, and force me to make comparisons to my job at Ashland that I didn't want to make.

"Yeah, maybe," I replied, and then we were just silent, listening to the cicadas and the distant squeal of kids' voices down the street, where someone was having a bar-becue and probably lots more fun than we were.

SIXTEEN

The hot and humid July turned into an even hotter, more humid August. Spending most of my time inside, however, I barely noticed. Between the house, Ashland, and Suzie's office, my only jaunts into the real world were the dog walking and my quickie lunches with Eve. The sounds of this summer were the hum of air conditioners and the *huh, huh, huh* of panting dogs.

At night, sometimes Meg would come over to watch a movie. She never invited me to her house. It felt like she needed a break from something, although I didn't ask her what.

Mr. Churchwell had arranged for me to take the Regents exams at a nearby high school, because our school district was too small to have their own summer testing. I'd taken a bunch of practice tests during the previous few weeks; they were a great way to make me drowsy late at night when I couldn't sleep. So for two mornings in mid-August, I sat in a gym filled with students I didn't know and lost myself in questions, answers, and essays.

When I was done and driving home, I thought of the phone call I would have made to my father.

Hey, Dad, I think I did well. I had to write a presentation on the benefits of weight-bearing exercise, so instead of celebrating with ice cream, let's go for a nice long walk. Just kidding!

The day after the exams, I'd just barely woken up when I heard the phone ring, then Nana call out that it was for me. She'd stopped coming into my room to deliver anything weeks ago.

"It's Eve," said Eve sort of breathlessly, with no "Hi" or anything.

"What's up?" I asked, confused. I wasn't supposed to be at work until ten, although the hospital opened at nine.

"Your friend is here, with his dog." She was practically whispering.

"David?"

"He wants to leave him here. Board him, I guess."

I was so shocked that I couldn't say anything.

"I thought you'd want to know ASAP. I'm stalling him, saying I have to do some paperwork. So he's here . . . if you want to . . . see him."

Now I could hear the restrained anger in Eve's voice. She'd been around enough people dumping their pets; she knew the signs.

"Give me fifteen minutes."

I jumped out of bed and threw on the previous day's clothes, which were still lying in a heap on my floor, and rushed downstairs, pausing just long enough to tell Nana there was an emergency at work.

The traffic lights were with me and I made it at the fourteen-minute mark. Mr. Kaufman's Jaguar was still in the parking lot, and I pulled up next to it, even though I was supposed to park in the back with the other employees.

I grabbed the front door handle and paused for a moment, trying to slow down my heartbeat. Things had happened so fast, I wasn't even sure what I felt. I just knew I needed to talk to David but didn't want to seem like a maniac.

Once in the door, I scanned the waiting room. Empty.

Then I saw him, behind the tall round rack of greeting cards in the corner, which the hospital sold as a fund-raiser for the ASPCA. He had dropped a card and was picking it up, dusting it off.

He raised his eyes to look at me and then stood all the way up.

"Fantastic," he said dryly.

I took a step forward, then held out both hands as if hoping to catch some answers.

"What the hell, David?" I tried to keep my voice even.

He shot a dirty look at Eve, who had sunk so low behind the front desk you could only see the top of her head, and gingerly put the greeting card back in its rightful spot on the rack.

"What the hell is that I'm leaving. I can't take Mash with me."

"I don't understand."

David glanced at Eve again. "Can we talk outside?"

I examined his face now. He seemed calm and resolved, in the saddest of ways. I motioned for him to follow me and led him out the front door, then around a corner of the building where there was some shade.

David took a deep breath, and although there were some steps behind us going up to the side entrance, he remained standing, and so did I.

"He's not going to wake up," said David. "My dad. That's what the doctors are saying."

I folded my arms across my chest in a *Go on* type of gesture.

"I can't stay by that bed anymore. I'll puke or something. And things are messed up with my cousins."

"Where are you going to go?" I asked, trying to make it sound challenging rather than curious.

"My buddy Stefan . . . he used to live here but moved to California. Maybe you remember him?"

I shrugged, even though I knew exactly who he was talking about.

"Anyway, I'm going to go check things out with him." He looked up at the brick wall of the hospital, and I could see him start to break down. Fighting it. "I have to be gone."

I wanted to sit or lean against the building or do something else besides stand there face-to-face with David with nothing holding me up. To make things worse, I had a split-second urge to reach out and touch him. I wanted to hang on to my fury, but it was already shrinking away.

To be gone.

I'd thought about it too. Sometimes my life here felt like a cage where I could never escape the pain. At other times, it felt like the only firm ground on earth. How could I fault David for tipping one way while I was tipping another?

"Why didn't you call me?" I said softly. "Why wouldn't you leave Masher with us?"

"That medication is a lot of work," he said, almost whining, but then pulled his face straight. "You have enough on your plate. I figured, if I boarded him here, he could still see you." David paused, looked at the wall again, and then added, "Plus, I didn't want you to know I was leaving until I'd already done it."

193

Now he forced a smile, adding, "Because, you know, we wouldn't want to have a scene or anything."

The thought of David being across the country, where there was no hope of seeing him occasionally, felt like one more thing to miss. I didn't expect this feeling. And I didn't like it.

"Please let me take him," I said, trying to focus on Masher so that sensation would go away. "You know he won't be happy in a kennel."

David bit his lip and nodded. Grateful, like he'd been hoping for this from the beginning.

"Can you go in and tell Eve? She has to hear it from you."

He nodded again, then headed into the building. Which left me standing by myself, not sure what to do next.

Since David was going to disappear without a trace, maybe I should beat him to the punch.

I checked my cell phone and saw that I didn't officially have to be at work for another half hour. It would be just enough time for me to drive home and change clothes before coming back, at which point I knew David would be already on the road.

And we would not have said good-bye, just like he'd wanted.

SEVENTEEN

The night before school started, I laid out my first-day outfit—jeans and an embroidered blue T-shirt—and Nana came in to see it.

"You'll look very pretty," she said, rubbing cream into her hands. This was a bedtime ritual for her, the spreading of lotion on all limbs and digits, and especially on the webby skin between her fingers. She had this idea that your skin got dried out while you slept, making you look older faster.

"I just want to seem, you know, okay."

"You will. Because you are."

Earlier that day, I'd had a session with Suzie.

"How do you feel about seeing everyone again?" she'd asked. "Especially the ones who were there that night, after the prom?"

I hadn't been able to answer her then, so she helped me create a "comfort zone" that I could go to in my head if I needed it at school. (I settled on the space at home, between the white couch and the window, wrapped tightly in a quilt from my bed.)

After Nana disappeared into her room, I opened my journal, waiting for something to kick in. The window was open and a breeze swam in, almost chilly enough to raise the hairs on my arm. Fall was starting, right on cue. The *starting* part of that made me uneasy.

As a family, we got collectively bummed out by the end of summer. Toby and I would lie around and watch a lot of television, relishing the feeling of not having any homework we should be doing. My dad would work late to avoid the quiet sadness in the house, and my mother would spend extra hours at the studio to catch up on wedding season portraits.

I began forming words with my pen, but they felt clunky and stupid:

I'm going back to school tomorrow. They will look and stare and whisper again.

I stopped writing and started drawing. Big round eyes, sharp and jagged eyes, eyes narrowed to mysterious, sneaky slits. Soon, I was fast asleep, the notebook balancing on my chest, the cats on either side of my legs. Dreams came fast and short, flickers of scenes that ran into one another like a silent movie.

When Megan's car reached the bottom of the school's driveway, she turned to me and smiled. "Here we are at last," she said, and I couldn't figure out why she was so excited to be done with a three-minute drive. But now she was turning left into the senior parking lot, and I got it. What she meant was, *At last, we're seniors! We're going to rule the school!*

Meg was no longer driving her mom's minivan. Her sister, Mary, had left for NYU the week before, and had bequeathed to Meg her very tiny but very cute red Toyota. She was so amped about it that you'd think it was a Mustang convertible.

We had timed our arrival to be early, but not too early. Other seniors were already there, leaning against their cars in groups, chatting. Meg drove over to them and pulled into the first open space. All heads turned, scanning the front seats to register first Meg, then me.

"Ready whenever you are," she said, pulling up the parking brake until it made a *grurt* noise. I gathered my stuff and got out quickly, wanting to appear ready, even eager. Still, it was an effort for me to raise my head from the pavement to see who was there.

Andie Stokes and Hannah Lindstrom were coming

toward me. Andie wrapped me in a hug.

"Hey," she said.

Hannah did, too. Now, suddenly, Caitlin Fish. They were practically lining up.

I was getting an air kiss from Lily Janek when I noticed three guys hanging out across the parking lot, hands in their pockets. One of them was Joe. He looked up at exactly the wrong moment and our eyes met. He just nodded. Not even a nod. Just a swoop up of the chin, then down. Our time at the coffee place had been nice, but I still wasn't sure where it left us, and clearly he wasn't either.

I took a second to check out the rest of the lot. Was I hoping to see David? Even though I knew he was surely in California by now, the familiar school setting caused a knee-jerk hope that maybe he'd be there. I'd have to get over that.

Now I smiled quickly at Joe, then someone touched my shoulder and I turned to see Meg ready to usher me inside like a bodyguard. As I walked toward the school entrance, feeling Joe's eyes on my back, maybe even on my swinging shoulder bag or my new shoes, I wondered how soon I'd get to see him again.

One car was missing from the driveway when Meg and I pulled up to my house that afternoon.

"Nana must be getting her hair done," I said.

"You sure you don't want to go with us to Vinny's?"

asked Meg. She was meeting Andie and Hannah and their crowd to celebrate the first day of senior year with pizza.

"Thanks, but I just need to chill." The day had been good. People had been nice. Mr. Churchwell tracked me down to check up on me, and Nana called at lunchtime to see how I was, but I didn't mind. Now, even the weight of my book bag as I heaved it out of the backseat had a reassuring, solid feel to it.

"Pick you up tomorrow?" she asked.

"Call you tonight," I said, then got out of the car.

I waved at Meg as she backed down the driveway but quickly turned toward the house. There was Masher in the front window, his ears forward and high, panting. When I opened the door, he ran past me into the driveway, then stopped and shot an intense look in my direction. "Yeah, just give me a few minutes," I said. I dropped my stuff in the house and changed into my sneakers.

Back outside, at the end of the driveway, I stopped to open the mailbox. Masher sat in the middle of the road, looking up the hill, then down the hill. I slid out the pile of mail and started walking, the dog a few yards ahead of me. Bills, the *PennySaver*, some junk mail for my dad. *National Geographic*, addressed to Toby. I touched my finger to Toby's name printed out in dot matrix, thinking *At least he's still alive in a computer somewhere.*

Then there was an envelope addressed to "Masher, c/o Laurel Meisner." I froze, staring at it, while Masher began peeing in the Girardis' ivy patch.

I tucked the rest of the mail under my armpit and opened David's envelope. Inside was a letter written on lined notebook paper.

Masher,

Sorry it took me so long to write. Things didn't work out with my buddy Stefan, so I'm headed back. But I think I'm going to take my time and check things out on the way.
Mash, that means you're gonna have to stay there for a while. I hope you understand.
I'll write or call whenever I can. I don't know when I'll be able to see you again, but it won't be too long. Promise.
Cya,
David

I read it twice, then folded it into my pocket. Masher took that as his cue to stop peeing and start walking again, and I followed him, past the Girardis' and every familiar spot after it.

EIGHTEEN

Every few days, a postcard from David to Masher would show up in our mailbox.

Hey Masher, the first person I saw in San Francisco was a guy with purple dreadlocks down to his waist. Masher, did you know that Seattle really does have killer coffee? Masher, you would not believe how many cows there must be in the world.

As he made his way slowly, zigzaggedly east, David told his dog that it was hard for him to get online and send an email, but he liked being able to jot things down on a twenty-five-cent postcard and mail it off when he got the chance. He told Masher about how being alone on a highway in the middle of nowhere gave him a sense of peace he'd never felt before, and how he'd had the best meal of his life late one night at a truck stop outside Salt Lake City, served by a waitress named Melba.

I read the notes aloud to Masher because it felt wrong not to, but secretly wished just one letter would come addressed to me. There was never a return address, so I couldn't write back to him even if I wanted to.

"How is David?" Nana asked one day as I turned David's latest over and over in my hands. This one told Masher all about what it felt like to ride a raft down the Snake River in Wyoming.

"He seems good," I said.

"His grandparents were up here last weekend from Miami." Nana paused. "They're talking about selling the house."

I felt something lurch in my stomach. "Why?"

"Well, nobody's living there, but somebody has to pay all the taxes. The house is worth quite a bit, and I think they want to put something away for David. Also," she leaned in to whisper, although nobody else anywhere could possibly hear us, "I got the impression that Mr. Kaufman's care is quite expensive."

I thought of how Mr. Kaufman drove the nicest cars

of all the neighbors and was always buying pricey electronic gadgets before anyone else had heard of them. Now he needed help to cover the cost of being only half-dead, and I didn't feel one bit sorry.

"What will they do with all the stuff?" I said, after a few seconds.

"I don't know, sweetie." Then Nana was miles away, staring out the window.

"Are you okay?"

She snapped out of it and looked back at me with a sudden determination. "Yes. But I have something I'd like to discuss with you."

I just raised my eyebrows at her, tired of asking questions.

"I need to go home in a few weeks, to take care of some personal business. How do you feel about that? It would just be for three or four days. I've already spoken to Mrs. Dill, and you can stay with them."

It was so easy to forget that Nana had a house full of her own furniture and uneaten food and *Reader's Digest*s piling up in the mail stack.

"What kind of business?" I asked.

"I'm thinking of renting out my house for the next year. I'd like to see Dr. Jacobs about my arthritis, too. And I need to meet with my lawyer about selling the condo." When Nana said "the condo," she winced like it hurt.

The condo meant Nana's deluxe two-bedroom

apartment at a retirement community in Hilton Head, where she'd been planning to move. My dad had helped her find the place just a few months before the accident.

Nana had had plans. She was old, yeah, but she still had a future. So what did she have now?

I looked at Nana trying so hard not to cry. "Is it okay with you if I go?" she asked. "You can come with me if you'd like, but I'd hate for you to miss school now that you've started again."

She had given up so much to be here. Did she ever resent it? Or me?

"Please go," I said. "I'll be fine. Please do what you need to do, Nana."

She nodded, biting her lip, wrinkling her nose. Then I watched her walk quickly out of the kitchen on her way to break down somewhere away from me, the perfectly centered back seam of her straight, straight skirt wiggling like a tail.

Andie and Hannah talked Meg and me into coming with them to Vinny's Pizza for lunch the next day. "We're seniors! We have to take advantage of our off-campus privileges!" Andie had argued. I was game. Tell me there's an alternative to sitting in the cafeteria with people stealing glances at me between Tater Tots, I'm there.

At Vinny's, we couldn't agree on toppings, so we ordered a large pizza divided four ways: pineapple

(Hannah), veggies (Meg), sausage (Andie), and plain (yours truly). Vinny himself was behind the counter and gave us a dirty look when Hannah placed the order, but later, after we'd squeezed into the booth in the window, he brought us over a free plate of garlic bread. I noticed his wife back in the kitchen, staring at me sadly.

"So Laurel," said Andie, peeling the crust off a slice of bread. "Do you see that bench out there?"

I looked out the window to a bench on the sidewalk. A young mom was sitting on it, desperately rocking a stroller back and forth with a defeated look on her face. I glanced back at Andie and nodded, then watched her eat the crust and hand the middle of the bread to Hannah, who popped it in her mouth. This seemed like a ritual for them.

"I was trying to think of something else besides planting a tree, because I realized that's a little tired, and one day I noticed that bench has a plaque on it," continued Andie. "Some person I've never heard of, but I called the town office and guess what? They're memorial benches. You can buy one. We can buy one, the senior class, for you know, you."

As gung-ho as Andie was about this whole memorial idea, she didn't seem capable of actually talking about the people it was for.

I thought of my parents' names, Toby's name, on a plaque on a bench. Sweaty backs and bra straps pressing against it, stupid kids sticking gum in the corners. I wasn't sure my family would have wanted to be remembered in any way that had to do with people's butts.

"What store would it be across from?" I said, because I couldn't think of anything else. Meg kicked me under the table, so then I added, "Because my dad always loved the sandwiches at the Village Deli."

Andie and Hannah looked at each other, both chewing their bread components. "That's a great idea!" said Hannah.

"How do you plan to raise the money?" asked Meg.

"We're going to do a bake sale at each of the home football games," said Hannah. "We'll ask the senior class to make cookies and brownies and stuff. It can really add up." She paused, then added, very seriously, "But don't worry. We won't ask you guys."

"And Laurel, you can get stuff at the bake sale for free," whispered Andie.

Just then, my cell phone rang. **HOME** it said on the display.

"Hello?" I answered, like I didn't know it was Nana.

"Hi, Laurel. How are you?" Her voice strangely formal.

"I'm having lunch in town."

"I just wanted to see how your day was going. You're with Meg?"

"And Andie and Hannah." The girls were trying not to watch me.

"Those popular girls?"

I lowered my voice. "Yes, Nana. What does it matter?"

"Mrs. Dill told me some things about those girls. I'm not sure I want you hanging out with them."

"It's fine. I'm fine. Can I go now? Our pizza's here," I lied.

I hung up. "My grandmother," I said to Andie and Hannah. "She's going a little control freak on me."

I thought of the last postcard I'd gotten from David. He'd written, *Masher, would you believe I can no longer keep track of what town I'm in? It's an incredible feeling.*

I could see why, sometimes.

Later, when Meg and I went to the restroom together, she asked me, "What was that about with Nana?"

"I honestly don't know." I wondered how much to tell Meg about what Nana said. "I think your mom has been trash-talking Andie and Hannah."

Meg sighed as she turned on the sink to wash her hands. "Yeah. She decided last week that they're slutty."

We paused, awkwardly, so I said, "And you're not?"

Meg flicked water at me. I flicked some back. Which meant we didn't have to talk about it anymore.

NINETEEN

Dear Student:

Your college planning appointment with
Mr. Churchwell has been scheduled for
MONDAY at 2:30. Please arrive promptly
at the guidance office and bring a list of
any questions you may have.

I had found the note taped onto my locker one day in early October, and as I was reading it over, I heard a voice behind me.

"Looks like we both got tagged!"

I turned to see Joe Lasky, waving his own note. A sight

that made me happy-nervous.

"They must be doing the *L*s and *M*s this week," I said.

We were a month into school and I'd barely seen Joe. We had no classes together, and when I saw him in the hallways he was always rounding a corner ahead of me, or walking the other way surrounded by friends. When we did come face-to-face, all we ever had time to do was say hi to each other and keep on moving. Fortunately, Meg was smart enough to stop asking about him.

"I remembered you'd be here between fifth and sixth period," he said, and it dawned on me: *He's been hoping to run into me like I've been hoping to run into him.* "And I was wondering if I could talk to you about a project."

I raised my eyebrows. "What do you mean?"

"I'm doing some caricatures for a little art show at the library, and I thought it might be cool if you drew some backgrounds for them. Like the one you did for BlowHard. We could put both our names on the finished pieces."

I thought of the stuff I'd drawn on Joe's sketch pad that day. I'd given BlowHard a really shabby basement apartment, like he was living with his parents.

I knew that kind of thing looked great on college applications, and I knew it meant Joe and me spending more time together. Even if it was just something he came up with to give us an excuse to hang out, I wanted to take the bait.

"That would be great, Joe," I said.

"I should be ready to show them to you in a couple of weeks. Is that cool?"

"Sure."

He smiled at me and then looked away, as if I'd caught him doing something.

"Then I'll be in touch."

On Monday, as instructed, I walked to Mr. Churchwell's office as slowly as I could. I hadn't spoken to him since the night of the prom; I didn't count the one-word answers I gave him when he asked me how I was doing, how the other kids were behaving toward me, and if he could help in any way (obviously, the answer to that last one was always *No, thank you*).

"Laurel!" he said, way too cheery, as he opened his door. I hadn't even knocked yet. He must have seen me, standing in the guidance office waiting area, picking something really important out of my thumbnail.

"Hi, Mr. Churchwell," I said, and waved my note at him like a white flag of surrender.

"Looks like you're up! Come on in and take a seat."

I did, and while he fumbled with some folders on his desk, I looked around the room. There was a poster on the wall for some college in Connecticut. Students sitting on a grassy lawn, books in their laps, gesturing intelligently. A tall clock tower behind them framed by an oak tree.

"So. College planning," said Mr. Churchwell, like I was

the one who brought it up.

"Yup."

"Do you plan to go to college?"

I looked at him, hearing that question for the first time. "Of course I plan to go," I said curtly.

"That's great news, Laurel, because I hear you did very well on your SATs."

"I did."

"And you've been a strong student since the beginning. Ninety-eighth percentile, officially. Your grades haven't suffered in the wake of the accident, which I find to be . . . amazing." He gestured to a folder on his desk, a red-rimmed label on its tab. Clearly, my File.

I shrugged it off. "I think the teachers are being easy on me." But even if that were true, I was working hard. I didn't know how not to.

David's last postcard, from just the day before, jumped into my head. It was a photo of Daytona Beach, all golden sand and empty sky. He'd drawn a stick figure lying on the beach and an arrow pointing to it next to the word "ME." Nothing else was written on the card except my address.

"I'm sure you started this process . . . previously," he said gently.

I remembered the pile of information packets I'd picked up at a college fair last winter. They'd sat on the coffee table in the den for weeks before my father dropped them in my lap one day while I was watching TV.

"Whaddya think?" he'd said. My dad liked to ask vague questions, soft lobs that left the ball in my court to return however I wanted.

"I like Brown and U Penn," I'd answered. "And Yale, of course."

"Of course."

"And Smith," I had added.

My mother had gone to Smith. That's where she'd met my dad, late one night at a party in her dorm. He'd tagged along with a roommate who was visiting his high school girlfriend there in order to break up with her in person. "If he hadn't decided to dump her," my dad liked to say with a wink when telling me this story, "you would have never been born!"

"Are you looking for something with a good theater program?" asked Mr. Churchwell now, opening my folder and sliding a clean lined sheet of paper into it so he could make notes. "I know you're very active in the Drama Club."

"I don't act. I just do behind-the-scenes stuff. Painting the scenery."

"So . . . are you interested in art?"

I shrugged, and he jotted something down.

"It shouldn't be hard to find a great art department. Have you thought about distance?"

"Distance?"

"Distance from home. Whether or not you want to go away to school, or commute."

Wow, I was just so completely unprepared for this meeting.

"No, I hadn't thought about it," I said.

"If you want to live at home, there are a lot of excellent schools within an hour of where we're sitting right now, especially in the city. Columbia, for instance, or NYU. You do have a support system here."

Stay close. I thought of Nana, making me pancakes every morning. And then I thought of Eve, living at home, with a purpose. Maybe I could have the same kind of purpose.

"But then again," Mr. Churchwell continued, tapping his pencil on my file, "I also think you might consider a . . . change of scenery. A lot of kids who come through my office want a fresh start somewhere."

When I was with Eve, I got by with white lies and omissions, never talking about my family in the present tense. Going away to school would be like diving into a world full of Eves. People who had no idea who I was, or what had happened. It sounded like pure, simple heaven.

Mr. Churchwell must have seen the confusion on my face because he said, "You don't have to make this decision now. Apply to a range of schools at a range of locations. Worry about it later after you know who's accepted you."

Procrastination. That worked. I took a deep breath.

214

Mr. Churchwell jotted something down in my folder and raised his eyebrows. "Do you have any particular schools in mind?" he asked.

"My dad went to Yale. It was his dream for me to go there too."

"Yale would be a good fit for you," he said, nodding and scribbling a note. "And it's not too far away. You could come home on weekends if you needed to." He paused, looked at me a little sideways. "It's tough to get into, but being a legacy gives you a better shot, for sure. We'll put that at the top of your list."

Then I remembered Eve telling me that once she got her undergraduate degree, she was going to apply to Cornell's vet school. "If you're at all interested in working with animals for a living," she'd said, "that's the place to go to college on the East Coast."

The only other thing I knew about Cornell was that it was cold, but I needed more names on my list.

"I've heard good things about Cornell," I told Mr. Churchwell. Then I rattled off the packets I remembered showing to my dad, and Smith for my mom, and Columbia and NYU because I could commute there. When I was done, Mr. Churchwell looked at the page he'd created in my folder.

"Have you visited any of these schools?" he asked.

"Just Yale, and the ones in the city. My father and I were going to do a bunch of weekend college visits last spring."

Dad had already arranged for the Fridays off from work and started booking hotel rooms.

"Ah yes, of course," said Mr. Churchwell sadly.

"Did I miss the boat on that?"

"No, not necessarily. Most schools offer interviews with local alumni, and you can always visit a campus after you get in to help you decide." He paused, making another note. "So with Yale, I recommend you take advantage of their Early Action application program," he said. "It means if you get your application in by November first, you could be in by mid-December, but it's nonbinding. You can still apply to other schools to keep your options open."

I acted like this was news but the truth was, I knew all about the Early Action thing. Dad had really wanted me to apply early. He loved the level of commitment it implied, and the whole ordeal being over as quickly as possible.

"Early Action sounds like a good idea," I said to Mr. Churchwell.

"You should download the materials and get cracking, especially with Yale, since that deadline is right around the corner," he said. "I think you'll have a strong application."

"Really?" I asked.

"Well, in addition to having great grades and SAT scores, your work with the Tutoring Club and your painting. You'll want to send them pictures of some of your sets. Your job at the vet's office goes a long way. And you're back in your school routine, working hard. In light of what's happened to you, that says a lot about character. It matters."

I thought about this for a moment, wrapping my head around what he meant. "So we should tell colleges about the accident?"

"I think your teachers should mention it in their recommendation letters, of course. But whether or not you write about it yourself, in your essay . . . that's your choice."

"So they might accept me out of pity."

"No. I didn't say that. They might accept you because among many other things, you've shown amazing strength and commitment in the face of adversity."

I considered what was being laid in front of me: The chance to really use my situation to an advantage that others didn't have.

"Think about it," he said, "and let me know."

TWENTY

Are you sure you don't want to come watch?"
asked Meg one day after last period. She
and Gavin were going to try out for *My Fair
Lady*, the Drama Club's fall musical.

Meg and Gavin were now a well-established couple.
Her first real boyfriend, and he was a good one to have. He
wasn't in Andie's crowd but everyone liked him; plus, he
had his own car. They had this habit of leaning together
against a wall with their hands in each other's back pockets, which I thought was just sickening. Sometimes I
pictured myself and Joe standing there with them, doing
the same thing, and that made it even harder.

Fortunately, I was scheduled to be at Ashland that day. Meg's face fell when I reminded her, as if she really wanted me to watch her French-kiss in the back row of the school auditorium. I knew she was trying to pull me back into my old activities ever since I'd reduced my hours at the hospital to just two afternoons a week. I needed the time to keep up with class work, but I missed the daily rhythm of the hospital, and being surrounded by people who didn't know anything about me. Now when I went, after a day of school and people staring sideways at me, it was almost more of a break than being at home.

Sometimes, when it was slow, I'd take a few minutes to sit on the rabbit bench out front and think of that day with David. Wondering where he was and when I'd hear from him next.

When I got to Ashland, all was chaos. A family had brought in their dog after he'd gotten into a fight. He was pretty beat up and bleeding, and Dr. B had been working on him for an hour. Which meant that the regularly scheduled appointments got delayed, and people were pissed. "He just pooped in his own carrier!" said a woman with a cat who was howling low and constantly.

"The doctor is handling an emergency at the moment," said Eve calmly. "You're welcome to reschedule, and we'll give you a discount on the office visit fee."

This placated the woman and Eve turned to me, made a face. "He's got to get another doctor in here full-time," she whispered. "There are just too many days like this."

I made myself as useful as I could. Dr. B and Robert got the injured dog stabilized, and we were able to start getting appointments in. After an hour, a man in a paint-covered jumpsuit walked in holding a dirty duffel bag with both hands. I saw Eve stiffen and found myself doing the same thing.

"Can I help you?" she said politely as he stepped up to the desk.

"I hope so. My crew was painting an empty apart-ment and we found this kitty in a closet. She seems sick or something."

Eve stood up and opened the duffel, peering inside. After a few moments she turned to me. "Get Robert ASAP."

I did what I was told, and Robert swooped in and took the bag as Eve whispered something to him. After he dis-appeared with it, Eve composed her face again and turned back to the man.

"You don't know where she came from?"

"I called the owner and he said the tenants who just moved out had a cat. Maybe it was theirs?"

Eve bit her lip. "We'll take care of her."

"Will she be okay?" he asked. "I'd . . . I'd take her, but my wife's allergic. . . ."

"I think she's about to give birth, actually." She leaned over and touched the man's arm. "You brought her to the right place." Then, when he didn't move, Eve added, "Do you want your duffel back?"

He shook his head, then looked around the waiting

room where three clients sat, having watched the whole exchange, staring at him. He bowed his head quickly to Eve and left.

After the remaining clients had been seen, Eve and I went in to check on the cat. Robert had set her up in a bottom cage and hung a towel over the front of it. Eve pulled the towel up gently and peeked in.

The cat looked up at us, a skinny, coal-black thing with haunting yellow eyes, still on her guard. She looked tired and spent as she nursed a mass of squirmy newborn kittens. Dr. B came in and Eve dropped the towel back into place. "So we have a new mom?" he asked wearily. "That's what, six weeks of that cage being occupied, until the kittens are weaned and you can place them?"

"I'm out of foster homes," said Eve with a pleading edge to her voice. "What am I supposed to do? Take her to the shelter?"

Dr. B just shrugged. "It's an option."

"She can't go to the shelter. She's already been dumped once, and if you bothered to *look* at her, you'd see how malnourished she is. They'd all get sick and die there."

Dr. B sighed. "Then you take her."

"My parents will kill me if I bring home any more." Eve was tearing up. She pulled up the towel again, hoping to force something in Dr. B. "Look at how depressed she is. All she wants is her family back."

As soon as Eve said that, I could feel my throat close up and a bolt of something hot and sharp behind my eyes. *For the love of God*, I thought, *please don't start crying here.* And then I saw something in my head. A bright place with a window and a soft bed that sat empty as wasted space on the planet.

Toby's bedroom.

"I can take her," I said, before I could think of the many reasons not to.

Eve put both hands on my shoulders, smiling wider than I thought her face had room for. "You CAN?"

I just nodded, looking at my palms. "I have room," I said after a few seconds. "I have plenty of room."

"Laurel, how can you do something like this without asking my permission first?" said Nana as we stood in the living room, a cardboard box full of cats at my feet. She was angry, her mouth pursed and her frown lines making cracks in her carefully applied makeup. I'd almost forgotten what that looked like.

"I didn't think you'd mind," I said, shrugging, not looking at her.

"Well, I do mind, but that's beside the point. This is my house too now, and I'm in charge, and if you want to bring in some homeless animals to live in your brother's . . ." She stopped as the word stuck in her throat, and turned away from me, finally spitting out, "Your brother's room . . . we have to talk about it."

"I'm sorry," I said. "Why don't you take your trip upstate, like you've been planning? That way you won't have to deal with it."

"I don't feel like going right now. Don't change the subject, Laurel."

She looked at me, her anger giving way to what seemed like confusion, like she was wishing she had a handbook she could check to figure out what to do in this situation.

"It was just something I needed to do." I thought of the cat's expression, imagined her alone in the empty apartment she knew as her home, wondering what she'd done wrong.

Nana saw that I was about to break down, but held her mouth in a firm line. "I understand that, and I think I understand why. I just wish you'd remember that you're not the only one trying to figure out how to get through."

Now that firm line fell apart, and she reached out to me. "I lost them too, you know," she said shakily.

I stepped into her and felt her arms grow tight around me, her crisp plaid blouse pressing against my chest. It was a place I didn't realize I wanted so badly to be.

Neither of us said anything for a little while. I pictured the kitty in the box, listening to all this, thinking, *I'm not sure this is going to be any better than the animal hospital.*

Finally Nana took a deep breath, stood back, and said, "Okay, but you feed them, you clean up after them. And you find them homes as soon as you possibly can."

I just nodded, and decided I would call my mama foster cat Lucky.

TWENTY-ONE

ne week before my birthday and two weeks before Halloween, the leaves hit their peak. I could stand on our front lawn and look south to see the quilt of browns and reds and yellows stretched across the hills. It was hard for me to drive because I'd always be staring up at the trees, which bent forward over the road like they were showing off their last bling of the season before going bare for the winter.

The memories hit me hard, squeezing my chest, every time I stepped outside and felt that snap in the air, the fall food smells drifting through our neighborhood. My dad and Toby and I raking the lawn, then jumping into the leaves. Mom and I shopping for sweaters and corduroys at the outlet mall. All four of us driving up north to go apple picking early on a Saturday morning. I'd always loved October because it moved things along, it kicked our butts into shifting gear. But now that things were moving along without them, it just made me cry a lot.

"Birthdays and holidays are very difficult when you're grieving, especially the first year," said Suzie during our latest session. "It's going to be a tough few months that way."

"I know," was all I said, playing with a loose button on my sweater.

"How's your college application coming along?" she asked. "You only have a couple weeks left to submit to Yale, right?"

"I'm almost done," I replied, glad to change the subject. I thought my application was pretty good. Or at least, good enough for my dad. I even had photos of my best set paintings over the years. They were photos Mom had taken, which at the time had seemed too embarrassing for words. Now the fact that she had taken them made the photos precious, and I had copies of them in a frame on my bedroom wall.

"Teachers are practically lining up to write my recommendation letters. That's pretty weird."

Suzie smiled. "Weird, maybe, but I'm sure not undeserved."

"I'm still stuck on what to write for the big essay." In other words, do I write about my family or not tell them anything about what happened? I was totally stumped and just kept putting it off.

"You'll think of the right topic, I'm sure."

I nodded. This was what everyone else had told me, including Nana and Meg. We were silent for too long, I guess, because Suzie jumped in with a new item. "And your birthday's coming up. Are you feeling like you want a big party, or just a small celebration?"

I just shrugged. Every time I thought about it, I got too sad.

"Because I think you need to empower yourself on this. You're old enough. If people do things for you and it's not what you want, it will really make you feel worse. What did you do in the past?"

"Usually Meg and I would go out to a movie and then have a sleepover."

"Is that what you want to do this time?" asked Suzie, making a note on her pad. Sometimes I imagined Suzie drawing squiggles and hearts all this time she was pretending to take notes.

I tried to picture Andie Stokes and Hannah Lindstrom in sleeping bags on the floor of the den. Like that was going to happen.

"No," I said. "I think it's time for a change. Maybe dinner at some cool restaurant."

Suzie nodded. "That sounds lovely."

Then I pictured Meg and Nana and Eve and me and

maybe Meg's parents, eating at a corner table at the Magic Wok. It did sound lovely.

"What about Halloween?" asked Suzie, bringing me back to reality. "There's a school dance, right?"

Man, she was in the loop.

"Yes," I said. "There's a dance and yes, I'm going. Andie and Hannah and a couple of their friends, and Meg and I, are going dressed as sushi. I think they said I'm yellowtail."

"Now *that* I would like to see," said Suzie, making another note (or another doodle). She looked at her notes again and, as if deciding I hadn't given her enough to write about, asked, "Anything else you want to talk about today?"

I had a new postcard from David tucked into the last pages of my history textbook. He was in Mexico. *Just for the weekend*, he'd written. *Just to see what it's like to have authentic tequila.*

I still hadn't told Suzie about anything that had happened with David; I wasn't about to start now. But I felt like I owed her some kind of new personal nugget.

"Joe Lasky wants us to do an art project together," I said, thinking of his open smile that day by my locker.

She smiled, way too pleased, but I was glad for it. Maybe she could get excited for me, since I wasn't allowing myself to.

"Tell me about *that*," said Suzie, and so I did.

It was after school and I was waiting for Joe. The day before, he'd sent me a text while I was in English:

superhero powwow 2mrw? no villains allowd.

I'd laughed, then texted back:

k, jst tel me whr d scret headquarters r.

Now the door, which I'd closed so nobody would see me sitting alone in the art classroom, started rattling. Joe's face appeared in the door's little window, his eyes confused.

"It's not locked!" I called.

Joe rattled a little more, pushed a bit harder, and suddenly fell into the room.

"I guess that's why Mr. Ramirez never closes this door," he said. His sketch pad was tucked under one arm and his bag slung diagonally across his chest. "Thanks for meeting me today."

"No problem." I shrugged, thinking, *Don't you know I've been looking forward to this?*

And: *You'd better not be doing this out of some obligation, to make up for prom night.*

Joe grabbed a stool and pulled it next to mine, then slapped his sketch pad on the table in front of us. "So, how do we do this?"

It felt like a bigger question, one that you could only answer with action. So I opened his sketch pad to the first drawing, a preteen-aged girl in oversize red boots and a perky minidress, her hands on her hips.

She was sticking out her tongue.

"Who's this?" I asked him.

"My little sister. SuperBrat. I've been drawing her in various forms for years."

"She's that bad?"

"You have no idea," said Joe, shaking his head. "When I was younger, I used to keep a list of ways she might die." He sucked in his breath and his face turned instantly white. "I'm sorry, I shouldn't have said that. . . . You . . ."

"It's okay," I said. But he looked so angry with himself. At that moment I realized how hard he must have been trying not to say anything to upset me. "You should definitely use this one," I added, coming to his rescue. "I could draw a room where everything is gigantic in relation to her. Tables and chairs and stuff. Like, she thinks she's a big shot but really, she's tiny in her world."

"I like that!" said Joe, nodding. Our heads were bent close to each other, and when I smelled his hair, it brought me back to prom night and almost overwhelmed me.

Joe, and this back-and-forth conversation. Not one-way postcards I couldn't answer, postcards that might as well have been messages dropped out of the sky and all I could do was try to catch them.

I grabbed my notebook and wrote something down about SuperBrat. "Okay, show me the next one."

A half hour later, we'd gone through all his sketches and picked out eight that should be in the show, and for which I could draw some backgrounds. Ideas came speeding through me, fully formed. It was as if they were traveling a highway that had been clogged with traffic but was now unexpectedly clear.

When we reached the end of Joe's sketch pad, we sat there for a moment. I didn't want to leave yet.

Then he said, "I hear you and a whole bunch of other girls have something fantastic planned for the Halloween dance."

I'd been wanting to find out whether or not he was going, but was afraid that if I asked, he'd think I wanted to go with him. Which I was sure would have been a terrifying prospect, given our history. Some things are just too scary even for Halloween.

"Yeah, it's a secret," I told him. "You'll have to see for yourself."

Joe looked down. "Unfortunately, I have to work that night."

I swallowed my disappointment. "I'm sure there will be pictures after the fact," I said casually, then started busying myself with my book bag in preparation to leave.

"I'm trying to get out of it." He still didn't look at me.

"Okay," I said, not looking back.

"Are you parked in the senior lot?" he asked, and when I turned to him and nodded, he made an *After you* gesture with his arm toward the door.

The hallways were mostly deserted, and only a few

people saw us walking out together. I knew it would be enough to start the rumor mill chugging again.

"Thanks again for agreeing to do this," said Joe as we approached my car.

"It's going to be fun," I said. "Plus, I can put it on my applications, if I don't get in early to Yale."

"I'll take photographs of the finished pieces so you can send them in."

"That would be great," I said. I stepped up to the car door and dug the keys out of my bag, then turned to wave good-bye, thinking that he'd stopped several feet behind me. But he hadn't, and now he was closer than I expected.

"Have a great night, Laurel," he said. Then he paused, and for half of a half of a fraction of an instant, I thought he might kiss me.

Kiss me, Joe. I won't shatter.

Instead, he leaned away from me, like he was afraid it might happen accidentally, and spread his arms wide. I copied him and we tilted into each other for the briefest of hugs. Not even a hug, really. More like a body brushing.

Seriously, Joe, you can touch me without breaking me. In fact, you might even put me a little bit back together.

Then he was stepping away from me and waving, and I waved back with the most normal smile I could muster.

As I drove home, I thought of Joe's lips by Adam LaGrange's pool, and how his hands had felt on me. Not this brushing nonsense, but planted firmly, with a sureness. How could I ever get that back?

And then I wondered about Mom. If she were waiting at home for me, would I ask her advice? Would we make tea and talk about what to do about Joe? I'd never gotten to the point with her of needing real boy guidance. But then, if she were alive, Joe and I would still be virtual strangers.

The sad and twisted irony of that made me suddenly furious. I turned up the radio as high as I could and then screamed into the oncoming traffic. It was a trick Suzie had taught me. Anyone outside the car would just think I was rocking out to a really great song.

Meg sat with me in the middle of the New York Yankees rug on the floor of Toby's room. Lucky lay purring crazy loud between us as I rubbed her belly and Meg scratched under her chin. She liked taking a break from the kittens, who were sleeping in a pile at the back corner of the dog crate Eve had lent me.

"She looks good," said Meg.

"I know, I can't believe how much weight she's gained in just three weeks. Eve gave me the recipe for a cat power meal that makes a big difference."

"Eve knows all," said Meg sarcastically, but I didn't respond and instead, glanced up to the solar-system mobile on the ceiling, which was twirling slowly and almost halfheartedly.

When I came into the room the day I saved Lucky's life, it was the first time it had been opened since Nana had to find Toby's good suit for him to be buried in.

While I had been able to go into my parents' bedroom a few times to look for things, neither of us could open Toby's door. We never talked about the *stuff* issue, even though Suzie occasionally asked me about that.

The air was stale but for a second, I thought I could smell that combination of Head & Shoulders and light sweat that would always be my brother. He had some new posters up: a few bands that he'd just started listening to and one of a blond model in a bikini, straddling a Vespa scooter, that made me laugh. There was a blank sheet-music book on the desk, with notes scratched out in Toby's crooked, struggling handwriting. I had glanced up at the electric piano in the corner, then back at the sheet music. All I could make out were the lyrics, *Tell me why, you want to cry.*

Toby was always good at making up songs, even if he had trouble writing them down. When we were younger, before my going to high school seemed to turn the three years between us into twenty, we'd put together shows for my parents. He did the music, I made the sets and costumes, and we just goofed through the rest of it.

Even though his room now smelled of cat, not teenage boy, I imagined Toby thought what I was doing was cool.

"Are you working on your Joe stuff?" Meg asked,

changing position and stretching.

She meant the drawings, of course, but those teased a larger, Joe Stuff world of possibilities.

"Yeah, a little. The show's not until December, so there's time."

"I'm glad you guys are . . . friendly now."

We paused, and I almost started to tell her about David's postcards. They weren't something I should be keeping from her, I knew that, but how could I explain them?

Then we heard Masher scratching and whining at the door, and the moment was gone. It drove him crazy that there were animals in here that he could smell but not see.

Lucky looked toward the door with disdain, then climbed into Meg's lap. "She must think you need a little sugar today," I said.

Meg frowned for a second and the tip of her nose twitched, like she had something to say about that, but then she just bent down and gave Lucky a big wet kiss on the head.

I wanted the Magic Wok for my birthday. I got the Magic Wok and the big round table in the corner, with the Lazy Susan on it, which I always loved when I was little.

Nana and Megan sat on either side of me. Meg's parents sat next to her, and Eve sat next to Nana. Everyone ordered the mai tais, which came in a ceramic Buddha with a ridiculously long straw, including Meg and Eve and me, although we got the alcohol-free versions that tasted like Slurpees.

"To Laurel," said Meg, raising her Buddha. "May this year be as awesome as possible."

Everyone raised their Buddhas. "To Laurel!"

We ate dumplings and egg rolls and everyone got along, except maybe Mr. Dill, who didn't seem to like Chinese food because he asked the waiter to get him a steak sandwich, and Mrs. Dill rolled her eyes and tilted her chair away from him.

Also there was the sadness. I could feel it right there under the table, about to crawl out on hands and knees into my party. Maybe if I kept my legs together and my feet pressed to the ground, it wouldn't have room to escape.

But it came anyway, no matter how loud everyone laughed at Eve's jokes or the way Nana tried for the first time in her life to use chopsticks.

It was my birthday, and I wanted my mom and dad. My mother always tried to do something a little alternative for my parties, like buying old hats at the secondhand store and letting my guests and me decorate them with felt flowers and beads. Dad gave me a book every year, inscribed inside the front cover. I'd always thought, *Why can't she just hire a magician or a bounce house like everyone else? Am I supposed to read this book and pretend that I love it even if I don't?*

Every time I felt like I was going to lose it, I took a sip from my Buddha and stared at the green cap of the low-sodium soy sauce bottle as it sat in front of me on the Lazy Susan. Or I just smiled and laughed and nodded whenever everyone else did.

It felt right, the people who were here (except maybe Mr. Dill). Fortunately, Andie and Hannah had an away field hockey game and couldn't come, and I knew that when I invited them. Things with Joe were still so unformed, shapeless. That was an awkwardness I didn't want in the mix.

After the appetizers, I got up to go to the bathroom, and Meg rose to go with me. As we walked away from the table and down the hall, I heard Eve ask, "So where are Laurel's folks tonight?"

A hush came over the table, but I didn't turn to look over my shoulder.

"Keep walking," said Meg, and she pulled me toward the restroom door.

When I was done peeing and Meg was done peeing and we had both washed our hands, I knew I was going to have to go back and look at Eve's face and see that she knew now.

Screw it. It was my birthday.

Meg went back to the table first, and I followed her. They were all talking about their favorite "food movie moments," and Mrs. Dill was describing some scene from a Jack Nicholson film where he was ordering an egg salad sandwich, and everyone made sure to keep the conversation going when I sat back down.

But as soon as I did that, Eve started crying. Nana put her arm around her as Eve raised her eyes to me, and I looked away. Then, fortunately, the food came, and soon everyone was too busy using eating as an excuse not to talk.

Later, they brought out a big cake and made the whole restaurant sing "Happy Birthday," and I opened gifts. For a second, I remembered the Tinker Bell bubble bath David once gave me for my birthday when we were little kids, and wondered where he was at that very moment.

TWENTY-TWO

I don't get it," said Meg. "This is supposed to be the rice part?"

"Yeah. Doesn't it look like rice?"

We were standing in front of the full-length mirror in her mom's room, with big slabs of white Styrofoam hanging off our backs. The Styrofoam was attached to straps that hung over our shoulders, which were attached to big colored sacks of material hanging down the front of our bodies. I don't think either of us was prepared to admit how moronic the whole thing was.

"No, and these don't look like pieces of fish."

"I think it'll be better once we put on the seaweed," I

offered, pointing to the green felt sashes lying on the floor, which we were supposed to wrap around our middles.

"Tell me again why we agreed to do this?" asked Meg, trying to make her rice slab hang straight.

"You're the one who likes them so much. And Andie said they really needed a full sushi platter. How could we do that to them? Make them go to the Halloween dance without *shrimp* and *yellowtail?* They'd be laughed out of town!"

Meg giggled, then gave me a sideways glance. "You don't like them?"

"I guess I do. I don't *not* like them. They're nice."

"Yeah, they are,." What she didn't say was, *and they're popular,* and she didn't feel the need to mention that *by hanging out with them, my social score has skyrocketed.* And I didn't feel like reminding her out loud that *this is all because they want to look like saints for befriending poor Laurel Meisner.*

There was so much that Meg and I weren't saying to each other these days.

"You're right," announced Meg, to her reflection in the mirror. "It'll look better with the seaweed. And Gavin will complete the effect."

Gavin was going as a giant pair of chopsticks. I just smiled at her and thought, *If things were different with Joe, what would he go as?* Maybe wasabi? Would a guy ever like me enough to dress up as wasabi? And how exactly would that work, anyway?

It was a Friday night and Halloween itself was the following Thursday, which meant I had just five more days to write my essay for Yale and submit it before the November 1 deadline. I still had no idea what to say, especially whether or not to write about my family. Without that, I was having a hard time finding something to say that mattered, something that would make the Yale admissions department think I was special. I knew I should have been home working on it, but all of this somehow seemed much more important.

"You'll come up with something in time," Nana had said confidently. "You always do."

Downstairs, Meg's parents and Nana waited with their cameras. Mrs. Dill had changed her mind about "those girls" when Meg brought Andie home for dinner one night, and they all got along famously. Nana had changed her mind the day after my birthday, when Andie came to the house with a card and a gift certificate for a mani-pedi at Happy Nails "from all of us." If there was a way to Nana's heart, it was through good grooming.

More photos in front of the staircase. Nana didn't really get the sushi thing, but she made a big deal out of us anyway. Then she took Meg into the kitchen, just the two of them, and I heard her whispering something about not leaving my side. The whole scene was such a flashback to prom—we all felt it, I could tell—that I couldn't blame

Nana. I was even a little grateful, and glad she'd post-poned her trip home yet again to be here.

We neatly folded the costumes and loaded them into Meg's car before driving to school for the dance. We were both wearing white head to toe, and glowed a little in the fluorescent light above the Dills' driveway. Before we climbed in, Meg and I stood on either side of the car, looking at each other over its glossy black roof.

"I feel like we're going to a mime party," I said, unable to hide the shaky nervousness in my voice.

"You'll be fine," said Meg, but she sounded uncon-vinced.

We'd been worried about being late, but as soon as we pulled into the school parking lot I realized we were going to be among the nerds who showed up first. There were only a handful of other cars there.

"It's okay, we need the time to get dressed," said Meg.

So we stood behind the Toyota, yet again putting on the Styrofoam and the green felt belts, hoping nobody saw us until we were together with the rest of our platter. And then we waited, huddled in the shadows between the car and a tree, just a pair of raw delicacies watching other kids arrive.

Meg offered commentary.

"Luke Trumbull is Frankenstein. That's old school. Oh, look! Somebody's Thing One and Thing Two from *Cat in the Hat.* Can't tell who yet, they're too far away."

Finally, we saw Andie's Beetle swoop in, and we made our way to where she was parking.

"You guys look yummy!" she said, then Hannah and two of their friends climbed out. We helped them get their costumes on, and together, we looked less stupid. Hannah had designed and made them, so she was extra proud as she herded us toward the school, snapping pictures of us from behind.

"Let's get a group shot before we go in," said Hannah as we reached the main entrance. We arranged ourselves on the steps, our arms around one another, while Andie flagged down a sophomore to snap the photo for us. He looked thrilled at the opportunity and made a big deal out of positioning the camera.

"Say 'sake'!" he said.

"Sake!" we all echoed, smiling.

He took a photo, then said, "One more, the other way." As he was turning the camera, something caught my eye off to the right, near where the squat, round auditorium building sat like a big tuna can in front of the school.

The bear statue appeared to be moving.

No wait. Not the bear statue. A person standing in front of the bear statue, shadowed in silhouette.

A person who looked like he could be David.

"Say '*sayonara*'!" said the sophomore, trying so hard to be cool.

I was afraid to turn my eyes away, in case what I saw disappeared, but Meg tightened her arm around me and I glanced at the camera long enough to get blinded by the flash.

Now I couldn't see anything by the auditorium except white sparks. Meg and the rest of the platter headed into the school, but I just stood there on the steps, watching the sparks fade from my vision.

The David-person moved again, and I started to move toward him, walking across the wet grass in my white sneakers, not caring about how muddy they were getting. Finally I reached pavement again, the walkway in front of the auditorium, and now I could see him unshadowed. He saw me, too.

"Laurel," he said simply.

His hair was longer now, brushing the tops of his shoulders, and the weight of it made it hang straight and shiny. He'd lost more weight and gotten kind of tan. He looked about five years older.

And then there was me, dressed as sushi.

"Hi, David."

His eyes swept up my costume, but stopped before they got to my face.

"Don't tell me. Yellowtail, right?"

"How did you know?"

David smiled sideways. "In California, there's sushi everywhere. I ate a lot of it."

"There you are!" I heard Meg's voice behind me and spun around. She was panting. "I thought you were with me, I'm sorry. It was so crowded it took me a few minutes to realize—"

Meg caught sight of David and her mouth dropped open.

"What the hell are you doing here?" she asked angrily. It was what I had planned to say, once I'd decided which was weirder: David showing up like this, or David knowing what kind of fish I was supposed to be.

"I'm here to see Laurel," said David, now raising his eyes to mine. They were perfectly round and completely open, telling me it was okay to let my gaze lock on. "I just got in tonight and I went to your house . . . to see Masher . . . and nobody's home. And I knew there was a dance here so I figured I could find you. . . ."

He wanted to see his dog. Well, of course. I dropped my eyes away.

"Laurel, maybe you can give him your house keys? Your grandmother's probably still at my place."

I looked at Meg, then behind her at the lights of the school as they seemed to quiver from the energy of the dance. Music boomed from the gym, where no doubt the rest of our sushi platter was looking for us, and Gavin was wandering around as a big pair of chopsticks with nothing to pick up. Joe was miles away ripping ticket stubs at the movie theater, and I had nobody hoping to see me.

"Meg, just go in," I said.

"What do you mean?"

"Just go. To the dance. I'll . . ." I glanced at David. "I'll go home with him."

"But you'll miss the fun," she said weakly.

"Not really," I said. "And you'll have more of it without me there."

Meg tilted her head as if she was about to shake it in denial, but stopped. She knew I was right.

"What do I tell the girls?"

"Tell them I realized I wasn't ready for a big social event yet. It's kind of the truth anyway."

"Let me go with you," she said hesitantly.

"No, I want you to stay."

"I promised Nana . . ."

"She'll be okay with this, I swear."

Meg narrowed her eyes. "There's something you're not telling me."

"Please just go. I'll fill you in later." I wasn't sure if that was true.

Meg gave me a confused, dirty look before walking back to school without saying good-bye. I watched her rectangle of white Styrofoam grow smaller on her way across the grass, then turned back to David.

"Thank you," he said. "I really can't wait to see Masher."

"He can't wait to see you," I replied, and started following David to his father's Jaguar, which was parked in the faculty lot and definitely not shiny anymore.

We drove to my house in silence. My costume was wedged in the Jaguar's backseat, and I fought the urge to climb back there with it. Anything to not be sitting silently next to David, dressed head to toe in white like a gigantic neon sign of dorkiness.

When we passed the Kaufmans' house on the way to mine, David craned his neck to look up at it, not bothering to hide the pain in his eyes.

We pulled into my driveway, the Volvo still absent, but he didn't turn off the car. He just stared straight ahead at our garage door.

"Sometimes I play that night over in my head, with things going differently," he said. It came out sounding distracted, dreamy.

I didn't answer.

"You know, like, instead of going to Kevin's to piss off my parents, I do the decent thing and go with them to Freezy's. We would have had to go in two cars."

He looked at me, and I tried to hide the shock on my face.

"It might have changed everything," he said.

I thought of my Wondering Well. It had been Suzie's suggestion. Every time I felt myself drowning in what-ifs, I wrote them down on a piece of paper, folded it up, threw it in an old mayonnaise jar, and screwed the lid back on tight. It was a way of getting them out, letting them go.

My Wondering Well was getting full, and I'd need to find another jar soon.

Swallowing hard, I finally said, "It might have. But it didn't."

David sighed and nodded, then turned the car off and sat there, his hands still on the wheel.

"I've been driving for so long," he said softly, "it still feels weird to stop."

Silence again. It felt like David needed me to take the lead here. *We're on my turf now.* So I just said, "Thanks for the letters."

He turned to look at me, expressionless.

"I mean, Masher thanks you. I think they smelled familiar or something."

David smiled wistfully. "I'm glad he liked them."

"Let's go see him," I said, opening the car door. We climbed out of the Jaguar, and now he was following me to the house.

As soon as I took out my keys and they jingled, we could hear Masher barking and panting inside, which made David laugh. In seconds the door was open, and Masher leapt through the doorway straight at David, a frantic blur, and had his paws on David's chest and his tongue on David's face. He'd known David was there, even though we hadn't said a word. Somehow, he was sure of it.

I stepped around them into the house, toward my room, so I could change out of all that white. When I got there, I walked into my closet and closed the door behind me, thinking of David's eyes laser-beaming at the place he'd always called home.

Sometimes I play that night over in my head.

It had never occurred to me that David was haunted by the wondering too. It was so simple, and so obvious.

I cried hard but quietly with relief in the dark.

TWENTY-THREE

n hour later, Nana was laying out some Pepperidge Farm cookies for us on the kitchen table, apologizing that she didn't have anything homemade.

"It's fine, Nana," I said. "Can you chill?"

"I'm just kicking myself because we had that pumpkin bread but I brought it all down to the Dills', and I should have kept some for us."

She smiled down at David, who was sitting with Masher's head on his lap, inhaling defrosted mulligan stew as if he hadn't eaten in days. I had to give Nana credit; when she got home about ten minutes after we did, she was unfazed by his presence at the house. She didn't even seem to mind that I was blowing off the dance. She just went straight to the freezer to see what kind of food she could offer.

When David finally took a break from the stew and reached for a cookie, Nana made her move.

"So, David, what brings you home?"

He flinched for just a second but continued his cookie grab. "Oh, didn't you hear?" he said lightly—too lightly. "My grandparents sold the house, and I have to go through my stuff to decide what to keep."

We were silent. I had driven or walked by the FOR SALE sign every day since it first went up, but still the thought of someone else living in that house never entered my mind. It didn't seem possible. I'd grown to see it as an empty, perfectly preserved memorial of my family's last night alive.

"Who did they sell it to?" asked Nana.

"Some married couple with a baby," said David, practically spitting out each word.

We were quiet again. There was really nothing to say to him that would be appropriate. It only felt right to stay in the small, here-and-now details.

"Do your grandparents know you're here?" Nana asked.

"No, not yet."

"I'm sure they'll be happy to have you home again."

David shook his head. "I'm not staying there. I . . . I can't. Stay there." He pulled his cell phone out of his pocket and squinted at the display. "I'm trying to hook up with Kevin to crash at his place, but he's not calling me back."

Nana glanced at me, and I just raised my eyebrows at her to let her know, *Go ahead.*

"Well, you can stay here if you want," said Nana. "There's a nice sofa in the den that I can make up for you."

"Really?" David's face lit up. "That would be great. I could bunk with Mash here."

He had a look I'd never seen before. Sincerity maybe, mixed with a little self-pity. I didn't know him well enough to pin it down.

I kept wanting to say something to him, but after my little closet episode, I found myself speechless.

"How's your father?" Nana asked casually. I'd been hoping she wouldn't ask that. I didn't want to know.

And it made David's face fall again. "He's the same."

"I'm sorry," said Nana.

"I'm going to go see him while I'm here."

"I'm sure he'd like that." Nana paused, then put her coffee cup down. "I'll go get the couch ready. You must be exhausted."

She left the room and I almost followed her, but David turned to me.

"Masher seems great. Thank you for that."

I looked down at the dog and couldn't help but smile. "He's a good boy. And he doesn't even mind the new cat."

"New cat?" David frowned.

I'd been hoping for a way to tell him what I was doing, what was going on in my life. Suddenly it seemed easiest just to show him.

"Come check it out," I said, then simply stood and jerked my head toward the hallway.

The next morning, I woke up late. I'd gotten used to Masher waking me up at a certain time to be let out, but there'd been no wet nose on my neck at seven. Then I remembered why.

The couch in the den was neatly made up, and David's army duffel bag lay on the floor next to it, its contents creeping out.

"Where is he?" I asked Nana, who was doing dishes in the kitchen.

"Well, look who slept in today! Good morning, lazy-bones."

"He's gone already?"

"Just to his house. Masher, too. He wanted to get an early start." She paused and shook her head. "I don't envy him that job. It's one of the reasons why I keep putting off my trip home."

I thought of David sitting in his room, with his dog beside him, surrounded by all the things he ever owned in his life. Trying to decide what was important enough to keep.

Then I remembered Suzie asking about what we were going to do with my parents' and Toby's things.

"Are we going to do that here? With *their* stuff?"

I regretted it almost instantly, as soon as I saw the anguish on Nana's face.

"I'm not ready to talk about that," she said sharply. It was so easy for me to forget that where I'd lost a father, she'd lost her only son; where I'd lost a brother, she'd lost a grandson ("My darling boy," she called Toby, which always made him cringe).

"I'm sorry . . ." I mumbled.

"Meg called," said Nana, turning back to the dishes. "She said she also sent you a message."

I found my phone and read Meg's text, which was the expected check-in to see if I was all right. I sent her a response that yes, I was fine, and I hoped she had fun. I knew I was supposed to call her and get a full report on what had happened at the dance, and I was supposed to tell her everything David said and did all night. But I didn't feel like it, and didn't think about why.

So I grabbed my journal and tried to brainstorm ideas for my Yale essay.

David didn't come back until dinnertime, although Nana acted like that was too early.

"Oh, you're not having dinner with your grandparents?" she said, pleasantly surprised, as soon as she opened the front door for him.

He looked tired and defeated, his eyes red. He just shook his head no and moved slowly over the threshold of our house, Masher behind him quiet but with tail wagging.

I was sitting in the living room doing English homework but not making much progress. I'd given up on my essay for the day, and had just read the same paragraph in *The Scarlet Letter* three times, listening for footsteps up the driveway. Now I put the book down and followed him.

David sat down at the kitchen table, and I wondered if he expected Nana to produce some food, but he just folded his head into his hands and took one, two, three deep breaths. Nana gestured that we should give him time alone, and we moved to leave.

"Don't go," said David behind us.

We turned and froze. Why had I been waiting all day for him to come back? Things were just weird when he was here.

"I had no idea how much crap I owned," he joked. "I don't want to get rid of any of it, but my grandmother says there's only so much room in the storage space they're renting."

"Oh, a storage space! What a smart idea!" offered Nana, like it was the most brilliant thing she'd ever heard.

"I thought so too, at first, but now the idea of all my

256

stuff, my parents' stuff, locked away in some concrete block somewhere depresses the hell out of me. My mom always thought those things were so ugly. She wouldn't have wanted . . ."

David stopped himself, his voice cracking. He ran a hand—dirty fingernails, callused knuckles—through his hair and sniffled quickly. Several seconds passed, and although he didn't look at me, I felt that somehow he expected me to speak.

"We can keep it here at our house," I said, the words taking the express route from my brain to my mouth, with no thought stops along the way. "We have a huge attic, and it's mostly empty."

Nana gave me a startled look, and I just shrugged back at her. Then she smiled.

"Really?" David asked, his eyes meeting mine for the first time that night.

"Sure," I said, staring back at him.

"Thank you." This came out sounding stiff and polite, and he put his head back in his hands. I took that as my cue to go back to *The Scarlet Letter*, which I grabbed off the couch and took with me into Toby's room, where Lucky waited with her deep purr and yellow, contented eyes.

Later that night, there was a knock on Toby's door.

"What?" I asked, cranky, sure it was Nana. I'd finished my reading chapters and was now working on calculus at

Toby's desk. It was creepy, I knew, but I loved how Lucky sat next to my arm, with one paw across my wrist, as I tried to write.

"Can I come in?" It was David. I turned quickly in the chair and Lucky, startled, shot across the room. Her toenails left a thick white scratch on my arm.

"Ow!" I yelled.

David now opened the door. "You all right?"

"Fine," I said, holding my arm. "Just got nailed by the cat."

David came in, although I hadn't told him it was okay, and closed the door quickly behind him so Masher couldn't follow. A couple of tortured protest barks came from the hallway.

David sat on the floor, and Lucky came out from under the bed to check him out. We were quiet for a few moments as David petted Lucky, and kitten mews drifted faintly from the dog crate.

When I'd brought him into the room the night before to show him what I'd been up to, he'd just smiled, satisfied and not surprised. Like he expected there to be homeless cats, like there couldn't possibly be anything else that made sense. Unlike Nana and Meg, he'd had no questions. He just liked it.

It felt fair now. I'd learned so much from his postcards about what he was doing on his way across the country, and now it was my turn to fill him in. The balance seemed about right. It made our silence more about comfort and less about itchy strangeness.

Finally, David reached into his back pocket and pulled out a folded piece of paper. "I found this today," he said, opening the paper and holding it up.

It showed a drawing of a rocky hillside with the opening of a cave smack in the middle, shaped perfectly into an upside-down U. The cave was black, except for two sets of wide eyes in the Magic Marker darkness. One set of eyes had long eyelashes. Purple letters along the bottom announced, "LAUREL AND DAVID EXPLORE THE CAAAAAAVE!"

"Oh my God," I said, then laughed.

"So you remember?"

I remembered just two moments from a day a long time ago. One was David leading me through the woods toward the cave in the woods behind our houses, a place where most kids in the neighborhood were afraid to go, as he held a big walking stick and I held a plastic bucket full of snacks like I was Little Red Riding Hood. The other was us in the darkness of the cave, me feeling proud that I had actually walked a few feet in until the top of my head brushed its roof. We were eight, maybe nine years old. So long ago and so improbable that at times, when I thought about it, I wondered if it had really just been something I'd seen in a movie.

To David, I just nodded and then smiled.

He folded the drawing and put it back in his pocket. "I was thinking of going there tomorrow morning. It's been awhile since I took Masher, and he loves it. Do you want to come?"

He made the invitation with his eyes fixed on the cat, but I could tell it was a serious one.

"Sure," I said, then to cut the tension I added, "Should I take my basket of snacks?"

Now David chuckled a bit and stood up. "Only if you think we're going to get lost and need bread crumbs to find our way back."

Then he left the room without saying good night.

TWENTY-FOUR

y eight o'clock the next morning, David and Masher and I were heading out the back door dressed in jackets and boots, since the forecast was for rain and the sky was already deepening into a dark gray. The wind blew dead leaves around our ankles as we walked across my backyard, silently, our hands in our pockets because it was just way too nerdy—even for me—to wear gloves in October no matter how chilly it got.

After we crossed Watch Hill Road and continued farther into the woods, David cleared his throat and said stiffly, "I know I said it last night, but I really do want to thank you for offering to store my stuff."

"It's fine, David," I said. "We have the room. Those storage places are yucky."

He paused, and I could hear him swallow hard even though our feet crunched loud along the ground. "Can I ask you something?"

"Maybe," I said, trying to sound funny.

"Why are you being so nice to me?"

"Am I?"

"My dog. My stuff. Honestly, Laurel, you'd think that I hadn't been such an asshole at that party that night. And you'd think that . . ." David stopped walking. It seemed like his throat was closing around something, and he took a quick little breath. "You'd think that my dad hadn't been the one everyone blames."

It seemed so fitting, suddenly, that David would be the one to say this out loud, this thing that so many people up and down our street and through the neighborhood and across town had thought to themselves, or maybe whispered to the one or two friends they trusted most. The thing I'd jammed into a place deep within me, because I couldn't figure out what to do with it. Not even Suzie had been able to pull it out, and she sure had tried.

"I mean, I don't give a crap what *they* think," he continued, waving his hand. "They can go stick it up their gossip-loving, SUV-driving, Bob-and-Pam-are-meeting-us-at-the-golf-club butts."

He reached out and actually touched my shoulder with two of his fingers. "But you, Laurel . . . You have the right to think the worst, and I have a feeling I know how bad that really is, because I think it too."

I thought back to prom night, and David's reaction when I told him his father was a murderer.

"Yeah, David. I do think the worst. But you told me your dad wasn't drunk. Now you've changed your mind?"

He looked down. "No, I still don't think he was drunk. I . . . I know he wasn't. But even if it was another car that drove him off the road, he was the one driving. He *made* this whole mess."

Now he glanced up at the trees, gave a tired sigh. He had no idea how it felt like he'd read my mind.

I asked, "When are you going to visit him?"

"Not sure. When I'm done at the house, I guess."

"Can I come with you?"

David reacted with surprise. My question had surprised me, too.

"Why?"

Yeah, Laurel. WHY?

"I don't know. I just thought . . ." I wasn't sure what I thought. Now that David was saying the things I'd been thinking, it seemed like something we both needed to do.

"No," he cut me off. "Not yet, at least. Okay?"

His expression was so pained, and I suddenly got how David struggled, feeling protective of his father while also hating his guts.

"We'll have to find some way for me to pay you back," said David.

"You don't need to pay me back," I said. "You don't owe me anything."

"Oh, come on, Laurel," he said, his voice rising. "Stop being so nice. Give it to me. Give it to me like you did that night after the prom."

Masher started barking. He didn't like people yelling at each other.

"I was drunk," I said softly, "and it was so soon after."

"So now you're not angry anymore?"

"Of course I'm angry," I shot back, but as the words came out of my mouth I wondered if I'd ever said them before. Was there anything I could add that would make me stop sounding like an idiot? "I'm furious, but I don't feel the need to take it out on you."

"Still trying to be the good girl," said David, shaking his head. "Going for that extra credit. You get a certain number of points for the dog, and a certain number for hanging on to his stuff. God, you still want to be their sweetheart no matter what!"

Now I *was* angry, but it suddenly occurred to me that he wanted this. He wanted me to get in his face, mean and honest like a tough, loving coach in an old football movie. Maybe this was the whole reason he was here.

I took a deep breath. "I did those things because I

wanted to. Because I thought of them and they made sense and they made me feel good. If that makes me somebody's good-girl sweetheart, then okay, that's who I am. I can live with that."

He looked up at me again and blinked away a glassy layer of tears.

"How can you be so normal?" he asked, a twangy whine in his voice. "I can't—I can't be like that, and you got it worse than me."

"I'm not normal, David. Believe me. People stare at me wherever I go, watching what I'm doing, listening to what I'm saying. They treat me like I'm made of glass."

David's face softened, and he shook his head. "We're both screwed."

He was silent then, like the subject was closed. I wanted so badly to hear more, to talk more. For the first time in months, I felt like I had had a real conversation with someone. Like someone had cracked me open and everything that was plain and honest had spilled out onto the dry autumn earth.

What else do you know, David? And how do you know it?

I fought back the nervousness I still felt around him and was about to give voice to these things. But just then, Masher started barking again, and we looked up to see him about a hundred yards away, running circles in front of a rocky slope.

265

"Good boy, Mash!" called David. "I would have walked right by it!"

We walked toward the cave, which was much more overgrown now. No way would I have gone into it back then, if it looked like this. You could barely see the opening because there were so many weeds in front of it, and one tree had filled in so much that its branches hung down like bars.

Masher was already digging his way inside. David called for him to wait up but he disappeared into the cave, so David went after him, swiping at anything that got in his way.

I stood there, knowing I was supposed to follow, but not sure I wanted to. It pissed me off that David thought he knew so much about me. I would have turned around and headed home right then, but (a) I wasn't sure how to get there and (b) I wanted to stay.

"Laurel? You coming?" called David, and I headed toward his voice.

It took me a few minutes and several scrapes from strange, itchy plants, but I made it to where David crouched in the darkness with his hand outstretched to grab mine. I took it, and it felt cool and hot at the same time. I could feel the creases of his palm, which made my heart race a bit, which then surprised me so much that I nearly fell over.

"Here," was all he said, and I took one last step into the

cave. We both had to crouch while my eyes adjusted to the lack of light.

"This is smaller than I remember," I said.

"Well, we're bigger, Einstein."

"Oh, right. Duh."

"There's a rock right in front of you that you can sit on."

I felt with my hands until I found the rock, and lowered myself onto it. I could now see David sitting across from me on a little shelf inside the cave, and Masher's tail at the far wall, wagging. I couldn't see his head but I could hear him clawing and sniffing at something.

"Don't you think this is peaceful?" asked David.

"Sure, if your idea of a vacation is being locked in a closet somewhere."

"I was wondering if maybe this is what it's like to be in a coma," he said, and I could see him close his eyes. "Like, do you dream, or is everything just dark and empty inside your head?"

I had no answer for him. He wasn't asking me, anyway.

We were quiet for what seemed like several minutes but was probably just a few seconds. Finally, Masher decided he was done digging and started making his way out of the cave.

"After you," said David, tilting his head toward the light. I got up and took a big step onto the wobbly rock, but he didn't offer his hand.

Once we were out, David suggested we walk a bit

farther, and I just shrugged okay.

"Do you really think we're screwed?" I asked him after we'd gone a few dozen yards in silence.

He laughed, a little *humph*. "I don't know. I guess that depends on how much good luck comes our way in life."

"Don't you think that we have something to do with it too? Like we can unscrew ourselves, if we do things a certain way?"

He laughed a little. "Unscrew ourselves. You mean I actually have to do some of the work? It's so much easier to be a victim!"

David said that jokingly, but something about the way he said it struck me. I could almost hear it *ping* off my forehead. He was right. It was easier to be the victim, but it didn't feel so great.

And I wanted more than that. I'd wanted so much before the accident—all the things most people do when they're sixteen, I guess. Why couldn't I want them now? Why couldn't I have them, still?

"I have to come up with one more essay for my Yale application," I said. "And I'm trying to decide whether or not I should write about the accident."

David raised his eyebrows. "It's probably something they don't see very often."

"I just don't know who to tell, and who not to tell. Mr. Churchwell says that wherever I end up going, he could make sure my roommates and RAs are aware of my 'situation.'"

He nodded. "More watching, more tiptoeing, more kid gloves."

"What would you do?"

David stopped walking suddenly, so I stopped too. He stared off at something in the distance, squinting a bit, then shifted his gaze to me.

"What are you more afraid of? That people won't treat you normally once you get there, or that they will?"

Another sudden truth, so clear. David was scary good at throwing these at me and having them stick.

Maybe I'd been kidding myself. I'd been thinking it would be heaven, a world of people not seeing me as a walking tragedy. But now that I saw that, it scared the crap out of me. I wouldn't be special anymore. I would have no excuses.

David just smiled, knowing the answer. "You don't need to be afraid of it. That's why I left town, to be anonymous to everyone out there. And I wasn't ready for it. I'm still not. But you, Laurel. You're strong enough. You know who you are."

"I do?" I wanted to add, *Then tell me! Who am I?*

"I think so," said David. He bent down to pick up a stick. It was a perfect fetching stick for Masher, just the right length and thickness. I was always looking for sticks like that, and I guess David was too. He yelled, "Hey, Mash! Fetch!" and tossed it as far as he could. Masher shot off after it.

When David turned back to me I put my hand on his

elbow, and it didn't take him or me by surprise. It just seemed the natural thing to do. "Thanks for the advice," I said.

"Thanks for asking for it."

We smiled at each other, and neither of us clicked our eyes away.

"Laurel," he said, his smile disappearing. But it wasn't the beginning of a sentence. It had no upturn at the end of it. He was just saying my name, and it reminded me that I was here, alive, with two feet connected to the ground and breath filling my lungs. I was me, and apparently I knew who I was.

Then David put one hand gently on the side of my head, his palm pressing lightly on my ear, his fingers pushing my hair back. The prickly feeling of his skin on mine shot through me and made me a little dizzy. I still wasn't sure what he was doing.

Until he kissed me.

He just leaned in and did it before I knew it was happening—I was distracted by the hand-ear nuclear reaction—and before I could think anything, I was kissing him back.

His lips felt softer than I thought they would. Softer than Joe's. And much more practiced, confident, even while I thought I felt him shaking. He tasted sweet, too, and I remembered he'd had Nana's cookies for breakfast.

Then he pulled away and dropped his hand and stared

at me, wide-eyed as if I'd been the one to kiss *him*. "Okay," was all he said.

I looked at his lips and remembered a moment from last year when I'd seen him hanging out in the senior parking lot, smoking cigarettes with his friends. I'd watched him drag on one and then open his mouth to blow perfect Os of smoke, and I'd been impressed. Now I'd just kissed that mouth.

"Okay," I echoed.

"We should probably get back. I have to go over to the house."

"Right."

We started walking again, and when our hands accidentally brushed, David moved a few steps farther away. It made me ache, but I didn't do anything about it. Would I ever in a jillion years have the courage to tell him I wanted him closer, more touching, more kissing?

Thank God for Masher. It would have been the longest walk of our lives if he hadn't made us laugh nervously as he nuzzled the leaves and barked at the branches and did a happy little dance every time he found a new tree or rock. His antics carried us back through the woods and away from the cave, and away from our kiss. Masher knew exactly where to go, and all we had to do was let him take us home.

TWENTY-FIVE

avid spent the rest of that Sunday at his house, and I stayed in Toby's room, playing with Lucky and the kittens, who were just starting to crawl around while their mom watched them, tired but vigilant. I couldn't deal with my Yale essay, so I broke out my sketch pad and started drawing some backgrounds for Joe's art project, thinking that maybe if I focused on Joe for a little while, I wouldn't feel like I'd cheated on him somehow.

My cell phone had four unread text messages, and I assumed they were all from Meg. Twice I started to call her back, to tell her everything that had happened in the woods, but stopped before actually pressing her speed-dial button. I wasn't ready to share yet. I didn't feel like giving up anything of what I'd collected from the day.

I stayed up late, waiting for David to come back, but at nine o'clock he called the house and told Nana that he'd be awhile, and she arranged to leave a key under the mat for him. I was both relieved and disappointed that I wouldn't see David that night.

When I woke up the next morning, I got dressed and showered and crept to the doorway of the den to see David and Masher asleep on the couch.

"He got back late," said Nana behind me.

"I figured," I said.

"Do you want cereal or toast?"

Nana knew nothing of how my world had shifted in the last twenty-four hours. It didn't seem possible that I could concentrate on a simple decision like that, that I could care about something as tiny as what to eat for breakfast. But somehow I was going to have to get through the day, so I had to start sucking it up.

"Cereal, please. Thanks."

After breakfast I left for school, calculating how many hours until I could come home and potentially see David. It wasn't that I was dying to be with him, but I was curious. How was he going to act around me now? How would the shape of his eyes be different when he looked at me, and how would his limbs move when we were in the same room together?

I just wanted to know what would happen.

At school, Meg was pissed.

"Did you get my messages?"

"It was a weird weekend." Evasive, yet not a lie.

"Well? What happened? Why was David here?"

I told her about how the house was sold, how he had to go through his stuff, and how we let him stay with us. I told her that I barely saw him but that he was nice to me. None of it untruthful, but none of it the kind of truth I should have been telling my best friend.

"Did you have fun at the dance?" I asked her, wanting to shift the subject away from me.

"It was a blast," she said curtly, then paused and added, "Joe came."

A punch in my gut. "He did?"

"Yes," said Meg, with a firm s on the end of it. "He came. Looking for you." I had nothing to say, and it seemed like Meg needed to let that hurt me a little. But then she smiled. "He went as half Spider-Man, half Wolverine."

I tried to picture Joe that way—walking into the dance alone, scanning the room for me—and felt a pang of regret.

"He even texted you from school to see if you were okay," added Meg.

I glanced down at my phone, realizing that one of the messages I hadn't bothered to read must have been from him. Now I felt even worse.

Andie and Hannah found me after third period to update me on the dance, like I'd been waiting all weekend to hear what they had to say.

"I'm sorry you missed it, it was really fun," said Andie.

"And we won the costume contest!" added Hannah.

Well, duh, of course they did. I wondered if they were genuinely surprised that the world handed them treats or if they just faked it for the rest of us.

Not once did they ask how I was, or what had happened to make me go home so suddenly. I felt angry, but then thought of David asking me if I was afraid to be treated normally. And then that thought led to the thought of David's lips, his hand on my ear, not afraid that touching me would break something. His "Laurel" in that flat, even, solid voice.

I thought of that voice at lunchtime when I knocked on Mr. Churchwell's door. He opened it with a big smile, way too happy to see me.

"Laurel! What's up?"

"I just wanted to let you know I'm almost done with my Early Action application to Yale, and I've decided not to write about the accident."

He nodded at me, with a trace of a smile. Had I given him the answer he wanted?

As I walked away I heard David's voice again: *You're strong enough, Laurel. You know who you are.* The voice stayed in my ear all day as I counted down the hours, and then minutes, until I could go home and see him again.

When the final school bell rang for the day, I jumped

into the car and drove three miles over the speed limit all the way home.

But when I got there, he was gone.

"What do you mean, he said to say good-bye?" I asked Nana, who was gathering David's sheets and blankets from the couch.

"Just what it sounds like, sweetie."

"What about his stuff?"

"It's here. He came by this morning with a carload of boxes."

I hurried down the hall to our attic entry, a door in the ceiling with a little rope dangling down. There was no evidence that anyone had been there. So I grabbed the rope and the door swung open, with its folding ladder attached.

"Laurel, I just swept up," said Nana, confused. "What are you doing? Do you think I'm lying?"

I stood on my tiptoes and grabbed part of the ladder, pulled it down, then climbed up. I still had my jacket on.

The attic smelled bad, but the air felt less musty than I remembered, like it had been moved around recently. I rested my elbows on the floor of the attic and scanned the space. There were the same assortment of cardboard boxes, plastic bins, garbage bags full of stuff.

But in the far corner, I saw them. About a dozen boxes labeled DAVID KAUFMAN in neat black Sharpie. Arranged in four perfect stacks of three, so straight and arrogant I wanted to knock them over.

"Laurel, please come down," said Nana in a very small voice.

I did. She looked at me, and I felt suddenly exposed.

"I'm not sure what happened. When he came in for breakfast, he said he had to leave town suddenly. There was some kind of job he could do with a friend's rock band."

"Did he say where he was going?" I asked, walking past her into my room so she couldn't see my face.

"No, just that the rock band was going on tour and he had to meet up with them." Nana paused, not sure whether or not to follow me in. "I'm sorry, sweetie. It must have been nice to have . . . some company."

"It was," I said, all garbled, before I closed the door gently. On my bed lay Masher, his eyes heavy and hollow with sadness, his body limp as though he'd been crushed. He thumped his tail when he saw me but was otherwise still. I collapsed onto the bed with him, then screamed hard into the pillow for several long, sweet seconds of frustration and then relief.

"Don't worry, buddy," I said into the scruff of Masher's neck. "He'll be back."

That night I opened up a fresh email and clicked on the TO field. I typed *D*, then *A*. Before I could type the *V*, my email program filled in the rest of David's email address, like it had been waiting for me to get up the nerve all afternoon to write to him. If only it could tell me what the hell to say, the first time I'd written to him as myself and not as a dog.

It took me what seemed like a year, but I finally came up with something that didn't sound too angry, or too stupid, even after I read it ten times.

> David—
>
> I'm not even sure if you're checking email, but in case you are . . .
>
> I'm sorry you had to leave again so quickly. I'm sorry you couldn't wait until I got home to say good-bye.
>
> Good luck with the band and safe travels and all that. Keep in touch if you can.
>
> We'll all be here if you need us—your dog, your stuff, and yours truly,
>
> Laurel

I counted to three and hit send, and as soon as I did, I felt like I could breathe again.

Then I remembered that David had planned to visit his father, but never got the chance. He wouldn't have let me come with him. But now he was gone and had absolutely no say in the matter.

TWENTY-SIX

Peach, peach, and more peach.

Light peach on the walls. Dark peach carpet. Even the lights in long rows on the ceiling shone a yellow-pink, peachy keen glow.

Maybe it was all supposed to distract you from the smell, which I think could have made me throw up if I took too deep a whiff. That was the smell of medicine and bad food and unwashed bedsheets and indoor recycled air. It was the smell of hopelessness and attempted dignity, and of life in limbo.

"Can I help you?" asked the woman at the third-floor reception desk. She was actually wearing a peach-colored nurse's tunic.

"I'm here to see Gabriel Kaufman," I said.

"Oh, yes!" said the nurse, her face brightening. "You called earlier." She opened an appointment book and I glimpsed my name, scribbled in the middle of a page. I got the feeling this was a part of the Palisades Oaks Rehabilitation Center that didn't get many visitors.

"Is it okay to bring these?" I asked, lifting up the bouquet of flowers I'd brought. Nana had insisted we stop to buy them before getting on the highway. I went along with it because she'd been so quiet and helpful after I told her what I wanted to do. She'd offered to drive and wrote a note getting me out of school and work for the day, and made sure she got excellent directions from David's grandparents. And here the flowers gave me something to do with my hands.

Now Nana was shopping at some nearby mall—she couldn't stand these places, she'd seen too many of her friends die in them—and I was alone in the Peach Palace.

"Of course, sweetie. They smell lovely. He'll like them, I'm sure."

The nurse got up and motioned for me to follow her, down another long hallway. At the very end I could see a huge picture window with sunlight streaming in, and I had a sudden urge to take off running, running, until I could crash through the glass headfirst into freedom.

"Here we are," she said. She knocked twice on a door that was slightly ajar, paused, then opened it all the way.

282

"I'll leave you two alone, but please let me know if you need anything. I'll be back in a few minutes with a vase and some water."

I peeked slowly around the door and first saw furniture—a dark wooden dresser, an overstuffed flowered armchair. Then a bright window draped in gauzy white curtains, the sun coming through so strong I almost had to look away from it. Next, a machine that whirred and beeped quietly but intensely, and the rising and falling chest of Mr. Kaufman, moving to the beat of what I realized was his respirator.

I came all the way into the room and looked at the carved wooden headboard of his bed, his navy blue pajamas with white piping, his closed, frozen eyes. The wedding band on his left hand and the framed photograph of himself, Mrs. Kaufman, and David peering down on him from the nightstand. I recognized it as their holiday card photo from two years ago, posed on a ski slope somewhere, all three of them making the kind of face that could either be a smile or just squinting into the sun.

I stood over him for a minute, watching this robotlike sleep he was in—the respirator even made it sound like he was snoring—and reminded myself of why I hated him. *This jerk*, I thought. This jerk who had all that scotch at seder and killed my parents. Killed my little brother, just a kid who still liked making fart noises with various parts of his arms. Ruined my life. Not to mention what he did to his own wife and son.

You got what you deserved, and now you're basically broccoli.

There was a knock on the door again, and the nurse came back in with the vase. She placed it on the nightstand behind the photograph and smiled at me as I handed her the flowers.

"You said he'll like them," I asked. "Can he smell?"

"That depends who you ask," she said as she lowered the flowers into the water. "A doctor might tell you no, Mr. Kaufman can't smell anything because he's in a vegetative state." She glanced up at Mr. Kaufman's face. "But if you ask me, he looks better when there's something new in the room. Something pretty or that smells good. I noticed it once when his mother came in wearing a very strong perfume."

The nurse moved to leave and I almost stopped her. But she was out the door fast and I was once again alone with the sleeping man and the loud machine. I'd lost the thread of that anger and now just felt nervous, so I sat down in the armchair and started saying the first things that came to mind.

"Hi, Mr. Kaufman," I said. "It's me, Laurel Meisner."

I paused, like I expected him to answer. Just one of those things you do because you're trained to do it.

"I saw David. He was planning on visiting you, but he got a job opportunity and had to leave really fast."

I considered adding, *Actually, your son ran away from something. I hope it wasn't me.*

What would David have told his father, if he'd come?

"Your parents sold the house. I hear it's a young couple with a baby. It's a great house for a family who's just starting fresh. I think there are some other babies in the neighborhood, so that'll be good, like a whole new generation of kids."

I thought of David and Toby and me, of Megan and her sister Mary, Kevin McNaughton, and the Henninger twins, who now went to some private Catholic school and nobody ever saw anymore. A whole crop of children on two little streets, getting big and moving on. We grew into ourselves and away from simply being neighbors who all liked lawn sprinklers and swing sets.

I was stuck again for something to say. *Just talk! He can't hear you anyway!*

"Did you know that for a while, the police were looking for another car? They thought maybe there was someone else involved."

Now I could grab hold of my anger again, more sure of my strength.

"Too bad you can't tell them. Because they couldn't find anything, and now they officially blame you. You were drinking that night; we all saw it."

We did all see it, but nobody thought to mention that perhaps he shouldn't get behind the wheel. God, how many drunk-driving videos had I seen? And where were my parents in all this? Didn't they have the guts to say something to big-shot Mr. Kaufman, the guy my dad would never admit he admired?

It had been so easy to think about blame when I wasn't sitting across from the very fingers that had been curled around the steering wheel when the car went off the road. The foot that had been on the gas pedal and the brake. Those eyes that had seen the world spinning past the windshield, and the ears that had heard the shouts and cries my family might have made as they died.

But it was like looking at a frog laid out for dissection in biology class. Everything I knew about what was in front of me was just truth and facts, with nothing behind them. All my fury didn't make a difference. We were both still in the same place, unchanged.

Except that now I felt a little lighter, unburdened, by having said these things to him. I got up and pulled my chair a little closer to Mr. Kaufman's bed, then folded myself back into it, cross-legged and ready to stay for a while.

"David kissed me," I said to him. Hearing the words out loud, feeling the breath it took to form them, made it official now; it had happened.

Mr. Kaufman's machine whirred and dinged, like a *Hmmm, tell me more,* so I did. I told him about Nana wanting to go home but not letting herself, and the secrets Meg and I were keeping from each other now, and the

Andie Stokes crowd. I told him about Joe and the way I sometimes caught him looking at me, like it stung. I talked about my job at Ashland and how it made me feel like I was not wasting the lucky draw of being alive, like I was finding something in myself that I wouldn't have found otherwise. And then I told him about how Dad always envied him a little for his fancy car and his well-kept yard and expensive cigars.

Then that reminded me of Mom and the cigarettes she kept hidden in two different spots in the house, so I told Mr. Kaufman about how I'd caught her once, and instead of giving me a lecture about "Do as I say, not as I do," she just said, "Laurel, I hope you find something like this, a little self-destructive habit you can turn to every once in a while, when you're tired of being good. It will keep you sane."

I told him about the band Toby wanted to start someday. It was going to be called the Dangling Participles, and they were only going to play songs about grammar and spelling.

It wasn't until I noticed the light turning a different shade that I realized how much time had passed. I turned to the window and saw that the sun was setting behind the hills, and took out my cell phone to call Nana.

"Did you get the job done?" she asked.

"I think so," I replied.

"Then I'm waiting downstairs to take you home."

TWENTY-SEVEN

*e live in troubled times, to be sure.*

What the hell was that? It had just come out, and now that it was on my computer screen it only made me want to slap myself.

I'd come home straight from school on Wednesday to work on my essay, the clock counting down the final thirty-six hours until I had to submit my application to Yale. Really, I had backed myself further into a corner by deciding I wouldn't mention my family in any way.

The weekend with David, the afternoon with Mr. Kaufman. I couldn't process any of it into something I could write about.

Nana kept coming into the den with a can of Pledge and a rag, pretending to dust, but I knew she was checking up on me. She'd already found out that straight-up asking "How's it going?" did not get a good response.

The blank computer screen was taunting me, the blinking cursor daring me to think up something meaningful and honest.

Suddenly, there was a noise from upstairs.

Bump. Clang.

A low screech, and then a loud bark.

In about two seconds I ran from the den, my heart pounding, afraid of what I'd find.

Sure enough, Toby's door was open. Masher crouched on the floor with his tail thumping, only his body visible because he'd jammed his head underneath the bed. Bits of fur floated through the air.

"Masher!" I yelled. Another screech and now a hiss from under the bed. He barked in response, and it wasn't his usual bark. This one was from the gut, all primal.

I clapped my hands twice and called his name again, with no results. Then I dropped to the ground and reached under the bed until I felt his collar, and tugged hard. He whined, and I knew I was probably hurting him.

After dragging Masher out of the room, I shut the door, making sure the doorknob clicked.

"Bad dog!" I shouted.

"Forget to close the door all the way?" called Nana from

downstairs, like she'd been waiting for that exact thing to happen.

"I've got it under control!" I called back.

I turned to Masher, who looked at me with irritation. I'd denied him some basic dog right.

"You can't just do that!" I yelled, swatting his muzzle lightly with the back of my hand. "This is not your house!" I took another breath and blurted out, "You're here because your owner is a crazy loser who doesn't know what he's doing with his life!"

Now he seemed bemused, like he knew better and I should too.

Did David teach you that look, or the other way around?

I grabbed Masher's collar again and pulled him into the bathroom, which I knew he hated. The toilet ran nonstop, and he always barked at the sound of it. I closed the door and went to check on the cats.

None of them were hurt, but Lucky seemed nervous. I lay down on Toby's bed and she hopped up onto the end of it, looking at me quizzically from above my toes.

"I know," I said to her. "I know."

Her eyes narrowed into smiling slits, and I realized she hadn't been nervous for herself or her kittens. She'd been nervous for me, what with all my yelling.

"Oh, I'm fine," I said. She stepped onto my leg and walked up the length of my body, not losing her balance for an instant, and poked her head into my armpit.

I stayed there for a while, petting her, and then it came to me.

I would write my essay about the cats and Dr. B and Eve and the different ways something could be hurt and healed, and what I'd learned from that. I didn't have to mention my family outright, but they would be there, between the lines. So I went downstairs and sat at the computer.

Lucky the cat is blinking at me with trusting yellow eyes.

The rest of it came out so fast, I had a draft before dinner.

Almost as if he'd known what had happened with Masher, that night David answered my email.

> *laurel*
>
> *thank you for writing. it's good to know that you don't hate me, at least not yet.*
>
> *i'm in richmond, virginia. the band's got a ton of fans here.*
>
> *this city has a lot of statues of confederate generals, which means i must really be in the south.*
>
> *keep in touch,*
>
> *david*

Keep in touch.

I suddenly realized how annoying that expression was.

Like, *Now it's* your *job to stay in contact with* me. It said,
I'm really just too lazy.

I started to write back, to *keep in touch*, but decided I'd
be lazy as well.

On Thursday morning I woke up early, did a final pass
on my essay, and submitted my application to Yale online
with more than twelve hours to spare. Hopefully somewhere my father was saying, *That's my girl.*

I gave myself a few minutes to feel relieved and proud,
then for the tenth time, reread the text Joe had sent me.

sry i mizd u at d dance, hope ur ok.

It had been days and I still hadn't seen him. I could have
done the safe thing and texted him back, but I wanted to
talk in real time, live. No backspace key.

I'd visited Mr. Kaufman. I'd finished my college application. I felt kind of invincible.

"Laurel!" Joe said when I called, sounding surprised in
a good way.

"Thanks for your message. I'm sorry I missed you that
night."

"Me too," he said. Then silence. He got stuck so easily
with me now.

God, Joe! Talk to me! I'm just Laurel!

"I've done a couple of sketches," I continued. "I'd like
to show them to you so I know if I'm on the right track."

"I'm sure you are, but yeah, let's get together." He

paused, but I didn't jump in. I'd done my part and it was his turn. "After school today? Are you working this afternoon? I don't have to be at the theater until four thirty, and I usually go to the coffee place to do some homework first."

"I usually show up at four, but I can be a little late. I'll see you then!" And I hung up, trying not to think of David in the woods, but of Joe. Joe at the dance, dressed like a glorious freak as two different superheroes. In pieces of whatever costumes he could put together at the last minute because he'd decided to come looking for me.

I arrived at the coffee place before Joe and got my chai, then picked a sunny table in the front corner. My sketch pad was tiny compared to his; I preferred to draw out my scenery small first, so I could decide what the important elements were, then let it grow in my head to the point where I had to move to the large canvas.

When Joe walked in, we smiled easily at each other, and I just thought, *Yes.*

Here was someone who was talented and smart, sweet and sensitive. Undamaged. Normal.

I showed him a few of the sketches I'd done over the weekend, and he held up his caricatures next to them to see how well they fit. Two of them looked pretty cool. One was a little off, so I made some notes about how to fix that.

Joe glanced at the clock, so I said, "Do you need to get some homework done? I can take off."

"I'll do it on my break," he answered quickly, shaking his head. "Here, I'll walk you over to the vet's."

On our way down the sidewalk that would lead us to Ashland, Joe was quiet, and the comfortable feeling between us was gone. When we reached the hospital parking lot, he stopped and turned to me.

"Listen, Meg told me that you left the Halloween dance with David Kaufman. She seemed pretty upset about that."

Well, yes. Clearly. So upset that she felt the need to tell Joe out of spite.

"Was that okay?" Joe continued. "I mean, it's none of my business. But the last time he showed up at a party, things did not—"

"Go well?" I interrupted him, raising one eyebrow. "No, they didn't."

Joe laughed nervously.

"Things are fine now," I said, and shrugged. "We're taking care of his dog, some of his stuff. As a favor." Using the word *we* made it seem more neighborly, less complicated.

I knew what Joe was asking. Was there anything going on between David Kaufman and me? There was no way I could answer that question.

The way Joe smiled now, relieved and protective, made me realize how much he really did like me. And how being with him made me feel the most like *myself* that I had in months.

But I had a question of my own. "Speaking of prom night . . ." I paused to take a deep breath, not looking at him. "When you invited me to the prom. Was that . . . was that something somebody set you up to do?"

Joe frowned, confused. "Like who?"

"I don't know. Maybe Meg . . ." When I said it out loud it sounded so small and stupid, and I wished I hadn't said it. "You have to understand that I would think about that. At the time, I didn't want to know the answer. But now I do."

Joe looked at me for just a second and had to flick his eyes away to some far corner of the sky. "No, nobody set me up to do that. But I will tell you that if what happened . . . your parents . . . if that hadn't happened, I probably never would have gotten the nerve." He paused, then looked at me briefly again. "I know that's messed up. But I wanted to. I'd wanted to for a while."

But inside, I started to feel so mad. If he'd just had the guts to ask me out when he first wanted to, maybe this part would have been long over by the time the accident happened. And maybe we could have been strong enough together—why wouldn't we have been?—to survive those first hellish months afterward.

"You should have gotten up the nerve," I finally said, trying to spin it with a smile.

"I know. I just kept telling myself I had time."

"Life is short, Joe."

A painful look crossed his face. After a few long seconds,

he simply said, "You'll be late for work, and I should get going."

He bent toward me and tilted his head a bit to glance at me sideways, almost in admiration. Again, that halfway moment when something could happen. That now familiar feeling of *More! More!*

Suddenly, I was just so sick of it.

When Joe started to wrap his loose, lazy hug around me to say good-bye, I turned my face up and kissed him square on the mouth. Too quickly, like I'd smacked him. His lips weren't ready and felt stiff, formal. They weren't the lips I remembered, but then again, there had been other lips since. Was it that hard to keep track?

Joe turned red and sputtered, "Whoa."

Then he smiled. So maybe these lips would stick around.

"I'll see you soon," I just said, then walked as fast as I could into work.

TWENTY-EIGHT

Two weeks went by. Fortunately, I had midterms to study for and my other college applications to start, and didn't have time to be obsessed with much else. For instance, Joe sending me a text message every afternoon with a proposed superhero identity for one of the teachers.

margulis = algeBrawn!

(Mr. Margulis in the math department was huge and a former bodybuilder.)

It seemed like his way of keeping the status quo, of reserving his spot for something.

At Ashland, Eve set out a straw cornucopia filled with

turkey-shaped chocolates on the front desk, and I strung up a HAPPY THANKSGIVING banner on the wall. I used the wrong kind of tape and the next day it fell down and got chewed up by a dog. Eve didn't say a thing about it; she just went out and bought another. So it was, now that she knew about my family. She had become less bossy but less friendly, too; we never went to lunch or even talked about ourselves anymore.

"The first holiday season since the accident will be a tough one, Laurel," said Suzie. We were down to once-weekly visits. "Let's talk about strategies."

So we talked, about trying yoga and me possibly going to some weekend camp for grieving teens. She asked me to start a list in my journal titled "Thanksgiving: Things I'm Thankful For," and encouraged me to write anything that came to mind over the next few weeks.

I hadn't told her about my visit to Mr. Kaufman or about smack-kissing Joe. The truth was, I was getting tired of talking about myself. Suzie knew it too. Our sessions were starting to end early, because we'd reach the point of me just shrugging and giving her one-word answers, and she'd say, "That's enough for today."

laurel

wilmington, nc now. 2 gigs but I think everyone's going to stick around for a couple of weeks bcuz of the holiday. they have to bunk down at friends'

houses but fortunately i can swing the comfort inn
for myself. swanky, i know. i found that if you open a
minibar beer bottle the right way, without bending the
cap, you can fill it back up with water and you won't
get charged for it.
david

The email caught me unexpectedly on a Saturday, when I was just doing a quick check before heading out to meet Joe at the library.

I started pulling together some phrases in my head to answer him with. Something witty and cute. A joke about minibars? Or beer bottles filled with cloudy hotel water?

But when I read it again, and then again, I realized the email was not asking for an answer. It was just there. A record of where he'd been, like dropped bread crumbs along a trail. So I just let it be, thinking that maybe there would come a time when I'd need to follow those bread crumbs to find him.

And I had Joe to think about today.

The library had scheduled our art show—I felt okay calling it *ours* now—for the second week in December. It was going to be eight pieces hanging downstairs in the community room, where they held story hour and Pilates for Seniors and the book club my mom used to go to.

Joe and I planned to meet there, during a one-hour gap

when nothing was going on, to go over sketches once more before committing to ink and paint. "This way, we can see how they might work in the space," he'd said. But really, it was just a square underground room with white walls and fluorescent lighting. I knew he'd suggested the location because it was neutral territory. Private enough so that nobody would be watching us, and public enough so that certain touching-type things were just not an option.

"Howdy," Joe said as I came down the stairs to the community room with my sketch pad under one arm. I'd finally gotten a large one like his.

I flashed on how David always began his emails with simply "laurel," without even a comma or proper capitalization. There was no "howdy" in David's universe.

Joe was standing with Ms. Folsom, the head librarian, who'd invited Joe to show his artwork. Now, suddenly, I realized that she was his neighbor. It was one of those useless, small-town facts I'd always known but stored away until now, when it explained why Joe was doing all this.

"Hi, Laurel," she said, smiling sweetly. "I was so happy to hear that you guys are collaborating on this project. We can't wait to see the results!"

Her eyes danced a bit, and I wondered if my involvement was some kind of extra selling point for her. Maybe she thought people would be more interested in coming to see the art if they knew half of it was by *Laurel Meisner.*

"Thanks," was all I said.

"I'll leave you two to work . . . let me know if you need anything!" She patted Joe on the shoulder but not me, and moved past us back up the stairs.

"Good day so far?" said Joe, holding out his hand to take my sketch pad from me. I handed it to him but noticed him cringing a bit. "I'm sorry," he added. "That sounded like a therapist or something. I was just, you know . . ."

I wondered if there would ever be a time when he'd be able to just talk to me, without worrying that it would come out strange, without his words getting snagged on the Tree of Unfinished Sentences.

"Don't worry about it. You could never sound anything like my therapist."

He raised his eyebrows involuntarily. *Oops!* I'd just told him I saw a therapist. As if he didn't already think I was some fragile Christmas ornament you had to hang up high on the tree so it was less likely to get knocked off.

"Can we put our stuff over there?" I diverted, pointing to a table at the front of the room.

We went through our sketches for the eight pieces. His drawings made me laugh, especially TurboSenior, who looked not unlike Joe himself, and fortunately a couple of my backgrounds cracked him up right back. For the Incredible Sulk—a goth girl with a sour expression doing a karate kick—I'd drawn a frilly pink and green bedroom.

With Joe being so tall, I kept feeling his breath on my

neck, smelling of spearmint gum. I was careful not to turn to look at him when I knew his face was close. I couldn't take the uncertainty of another near-moment.

"I think it's safe to take this to the next level," said Joe when we were done.

Now I let myself look straight at him, surprised. *This?* Did he mean, *us?*

"Ink and paint," he stammered, realizing.

"I'm ready if you are," I said as lightly as I could.

I heard Joe swallow hard and looked up again. *Don't be afraid*, I thought loudly, and wondered if I was saying it to myself, or to him.

"There isn't going to be some chic gallery opening or anything like that," he said. "But my parents want to bring in some sparkling cider and cheese and crackers on the first night. I thought it would be fun for us to be here, you know, together."

Joe nervously bit his lower lip. We'd already made out and then I'd kiss-tackled him. Why did this have to be so hard? This was like baking cookies from a premade mix, not from scratch. All the hard work was already done.

"I mean, I'd pick you up, and take you home after," he finally said.

I smiled at him, saying nothing.

"Like a date," he added with a smile back at me, then we both took the deep breaths we needed.

When I got home, there was a stack of unassembled cardboard moving boxes sitting outside the front door.

"Nana?" I called, walking into the house.

"Can you grab some of those boxes?" she said, coming down the stairs to meet me. "I had them delivered, but I need your help carrying them in and putting them together."

After I brought them inside, I watched Nana as she examined the boxes, waiting for her to provide more information. But it seemed like she wanted me to ask.

"What are they for?" I finally said.

"Coats," she replied matter-of-factly. "You know I do that every year, up in Johnstown. We collect old coats during the holidays and distribute them at the Rescue Mission."

"Oh, right."

"So I thought we'd do the same here." She paused, and swallowed. "With your father's. And your mother's. She had so many." I didn't say anything, so she also added, "I found a foster children's group that will gladly take your brother's."

Nana went straight to the front closet, opened it, and started rummaging around. "You can keep anything of your mother's that you want, of course. You should. Some of it was expensive, and it would look nice on you." She pulled out a long brown cashmere coat that Mom often wore into the city and handed it to me. "Like this one."

I took it silently, the fabric collapsing into my hands. I raised it to my face and inhaled.

Musty, but laced with flowers and some kind of sweet spice, like cinnamon.

"I don't think I can do this, Nana," I said.

She was holding one of Toby's down parkas, petting it. "I don't know if I can either, sweetie. That's why we should do it together and do it fast, before I change my mind."

"Just the coats?"

"Just the coats. For now."

I nodded, biting my lip as the tears came burning through, and laid the cashmere coat on the dining room table.

I said, "This will be the Keep pile."

TWENTY-NINE

n Thanksgiving morning, Nana and I were prepping to make stuffing by hand and sweet-potato casserole, when she discovered, with horror, that she was missing something.

"How could I forget the marshmallows?" she asked, planting her arms on the kitchen counter as if she might faint from shock. "I've been making that casserole for forty years!"

"Nana, relax. The store's still open, and I'll go get some," I told her.

"And why doesn't your mother own a Dutch oven? Did

she never make anything for more than four people at a time?"

"What do *you* think?" I said, trying to make her laugh, but she didn't, so I added, "I'm sure one of the neighbors has one you can borrow."

I knew Nana was mostly stressed because she'd hoped to do her trip home during the past week, to get it done before the holidays. We'd spent a half day rounding up every coat we could find and donated eight boxes' worth to people who'd need them. She felt like she was on a roll, and ready to do the same thing at her own house. But at the last minute, she said she wasn't feeling well and didn't want to travel. "Besides," she'd told me, "nobody's going to rent a house or buy a condo before January anyway." I agreed with her but knew it was because she didn't want to leave me alone.

We were going to the Dills' for Thanksgiving dinner. It was never discussed, just simply assumed.

Last year, I would have been thrilled to be invited to the Dill Thanksgiving. My family didn't do the holiday well. I guess with no aunts or uncles or cousins to share it with, the pressure was off. Usually we drove up to Nana's and ate at the Holiday Inn, where Toby and I could hang out in the arcade until the turkey arrived. Or on rare years when I could convince my mother to have dinner at home, she always went upstairs to lie down for fifteen minutes before dessert. We never played games and we never had

308

friends over, or even went around the table saying what we were thankful for. Traditions like that never seemed important to my parents.

But down at Megan's, Mrs. Dill was serving up dinner for twenty-five, and I was ready for the Great American Thanksgiving I'd never had.

"If you leave right now," said Nana, "you can pick up the marshmallows. I'll go down to the Mitas' and see if they have a pot for us."

Twenty minutes later, I was driving home from the grocery store with two bags of marshmallows on the passenger seat, thinking about how the checkout clerk had laughed at my purchase and said, "Thanksgiving is just awesome."

I came up our hill a little fast, not paying attention, and swung into the driveway.

But where I was going, there was already another car parked.

I had to swerve to avoid hitting it, and once my car stopped, I sat for a moment, letting that adrenaline subside.

The day was overcast and with no sunlight, at first the car looked colorless. As I caught my breath, I could see what it was.

Mr. Kaufman, I thought, blinking hard.

No, you idiot. Mr. Kaufman's car. Which means David.

A new adrenaline shot through my body, this one a little different, and I forced myself to sit there for another few moments, wanting yet not wanting that excitement.

Finally, I checked myself in the mirror—unshowered, wearing sweatpants, but I'd looked worse—and got out of the car. The Jaguar was splattered with fresh mud, and as I approached it I touched my finger to the rear bumper. It left a dirty wet smudge on my hand that I didn't wipe off.

Through the window, I could see David passed out in the front seat, his hands still on the steering wheel.

I watched him for a few seconds, wondering what to do next. Finally, I knocked twice softly on the window.

It was strange to watch him wake up. David's eyelids fluttered, and I noticed for the first time how long and thick his lashes were. Then his eyes popped open, that surprising roundness. He saw me and startled, and a laugh jumped out of me that I instantly regretted.

David sat up and threw open the car door. "Not funny!" he whined.

"What are you doing here?" I asked.

He scratched his neck for a moment, looking confused.

"What time is it? When I saw nobody was home, I decided to crash for a bit," he said slowly. I stayed quiet, hoping he'd find his way to an answer. But he just added, "I was driving all night."

"Driving all night, from where?"

"Somewhere outside Washington, DC." He scrambled out of the car. I stepped back to give him room. Maybe now that he was standing up, he'd be able to make more sense.

"I was going to have dinner with the band at a Cracker

Barrel," said David. "But I woke up in the middle of the night and started thinking about . . . things . . . my parents . . ." He choked on the word and took a deep breath, then looked at me. Then put his hand on my shoulder and breathed out. "I didn't want to spend Thanksgiving with a bunch of guys I barely know, eating something barely edible, at a place that stays open just for all the losers who have nowhere else to go."

He took his hand off my shoulder, but I could still feel the weight of it.

"I remembered that I did have somewhere to go," he said, then glanced at the house. It was a hungry look.

I didn't know what to say, but fortunately David started talking again, faster than I'd ever heard him.

"I'm sorry I didn't call . . . I just hopped in my car and drove and it was the middle of the night and I didn't want to call and wake anyone. And then before I knew it, I was here. The car was gone and there was no answer at the door. I still have a key, but that felt creepy to walk in so I figured I'd just wait. . . ." His voice trailed off.

And then he gave me the same look he'd given the house. It was pure want. He must have sensed how desperate he seemed, because he added a sheepish grin and a head tilt, like he couldn't dare offer a hand again.

It felt safest to stay with the facts.

"You came to spend Thanksgiving with us?" I asked carefully, with no emotion.

"Yeah," said David, almost surprised. "I guess I did."

I just pointed down the hill for a moment, then said, "We're going to the Dills' house, but I can call Mrs. Dill. . . . I'm sure you'd be welcome there."

In an instant, David's eyes narrowed into disappointment.

"The Dills'?" he said with distaste.

"Yeah, it'll be fun. There's going to be a whole bunch of people there."

Now he gave a bitter laugh.

"Laurel, I didn't come all this way to have dinner with people I don't know."

"You'll know us, and the Dills. . . ."

David shook his head. "Forget it," he said, then moved back toward the car.

"So you're leaving?" I asked, trying to be calm, but it came out high and squeaky.

"If I go now, I can still make it to the Cracker Barrel."

David opened the driver's-side door and slid into the seat. Away from me.

Wait! A minute ago you were touching my shoulder!

I thought quickly of calling Mrs. Dill, explaining why we needed to cancel. Nana would go along with it. We could buy one of those depressed last-minute turkeys at the store and cook it in time for dinner . . .

No. We had an obligation. Meg would never forgive me. And then I looked at his face, indignant and insulted, and suddenly just felt angry.

"David—"

"I said, forget it!"

Now I was angrier. Actually, furious. "Let me finish!" I barked at him. He jumped a bit and looked up at me, genuinely surprised. "How can you show up here and expect us to have a table set for you, with a complete Thanksgiving dinner? Without calling, or emailing . . . You just can't do that."

David stared at me, his surprise turning to simple sadness, his mouth twitching.

Then he just said, "This was a mistake."

With that, he slammed the door and started the car. I only had time to step back before he sped backward out of our driveway, leaving a dirty cloud of dust behind him.

"I put rum in these Diet Cokes," whispered Meg, her breath spicy with onion dip.

We were seated next to each other at one of three large tables Mrs. Dill had set up in their dining room and foyer. Meg was psyched because it was the first time they didn't have a kids' table in the kitchen; she was with the grown-ups now. Nana was across from us, next to an elderly uncle, and I wondered for a second if it wasn't a setup.

Some part of my body was still shaking from that morning. Every time I blinked, I could see David's face changing from earnestness to regret, sliding away from me in a second. And I'd let it. I'd let it go.

I hadn't told anyone about David coming. Not Nana, who came back from the Mitas' just five minutes after he tore off, whose day I just could not complicate any further. Not Meg, who seemed preoccupied as usual with something of her own.

I remembered that I did have somewhere to go, David had said. His voice and face, open and honest, and trusting. I cringed at the thought, and tried to be happy he'd come in the first place. It was like he'd opened a window. Maybe in his rush to leave, he'd forgotten to shut it.

I took my Coke and sniffed it. The rum made it smell like the ARCO station. Mrs. Dill, at the big table across the room, stood up and raised her glass.

"Before we dig in, I'd like to thank all of you for coming. Every one of you means so much to me in your own way . . . and seeing your faces here in my house . . ." She started to choke up, and Mr. Dill reached out his hand to her elbow, but she shook it away. "I'm fine, honey. I'm just . . . happy. So happy! To being together and being thankful!"

Everyone took their cue to clink, then drink, although I only took a tiny sip of what tasted like gasoline with bubbles. *To being together.* I thought of David, eating a chain restaurant turkey platter somewhere near Washington, DC. I hoped he was with people he liked.

As Mrs. Dill sat down, neatly wiping a tear from each eye, I noticed that Meg was staring at her, frowning.

"Is she okay?" I asked.

314

Meg shrugged, then lowered her voice to a whisper. "I hope so. She just went on new medication, and I think it's making her a little loopy." She glanced at me with a look of relief, and added, "She's being treated for depression."

Then she turned away and began to eat, knowing that what she'd said just created more questions.

After dinner, I offered to help Meg load the dishwasher while everyone else took a pre-pie break. I wasn't going to let her drop some major info in my lap and then leave it there for me to stare at, like something gross that fell from a tree.

"I had no idea your mom was depressed. How long has that been going on?"

Meg stood rinsing at the sink and handed me a plate to rack. "I don't know. Awhile. It's only gotten bad in the last few months."

If we were running this conversation by the book, my next question would have been, *Why didn't you tell me?* But I knew the answer to that. Besides, I had my own secrets. What could I say to make things feel less icky between us?

I thought of Mr. Dill, his firm hand on his wife's elbow, the flat line of his mouth as he looked at her, like he was bracing himself for something.

"How's your dad handling it?"

"Not well." Meg handed me another plate without looking at me, and I knew the subject was closed.

That night, back at the house, Nana wanted me to sit with her and watch *The Wizard of Oz* on TV. When she fell asleep sometime before Dorothy met up with the Tin Man, I went over to the computer and opened my email. David's last message was still there, although it had slid dejectedly to a spot halfway down the page. It felt like by just clicking on it I could open up a hole to climb into, shout to the bottom of.

So I hit reply and told David about Thanksgiving dinner, about the old uncle with the sweet potato in his mustache all night and the friends from Connecticut, a married couple, who wore identical green sweaters with turtles on them. I told him about the cornucopia centerpiece that smelled like rotten fruit, and the plates with turkeys dressed like Pilgrims on them. I started to tell him about Meg's mom, too, but then changed my mind.

Finally, I just ended the email with this:

> *So I'd like to hear how Cracker Barrel matched that in the Weird Holiday department. Next time you come back to town, call first, and we'll be expecting you.*
> *Laurel*

I hit send before I could tinker with it, and went back to the couch, and to Oz.

THIRTY

ello? Is this Laurel?"

My cell phone rang at 9:07 the morning after Thanksgiving, while I was walking Masher in the woods.

"Yes. Who is this?"

"It's Robert? From the animal hospital?"

As soon as he said "hospital" I heard barking, far away and hollow, on his end.

"Oh, hey." I tried not to make it sound like, *Why the hell are you calling me?*

"Listen, I just talked to Eve. She's still with her parents in Vermont for the holiday. She said I should call you?"

Everything he said came out like a question.

"What's going on?"

"We got a call from Eve's connection at the shelter. They've got a cat who's scheduled to be put to sleep today, so she's calling around to see if anyone can take her. Dr. B says we have room, but it's really busy here today and I can't leave. So Eve said maybe you could pick her up and bring her in."

Me. The missing link in the chain that needed to come together to save an animal's life.

"Tell them I'll be there in twenty minutes."

When I told Nana why I was scrambling to the car, she just nodded and said, "As long as this one doesn't end up in your brother's room, do whatever you need to do."

I was just a few minutes from the house when my cell phone rang and I answered it.

"Hi, it's me." Meg.

"Hey! You're up early."

"Couldn't sleep."

"Too much excess?"

"No, my parents were arguing all night long, and I could hear every freaking thing. My mom crying. My dad punching pillows. Seriously, it was like listening to a soap opera."

"My God, Meg. I'm sorry." And then, because I thought of that "why didn't you tell me" feeling from the night before, because it seemed like something I should say, I added, "What can I do?"

"I just need to get out and go somewhere. Can we go to the mall where it will be crowded and obnoxious and I can forget about it all?"

"Um . . . sure. I can meet you there in a couple of hours."

Silence on the other end of the line. "I was hoping I could pick you up in, like, a minute and a half."

"I'm on my way to the animal shelter to save a cat." It came out like I was heading to the grocery store to buy toilet paper.

"What do you mean?"

"I got a call from work. They need my help."

"Well, *I* need your help." Meg's voice sounded echoey, louder, a little girl with her hand cupped over the phone receiver so nobody else could hear.

"You got it. Just tell me where to meet you."

"In two hours?"

"Maybe less. I have to pick up the cat, bring her to Ashland, and get her settled."

"Laurel, I don't want to be alone right now."

I thought about saying *Yes, of course, Meg*. I thought about calling Robert and telling him I had to come later. But the road was pulling the car so swiftly and purposefully toward the shelter, tugging me to an animal that would be dead if I wasn't on my way. It didn't seem possible that I could slow down and turn around, even if I wanted to.

"Why don't you come meet me at the hospital?" I asked.

There was a pause, and Meg sucked in her breath, and I could almost hear the anger and hurt she was vacuuming into her chest.

"Silly me, I forgot that it always has to be about you."

It was like a dart thrown right at my face. Quick and direct, with unexpected velocity. My defenses weren't fast enough.

"It's not about me," I said. "It's about saving an animal that's going to be killed! Could you really live with yourself if you knew this cat got put to sleep because you didn't want to go to the mall alone?"

Silence, worse than the anger-air-suck. More silence, worse than the dart.

"Laurel, there are a lot of things I can say right now about the last six months, but I think you know them all." She paused, and I wasn't sure if I was supposed to respond, but I didn't think so, because the next thing she said was:

"I'll see you around."

And the line went dead.

THIRTY-ONE

arly Action: Get your admission decision

The words on the Yale website sounded so *ho-hum* about it, without an exclamation point or even a period to punctuate what it meant to those of us who'd been waiting to see them appear. Everyone else who'd applied early somewhere was counting the days, marking them as little sticks on their notebooks or with big Xs in their locker calendars. I refused to keep track but still found myself checking the Yale admissions page online every day.

All I had to do was follow that link, and log in, and there would be an answer on the other side. It felt so strange to have that guarantee.

I got up, walked around the room, sat down again. Checked the weather.

Arrrrgh, just do it!

So I did, wondering if they'd be standing behind me, watching. Mom and Dad, maybe Toby, too. No, I'd make them stand outside with the door closed.

"Ha!" I said out loud to nobody.

I'd gotten in.

I thought of how my dad's face might have looked at the news. He was good at the knowing smile; I think he would have done that. And he got misty so easily, never afraid to leave the tears there and not wipe them away.

What about Mom? She'd be surprised, first. Genuinely surprised, and that would piss me off a little. And then she'd look relieved and laugh, and I'd just laugh back to forget the pissed-off part.

They're with you right now, I told myself. *They're here.*

When Nana came to find me ten minutes later, I was still crying.

"I remember when your dad got his letter," said Nana over our celebration half-plain, half-veggie pizza at Vinny's. "He wasn't sure he wanted to go, but he heard the girls were particularly pretty there." She paused, the corners of her eyes glistening. "He would be so proud, you know."

I nodded and looked down, then decided, to hell with

it. No time like the present.

"Nana, I'm not sure I should go."

She put down her slice of pizza, taking a moment to arrange it neatly in the center of the plate, and frowned at me. "Why wouldn't you go?"

"I mean, maybe I'm not ready to live away from home. Instead I could go to Columbia or NYU, which are both great schools, if I got in. And I could stay here." Then I added, because I thought maybe it would help, "With you."

How could I tell her the things that had been swimming in my head all afternoon? The things I didn't even want to think about before, because I didn't have to, but now I had to. It would have been easier to get rejected from Yale so I could keep on not thinking about them.

What about the animals? Not just Selina and Elliot and Masher, but the patients at Ashland and the future Echos who might need me to be on the other end of a phone call. Echo was the cat I'd picked up from the shelter and brought to Ashland that day after Thanksgiving. Eve already had a possible home for her.

But there was another thing. It had come up during a session with Suzie the previous week.

"Are you excited to hear about Yale?" asked Suzie, looking at her notes.

"I guess so," I'd answered, looking out the window. It felt like small talk.

"You're not sure?"

"No, I'm sure." I hated these idiotic conversations we had sometimes.

"Laurel," said Suzie, pausing carefully, "do you feel you're ready for your future?"

I'd just looked at her.

"Because that's normal. To feel anxious about moving on, continuing with your life, when people you love are gone."

All I'd said was, "Okay, I get that." I found that Suzie got quiet and satisfied after I said this. Our sessions had less talking these days, and we were always ending early.

Finally, I thought of an answer for Nana.

"I'm just worried about you. Won't you be lonely if I go away?"

Nana had picked up her pizza slice, but now she put it down once more. "I will miss you, yes," she said. "But honestly, Laurel, if you're in New Haven, it means I can spend the fall and winter in Hilton Head. I won't have to sell the condo."

"So you want to get rid of me?" I asked, trying to make it sound jokey.

"No. I want you to go get the terrific education your parents always dreamed of for you."

She choked up, which made me choke up, and we both took bites of pizza in silence.

At home, I picked up the phone to call Meg to tell her the news, then stopped myself. It had been three weeks since that morning, the Morning of Save-a-Cat-or-Meet-Meg-at-the-Mall, and when we were together, we were like actors in a play. At school, in the hallways or in the classes where we still sat next to each other out of habit, we played the scripted roles of best friends. Lending each other pens, waiting for each other in doorways and by lockers. Making small talk about how hard the math test was and how awful our hair looked.

But outside of school, that phone line was still dead. Meg no longer offered me rides anywhere. She didn't stop by to hang out, or invite me to her house. She didn't call or text me late at night to tell me about Gavin or Andie or especially her parents.

I missed her like crazy, but I was also stubborn. I knew I had been right. Echo had been more important. Echo, with the wide black stripes like she'd been painted with a thick sponge brush, who liked to lick your forearm while you petted her. Living things died forever. Friendships could be resurrected.

So I put away my cell phone and figured I'd tell her in the morning, at school. But I still felt really lonely. Maybe I could tell Joe. Yes, that would work. Joe would be happy for me.

I signed on to my email, and when I saw my in-box, my heart leapt.

A message from David.

laurel

  just for the hell of it i've started introducing myself
as leon. it seems totally hilarious to me. do i look
like a leon? no way. but i say, "hi, i'm leon" and
people just nod and say, "nice to meet you, leon!"
so i can just be leon for a while. leon needs some
background. i was thinking he could be the son of
circus people, like world-famous elephant trainers.
that's something you could say and nobody would
be able to check up on it, because who ever hears of
circus elephant trainers? i mean, the circus is totally
cliché but people eat that stuff up. that could get me
freebies and favors. and my life right now is all about
freebies and favors, as you well know.
david

Before I'd kissed David, I would have thought that was
him, flip and funny trimmed with badass on the edges.
But when I read this, I thought about the softness of his
lips and the way I could feel his heart beating fast that day
in the woods, and I knew he was hurting. Maybe all those
years of attitude, from the time he gave me the Tinker Bell
bubble bath until the night of the accident, were just one
long David hurting.

No mention of Thanksgiving, but there didn't have

to be. My email had been a peace treaty, and with this, it seemed like he'd signed it.

Come home, I thought. *Just come home.*

I started a reply to him.

Hey David, I mean Leon,

The circus works. Tell them you were being groomed to follow in their footsteps, or hoofsteps in this case, but wanted to be a tightrope walker and that created this whole scandal so that's why you left and can't go back.

I got into Yale. I'm not sure if I want to go.

And also, my best friend hates me right now. I have no idea how to fix it.

Maybe someone who grew up around elephants might have some answers?

Laurel

THIRTY-TWO

EROES AMONG US, read the art show flyer in big blue letters.

Then, underneath:

A COLLECTION OF COLLABORATIVE
PAINTINGS BY JOE LASKY
AND LAUREL MEISNER

My name on its own line.

Nana picked up a few extra copies at the library and distributed them to the neighbors. "Ms. Folsom says there's a mention in the newspaper!" she added as I sat in front of my dinner, trying and failing to eat. "I'll have to get a copy for my scrapbook."

"Uh-huh," I said, watching my hand shake as I lifted my fork.

Nana noticed. "Are you nervous?"

Judging from the buzz I felt under my skin and that "I might have to go to the bathroom" feeling, I would say yes. Definitely nervous. I wasn't sure how much of that was the art show and how much was the "date" status of my impending evening.

"I'm just excited," I said, which was half true.

"So am I." She checked her watch. "Well, your Joe should be here in about five minutes." I winced at the "your Joe" and Nana added, "He's a nice boy . . . I'm sorry, nice *guy*!" She looked at the clock again. "I'm picking up Ed and Dorrie at seven, so we won't be too far behind you."

Nana and the Mitas had planned a big night out, to visit the art show and then the diner for coffee and dessert. It was kind of funny and kind of wonderful that she was making her own friends now.

Other neighbors had pledged to stop by. Aside from our families, Joe and I had no idea who else might come to the "opening." He'd told only one or two friends at school, and I hadn't told Meg, and certainly not Andie or Hannah. "It's kind of cooler if people find out about it on their own," he'd said that day at school, stopping by my locker to say hi. "Otherwise it seems like you're bragging."

Fine by me. I didn't want any more attention. At first, I'd thought I was doing the paintings for Joe and college applications and because they needed to be created. When I saw them finished, I realized I'd done it for my mother, too. Because she would have been brimming with pride, and because she wouldn't have been afraid to tell me what she really thought of my work. The fact that anyone else would see them was just a footnote.

I forced myself to take one more bite of chicken and set off for a final bathroom visit and mirror check. I'd put my hair in a headband, careful to seem casual, yet a little dressed up.

And then we heard Joe knock on the door.

I looked down at the road from the window of Joe's truck and realized why people got cars like this. They made you feel safe in an exclusive, almost heady way. Like you were so far removed from the ground and everything around you, how could anything touch you enough to do damage?

"When my dad decided to get an SUV," Joe said as if reading my mind, "he sold this to me for a dollar."

"Bargain," I said.

"But I have to pay for the insurance."

We were silent again, for maybe the tenth time since he'd picked me up. I was beginning to accept that this was our thing, this start-and-stop way of talking.

I could just say, "Guess what?" and spill my news about

Yale, and the conversation would roll forward so easily. But for some reason, I couldn't form the words.

Maybe someday soon I would be able to tell him everything, about all my doubts and questions, with fingers crossed that he would get it. Not tonight, though. Not here, with just a few more minutes until we reached the library, when I didn't know what the night was supposed to bring. To change the subject, I almost told him about Meg and me and our fight. Again, something stopped me.

My mind jumped back to the email I'd gotten from David the night before.

> *don't sweat it about megan dill. doesn't sound like you're ready to fix things yet anyway. i've found that letting something stay broken for a little while helps me understand it.*

What David had said made sense to me. There was no point opening it up to other opinions.

Joe made the final turn onto the street where the library was, and I dug my hands, still shaking a bit, deep into the pockets of my parka.

"This one is my favorite," said Mrs. Lasky, Joe's mom, to Ms. Folsom. It was SuperBrat, of course. "Joe says he'll give it to me when the show's over."

I stood next to the snack table and peered across the

room at the two walls where the paintings hung. Joe had framed them himself with simple black wood frames and white mattes he'd gotten at Target. The two layers, Joe's caricature cut out and laid against my background, gave each one a 3-D effect. They looked great.

I scanned the artwork and wondered which would have been Mom's favorite, or Dad's, or Toby's. But I had no idea, and a sadness washed over me. Were they already that far away?

Joe was busy taking pictures and chatting with Ms. Folsom. Every time some new person ambled down the stairs into the room, Joe walked up to say welcome and introduce himself. Nana and the Mitas came through. Mrs. Mita hugged me too tight and left a lipstick mark on my cheek, and I let Nana take one photo of me in front of the paintings.

"Let's get one of you and Joe!" she said.

Joe heard and bounded over before I could refuse, and then Mrs. Lasky appeared with her own camera. So we posed, smiling, and as soon as all the cameras had snapped—I think Ms. Folsom got hers in there too—I made a beeline for the bathroom. On my way out, I heard Joe asking Nana which painting she wanted to keep.

I washed my hands and rinsed, then washed them again just because it was something to do, and I wanted them to smell nice for Joe later.

Even though I wasn't sure how soon I wanted *later* to come.

"Is this any better?" asked Joe, as I felt a blast of hot air coming from the vent in front of me. The temperature had dropped sharply, and Joe spent the entire drive from the library to Yogurtland fiddling with the dashboard temperature controls.

"Yes, thank you," I said, my teeth chattering.

"It'll get better in a minute," he said. "Maybe fro-yo isn't such a good idea. I just thought we should celebrate."

"They sell hot chocolate," I suggested. Celebrate or not, I wasn't ready to go home yet.

Joe pulled into the parking lot outside Yogurtland, which shared a small shopping center with two other stores. As he stopped the car, I noticed a bunch of kids going inside. Joe recognized them too.

"Kevin McNaughton," said Joe, a simple observation.

The Railroad Crowd.

"Jesse Pryde. All those guys," I said, trying to match the matter-of-factness in Joe's voice.

Joe started to turn off the truck's ignition, but I grabbed his arm and blurted out, "Let's not go in." He gave me a puzzled look, so I added, "The car just got warm, and it looks pretty crowded at the moment."

He glanced at the bright yellow and pink lights of Yogurtland, which wasn't really crowded at all, then took his hand off the ignition and looked earnestly at me.

"Do you want to listen to some music? I just burned

a new CD I think you'd like," he said. I nodded, and he grabbed a leather CD case, flipping through the sleeves until he found what he was looking for. "It's a mix," he said, and slid it into the player.

I didn't recognize the first song but liked it immediately.

"I like to drive dance to this one," said Joe. He grabbed the steering wheel and started moving his head and shoulders in a hopeless white-guy attempt at grooving out. I started laughing.

"What?" he asked. "You can't tell me you don't have a drive dance!"

"Of course I do," I said. "But mine has rhythm."

He reached out his hand and swatted me playfully on the head. Then he kept his hand there, hovering above me. Like now it had crossed into my territory and wasn't sure whether to head home or forge on.

It forged on. Slowly, Joe lowered his hand to my head, his fingers warm on my scalp. He ran them along a chunk of my hair that had escaped the headband, then tucked it behind my ear.

It was still cold enough in the truck that I could see my breath, and I looked over to see Joe's breath too. It was coming out of us at the same time, the same pace, and meeting in the space between us. I could see the molecules twirl around each other. So now I fixed my eyes squarely on Joe, who looked terrified.

"I really want this, Laurel," he said, then audibly

gulped. "You want this too, right?"

I nodded, but stayed still, determined that he should make the first move this time.

Joe leaned all the way toward me but kept his hands to himself now, offering just his face. I wasn't sure what he was doing until I felt his forehead on mine. We stayed that way for a few moments.

Finally, he kissed me, his lips warm and hesitant. Then I could feel him relaxing and giving himself over. I tried to do the same, coaching myself. *You do want this! Now it's happening! Enjoy it!*

I wasn't getting those fireworks I remembered from prom night, but we were touching again, and that was enough.

Joe twisted his body a bit, to get into a better position, then stopped and said, "This truck was not made for . . . this. The seats are too far apart."

"That's a design flaw you should write the company about."

He laughed, then reached for my seat belt and released it. "Can you come over here . . . with me?" he asked.

In three seconds I'd climbed over to his side and was sitting in his lap.

"So much better," he murmured. I felt Joe's arms completely around me now, cradling.

Yes. That's what I had in mind.

I almost sobbed from relief, but choked it down.

Joe blinked quickly, as if not sure I was really there, and said, "I would like to start doing this more often, if it's okay with you."

"It's okay with me."

He smiled. A pure, joy-filled smile, like a little boy opening a gift and discovering it was the one he desperately wanted.

"You're amazing, Laurel."

Something in the way he said this made me uneasy. I shook my head.

"I'm really not."

"Yes. You dazzle me. With everything that you've been through, you . . . you just keep . . ." Stuck again. He reset himself with a deep breath. "I should have done a painting of *you*."

The uneasiness grew. To make it go away, I kissed him, and we started again, his hands moving gently over my back. After a minute, there was Joe's tongue on my lower lip. The tickle of it took me by surprise. I giggled and he stopped.

"Are you all right?" he asked, a pleading edge to it.

"Nothing will happen this time, I promise." Then I added, "There's no swimming pool in sight."

Joe smiled. "Or David Kaufman." He leaned in again.

But I jerked away. "What?"

The sound of David's name, here in Joe's truck above the sound of the heater and the engine. With Joe's arms wrapped around me. David's name, like some kind of Molotov cocktail thrown through the moonroof.

What did Joe know? How?

Instinctively I crawled out of his lap and back over to my seat, staring out the windshield. When I finally had the courage to glance at Joe, he looked stricken with panic.

"David Kaufman . . . you know, I just meant, prom night," he said. He smacked himself on the forehead with a fist. "I'm an idiot, even mentioning that."

I felt a *phew* flow out of me.

But now David was somehow here, and Joe and I were so far apart, not even our breath was mingling anymore.

"It's okay," I told Joe. "There's time. Can you just take me home now?"

now was coming, everyone said. And they were making a gigantic deal out of it too. First snow of the season, a White Christmas, and all that.

"They say eight to ten inches," announced Nana over the buzz of the TV as I was leaving for school.

"Maybe we'll get a snow day tomorrow and I won't have to take Ms. Pryzwara's physics test," murmured Meg at her locker. She was just saying it to anyone, although I was the only person there.

snoball fight n d parking lot, pass it on, read the text from Joe. I answered him back (cool) but didn't pass it on.

Suzie called me that afternoon to cancel our session

that day. "Just to be safe, with the roads," she said.

We went home and the sky was still that teasing gray color, and everyone was bummed out. Even at night, I kept peering at the streetlamp at the end of our driveway, to see if there were flakes twirling in its little spotlight, but there was nothing but black night air. *Oh well*, I thought as I climbed into bed. *It'll probably just be a little showering of rain and everyone will shut up about snow for Christmas.*

But when I woke up the next morning, I knew instantly that it had happened. It was the quality of sound that gave it away—everything was just *muffled*. Tires passing on the road, birds chirping, and maybe somewhere off in the distance, a snowplow. I bolted up in bed and peeked through the blinds, and there were my woods, my trees and my rocks and my sloping ground, blanketed in bright, glaring white.

I heard Nana turn on the television news downstairs, the sound that Toby and I used to get all excited about on days like this. He'd come in and scramble onto my bed and we'd cross our fingers in as many ways we could think of, and perk up our ears for Mom to shout the official snow day announcement.

The thought of Toby on my bed in his dinosaur pajamas sent me all the way under the covers, where it was dark and sweaty and tears didn't count, until a minute later when Nana poked her head in to say, "No school today, sweetie. Stay in bed as long as you like."

But even deep in the bed, the memories came to me, and when Masher barreled past Nana and did a flying leap onto my stomach, I took that as a cue to get the hell out.

In my boots and ski pants and big puffy parka, I left the day's first set of footprints up the middle of our unplowed street, alongside Masher's as he bounded from one little snow pile to the other. Suddenly, none of the rules of the world applied. I didn't have to make way for cars and I didn't have to go to school, and all the neighbors in these houses with the smoke piping out of the chimneys didn't have to go to work. And maybe I didn't have to think about Mom and Dad and Toby, like I could get a snow day for that, too. And for worrying about Meg and Nana and college and what happened in Joe's truck and of course, David's emails.

I thought about my canceled Suzie appointment and felt so very grateful that I'd already gotten my snow day for that. I knew she was going on vacation for a couple of weeks, and I wouldn't see her until after the holidays.

The crystals of the snow glistened in the sunlight. It was light, powdery stuff. Not good for snowballs or sledding, but prettier and sweeter, like sugar. I walked a big loop up and down our street and then past Meg's house. I wanted desperately to go in. To pull her out of bed and pile into the family room to watch DVDs by their fireplace, drinking hot cocoa. But that was on the other side of a line I felt too wimpy to cross, so I kept walking, hoping Meg had been watching me from her window.

Once back inside, I went into Toby's room to see what was up with the foster cats.

I crouched down to peer into the big dog crate. Lucky, who'd been curled up with her babies, got up and stretched, then walked out of the carrier without them. They were getting big now and wanted to move, move, move, so they followed their mother out of the carrier and into the room.

One, two, three fluffy bodies, all striped, bounded past me. But there were four kittens in the litter.

I poked my head into the crate. One kitten, the white one, was still lying there, sleeping.

Or maybe not sleeping.

My hand shook as I reached out to pet it, expecting to feel it wake up under the warmth and pressure. But it was cold and stiff.

"Oh my God," I said aloud.

I looked at Lucky, who was sitting under the desk, licking herself. She glanced back at me, and if a cat could shrug, that's what she did. She just twisted her head and narrowed her eyes as if to say, *Stuff happens.*

I wasn't sure what came next. What was I supposed to do? It was a snow day and I was sitting on the floor of my dead brother's room with four cats that weren't mine.

Nana was shaking her head, trying not to seem as completely repulsed as she was. "Did it even seem sick to you?" she asked. She was doing a great job of hiding the *I told you so* threaded between her words.

"No. I don't think so. I mean, there was some diarrhea in the litter box, but I had no idea whose it was. It seemed like she was eating, but maybe it's hard to tell." I felt like I saw her playing with the others yesterday. But maybe that was three days ago.

I held the kitten wrapped up like a mummy in a towel, so it looked like I was cradling some old rag. It was easy to pretend there was nothing inside.

"What are you supposed to do with it?" asked Nana.

"Eve said I should just bring it in to Ashland. They have an incinerator for that purpose." I winced. "But they're not open yet because of the roads."

Eve had not been surprised, or accusing. She had just sighed and said, "I hate kitten death." She reminded me that it happened a lot and sometimes there was nothing you could do about it. But I knew from the heavy, sick feeling in the pit of my stomach that I should have been paying more attention.

"You took on too much," said Nana, reading my mind, reaching out to stroke my hair. I just nodded, biting my lip.

At three o'clock, Eve called me from Ashland to say that they were finally open and I could bring the kitten in.

"Laurel, the roads are still bad," said Nana. "Can't you put your . . . bundle . . . in the garage and take it in tomorrow?"

"I have to do this now. I owe it to her." I placed the towel in a big shopping bag and grabbed the car keys.

"Please drive carefully," she said.

"Nana, just for the record, you can pretty much assume that for the rest of my life. You don't have to say it."

I rushed out to the car without saying good-bye. It had gotten cold now that the sun was sinking out of sight, and the snow that had been brilliant white that morning was already looking dingy, the color of old underpants.

I drove about ten miles an hour to Ashland, tapping the brakes when I went downhill like my dad had taught me to do on slippery roads. The car fishtailed once at a traffic light, but I got it straight again the way he showed me, by letting go of the wheel for a second.

When I got there, the parking lot was empty. Inside, Eve smiled sadly at me.

"Nobody here today?" I asked.

"Most people canceled their appointments, but we did have a couple of emergencies. A dog who got hit on Spinner Avenue—he's in surgery right now." She zeroed in on my shopping bag. "Is that it?"

"Yes . . ." I was going to tell her what happened; I had a whole story complete with an apology. But she stood up and took the bag from me, then glanced into it.

"Do you want to come with me?" she asked.

I shook my head.

"Do you need your towel back?"

I shook my head again. Eve disappeared down the hall, and then reappeared about ten seconds later. "Okay. We'll take care of it," she said, sliding back onto her wheeled stool.

"Should I talk to Dr. B? Should we try to figure out why it died?"

"No. It'll be okay." Eve stared at me in a sad, kind way that she usually reserved for clients.

I wanted more from her, or from someone, but I wasn't sure what that was. So I said, "Do you need me to stay and help?"

"I think we'll be okay," said Eve. "But we'll need you tomorrow. It'll be busy with all the catching up."

"Okay. I'll come in after school."

"Take a candy cane," said Eve, nudging the jar toward me, and I did.

I got back in the car and started driving home. To get my mind off the kitten, I started to make a mental list of all the things I had to do before school the next day. But the feeling of cold white fur, the image of stick-straight legs that ended in stiff little paws, kept swishing back into my head.

When I felt the tears starting to come, I knew I had to pull over somewhere. Before I even knew what I was doing I was making a right turn into the train station parking lot, which was practically deserted. I stopped the car diagonally across the two best parking spaces—the ones my father had been ecstatic about getting on a few rare occasions—and put my forehead on the steering wheel, and cried.

After a few minutes, the car felt hot and the windows fogged up, so I climbed out to lean on the hood and get some fresh air. It was getting even colder and darker now, harder to see my breath. I peered down onto the train platform, where a handful of people stood waiting for the train into the city. Most of them were huddled in the cold-weather shelter that burned heat lamps, but one girl was waiting by herself with a backpack, near the steps.

Meg.

I opened my mouth to call to her, but stopped myself. Instead I walked over to the steps and walked down them as quietly as I could, hoping she would turn around and see me without me having to say her name. Finally I was about five steps above her and whispered, "Meg?"

She turned to look at me, her eyes red and swollen. "Laurel, oh my God. What happened?"

I was confused for a second and then realized that my eyes, too, were red and swollen. What a pair we made.

"Nothing. Long story. What happened to *you?* What are you doing here?"

Megan looked away, across the train tracks to a bill-board for vodka, her chin trembling. "My parents are splitting up."

"What?"

She nodded her head yes and lowered herself down onto the next-to-last step, which I knew was ice-cold, but I walked down to sit next to her anyway.

"They've been fighting all night and sometime this morning, my dad told my mom that he's leaving."

"Oh, Meg. For real?"

"Total *sayonara*, au revoir, and all that jazz. Apparently he was going to wait until next fall when I went to college, but he can't make it that long. Isn't that charming? *He can't make it that long*, like it's a living hell to be in our house."

I put my arm around Meg, and she leaned her head on my shoulder, sniffling.

"Are you, like, running away?" I asked.

"Just a little. I was going to go stay with my sister. I can't be near my dad until he packs up and goes to some hotel. I'll vomit if I see him."

We were quiet for a few moments. The northbound train pulled into the station and let some passengers off.

"I'm sorry about that day," I said. It was like pouring water into a curved vase. The empty space between us was there, waiting, the perfect shape and size for those exact words. "I should have been there for you the way you've been there for me."

Meg nodded, her head still on my shoulder. "I was so mad, but then I felt so bad about being mad. Then I felt mad about feeling bad."

347

"Isn't that from a Dr. Seuss book?" I said, and that made Meg giggle. "No. That makes perfect sense to me. I just . . . I was just somewhere else. But now I'm here."

"I really missed you."

"Me too." I paused. "I kissed Joe, like, a lot. And I got into Yale."

Meg lifted her head and stared me square in the face, straight and serious. "Really?" I wasn't sure which piece of news was more amazing to her.

I opened my mouth to elaborate, thinking how strange it was that I could tell her about Joe but not David Kaufman. Suddenly we heard the familiar faint rumble that meant the train was rounding the soft bend toward the station. Meg stood up and grabbed her backpack.

"Are you sure you want to go to Mary's?" I asked. "Because you could come back to my house and stay with me as long as you need to. That way you wouldn't have to miss school. Or put up with your sister."

Meg glanced at the train, all noise and slick metal, as it chugged up to the platform. Then she smiled at me and threw her backpack over her shoulder, leading the way back up the stairs to my car.

THIRTY-FOUR

wo days later, Meg and I had just gotten home from school when Mr. Mita knocked on our door, holding a four-foot-tall Christmas tree in a pot.

"I remember your mother always got these live ones," he said, and we all glanced out the window toward the edge of the front lawn, rimmed with Christmas Trees Past in various stages of survival.

Christmas was my mother's holiday. Although she was half-Jewish, it was what they'd celebrated in her family, and she just loved it. Christmas music, all the TV specials, even eggnog. Toby and I got eight utilitarian gifts for Hanukkah—socks, sweaters, new parkas—and the good stuff on December 25. My dad was okay with that, and if Nana wasn't, she never let on.

When it came to the tree, Mom couldn't stand the thought of one being grown just so it could be cut down and die slowly with pretty gifts beneath it, then put out on trash day. We planted our trees on New Year's Day, and although I always thought it was ridiculous trying to dig a hole in the frozen ground every January 1, now I was so grateful we had.

"That's very sweet, thank you," said Nana, but I couldn't tell if she meant it. Mr. Mita put the tree down in the living room and after he left, with a plate of Nana's cookies in his hands, Meg and I went into the garage to look for our Christmas decorations.

"Do you have a tree at your house yet?" I asked.

"Mom put up the fake one weeks ago. Which is a good thing, because now nobody even cares."

"What did she say when she called this morning?"

"The usual. She wants me to come home. She swears my Dad's leaving tonight, so we'll see."

I scanned the shelves of the garage until I saw the two big red plastic bins labeled XMAS and pointed. Meg grabbed the stepladder and moved toward them.

"Is she mad at you for not being there for . . . you know . . . *her*?" I asked.

Meg paused, then said simply, "Yes." In a series of quick

motions, she hopped up on the ladder, grabbed each XMAS box, and handed them down to me.

Ironically, the first thing we saw when we opened the first bin was our electric menorah. When Toby was little he broke the nice ceramic one my parents had received as a wedding gift, and Mom went out and found the plug-in kind at half price during a post-holiday sale. During Hanukkah she kept it on the kitchen counter between the spice rack and the paper towels, and she and Nana had a fight about it every single year.

I showed the menorah to Nana, who actually smiled a bit when she lifted it up, then placed it on a table by the Christmas tree.

While Nana and Meg unpacked the rest of the bins, I took a break to check my email, which was something I did compulsively a little too often since David and I had started writing again.

My in-box contained one new item: a picture message sent from a cell phone. I knew you weren't supposed to open stuff like that if you didn't know the source, but I couldn't resist.

First, the words **i thought this might remind you of something.**

Then, a photo of a van parked alongside a road somewhere. It was an older model, with a small round bubble window near the back, painted with a purple and pink desert scene complete with howling coyote and cactus.

I laughed out loud, and remembered.

One painfully hot summer day years ago, Toby and I were sitting in a small patch of shade in our front yard, trying to come up with something to do. None of the other neighborhood kids were around because of the heat, but we'd spent the morning squabbling in the house and Mom had ordered us outside for a while. We were bored and grumpy and pretty much ready to kill each other when David suddenly appeared in our driveway.

"Oh cool, you're here," he'd said. "My uncle is visiting and he's going to put on a magic show, but I can't find anyone. You guys wanna come down and watch?"

Minutes later the three of us were sitting on the back steps of the Kaufmans' house, the concrete blissfully cool against our legs, watching David's uncle James do card tricks. He was David's father's brother, and everyone knew he was kind of a wandering soul. He'd dropped out of a PhD program and was taking magic lessons. But the thing we knew best was that he had this awesome vintage van with a bubble window, a mural of planets and stars airbrushed on the sides, which was then parked in the Kaufmans' driveway. It served as a perfect backdrop for his act.

Eventually Uncle James went back to school, got married, and moved to Virginia, but I always thought of him with that van and space scene behind him. Maybe David did too.

The memory of Uncle James's voice cutting through the humidity and the emptiness of our neighborhood that day, of giggling at his jokes and gaping at his "magic," of the perfectly sweet lemonade Mrs. Kaufman served to us afterward, came back to me so sharply I had to put my hand over my heart.

"What's that?" Meg asked from the doorway, startling me. She was peering over my shoulder to the photo of the van on the computer screen.

I could have made up a lie right there, and I could have made it sound convincing. Instead, I just opened my mouth and told her, easily, calmly, the truth. About David, about the kiss in the woods, about his emails, about Thanksgiving morning, and now, about the picture of the van.

Meg didn't get mad that I'd kept these things from her, or even seem confused. She just took it all in, shook her head slowly, and said, "Whoa."

An hour later, Meg I were stringing lights around the dwarf tree when we got a call from her mom.

"Okay," said Meg, expressionless, into the phone. "Good." She hung up and looked at me. "Dad's at the Holiday Inn, so . . . I guess I should go back. She sounds lonely."

"I'll walk you home," I said.

We were silent as we made our way down the hill in

the near dark, Meg with her backpack and me carrying her school bag. It was close enough to Christmas now that everyone on our street had put their decorations up, and the leftover snow sat so delicately, it looked painted onto the doorsteps and windowsills.

We live in a nice place, I thought as we walked. You'd never know by looking at it that behind any one of these doors there was depression and drinking and parents who don't love each other anymore. And surely there were other houses that held a roof over death and grief and tragedy. It was just that mine got all the headlines.

When we got within sight of the Dill house, Meg asked, "Do you think we'll be okay?"

I thought about it, and how David might answer that question, and then said, "We will if we choose to be."

Mrs. Dill opened the back door for us and wrapped Meg in a big hug. They didn't move for a full minute.

The next day was the last day of school before Christmas break. For the past week, all anybody had cared about was who had gotten in where on their early college application. Everyone else who applied had received their decisions, so they knew I had to have mine. But I wasn't talking, and it was hilarious to watch them be too scared to come right out and ask me. In the end, it was Mr. Churchwell who spoiled the fun.

He pulled me aside as I was walking past the main

office at the end of lunch period. "Did you hear from Yale yet?" he asked me, trying to sound professional.

I couldn't bring myself to lie to him. "Yeah. I got in," I said casually.

"That's fantastic! I'm so proud of you!"

"I'm still working on my other applications, though."

"You'll have lots of options, I'm sure." And then he patted me on the shoulder, the kind of pat that wanted to be a hug but knew better.

Later, on the way out of seventh period, Joe touched me on the shoulder and I turned around.

"Congrats!" he said. "I heard about Yale!"

News traveled fast.

"Thanks!" I said, trying to match his enthusiasm.

Joe looked at me nervously, then said, "Listen, I'm sure the holidays for you are . . . well, they're not . . ."

"They're going to suck."

"Yes, they're going to suck," he said, smiling in relief, and I couldn't help but smile a little too. "Do you want to get together over break? We could catch a movie. Or go into the city and see some of the decorations."

I pictured myself standing with Joe underneath the big tree at Rockefeller Center, eating roasted chestnuts from a street vendor, holding hands. Why did that kind of moment have to exist only in movies, or lucky people's lives? It couldn't be that hard to get.

"I'd like that," I said. "Just call me. I'll be around."

"Good. So . . ."

"Merry Christmas, Joe."

"You too."

Then I watched him walk down the hall in that bouncy way that was both awkward and graceful, thinking about how he was more than just a little bit mine now.

Christmas morning, Nana woke me up early and marched me to the tree so I could open what seemed like five hundred gifts. Clothes, jewelry, gift cards, socks, underwear, skin lotion, magazines. Nana had even gone to Victoria's Secret and bought me three satiny bras. It was more than I ever would have gotten from my parents, and nicer stuff, too. I could picture Nana at the mall with a list, asking herself over and over again, "What would Deborah do? And how can I do it better?"

Each box I opened made me more anxious for Christmas to be over with. Nana seemed to feel the same way, and it occurred to me that this was possibly the first Christmas she'd ever celebrated.

The only thing I was looking forward to was Nana opening her gift from me. Meg and I had gone to the Bead-iful Boutique, where we could make our own jewelry, and I'd sat for three hours carefully stringing a necklace of pearls and onyx. I tried to fake Nana out by putting it in a big, sweater-sized box. She frowned, puzzled, as she opened it and sifted through the tissue paper. And then she found the little box inside and said, "You sneaky girl!" with a sideways smile.

The necklace made her tear up and she asked me to put it on her, and I had to admit it looked pretty nice. So I did one thing right for my grandmother. A tiny superficial thing, but hopefully it counted.

"What can you give your parents and Toby for Christmas?" Suzie had asked me a few weeks earlier.

"*Give* them?"

"I don't mean a traditional present. More like, some way to honor them. Or honor the gifts they've passed on to you, as a person."

I'd thought long and hard. It was the toughest shopping list anyone could hand me, but I wanted to do this.

For Toby, I emailed Emily Heinz to tell her I wanted to come back to help her run the Tutoring Club, and asked her to look for a student to match me up with.

For Dad, I bought an intermediate crossword book and started on the first one, with the goal of eventually completing every puzzle without looking at the answers.

For Mom, I began work on my first-ever portrait of someone I didn't mind mangling in the process: myself. So far it was just a sketch of the shape of my face and my hair, done while leaning over a mirror on my bedroom floor. *Don't erase too much as you go,* Mom said in my head. *Let your hand channel your impressions of what you see.*

Joy to the world, a little.

We had several invitations from neighbors who didn't want us to be alone on Christmas, and Nana accepted them all. Meg had gone with her mom and sister to her aunt's in Philadelphia, so I couldn't even drag her along for backup.

"We need to keep busy today," Nana said, straightening a stickpin in the shape of a rhinestone star on her red cashmere sweater. She had already been busy. She'd made about four thousand cookies and brownies in the last week, then divided them up onto paper plates covered in red or green plastic wrap and a bow. I helped her load them into a gigantic shopping bag, and we each took a handle as we stepped carefully around patches of ice on the driveway on our way to our first stop, the Mitas' house.

I wasn't looking forward to it, but I wasn't looking forward to anything that day. Sitting on the neighbors' couches with eggnog and a smile didn't seem any better or worse than lying in bed at home or getting my eyes poked out with hot needles. I had planned on checking out, on being there but not being there, but as I walked into the Mitas' living room I found myself making mental notes to share with David.

Later, back at home, I wrote this email to him:

Hi David—

I had a Blew Christmas. How about you?

*Here's what I learned from the three different
dinners I just attended in our neighborhood:*

*Mrs. Mita is tiny, sure, but she can eat her weight
in shrimp cocktail. She put it out for her guests, then
wouldn't let anyone get near it!*

*Alex Jeffrey spends most of his time in college
completely high.*

*There's a whole third floor of the Girardis' house
that I had no idea existed.*

*Nobody's sure if that old guy Mr. Hirsch actually
still lives in his house anymore. He hasn't been seen
in months.*

It's been an educational holiday over here.
Laurel

When I woke up the next morning, David had already
sent me a reply:

*ate chicken and waffles for christmas, then saw two
movies. it was the best day i've had in a long time.*
david
p.s. it's "your" neighborhood, not mine anymore.

I read the last line over and over again, as it went from
sounding pissy and then arrogant to just plain sad. The
sad version of it was still glowing on the computer screen
when the phone call came from Etta, David's grandmother.

THIRTY-FIVE

He's awake," said Etta. "Just this morning." Her voice was tight but breathy, and for two seconds I had no idea what she was talking about. She took my silence as an okay to keep talking. "He's been showing signs for several days, but they said not to get our hopes up, so I stayed in Florida. My husband, Jack, has had pneumonia and can't even travel to see our son."

"Mr. Kaufman," I said dumbly. Finally figuring it out.

"Yes, honey! Awake!" Her voice stumbled now. "He's only halfway there, if you know what I mean. But we'll take it."

"Has anyone seen him yet?"

"No, there hasn't been anyone. Laurel, I need your help. I need to reach David. Do you know where he is?"

"Where he is?" I echoed, thinking about David eating chicken and waffles somewhere in the Midwest.

"I thought you might know, since he stayed with you that time. I tried some of his friends, but they haven't heard from him."

Etta started to break down, and I heard her sniffle.

"It's going to be okay," I said. "I can help you."

> David—
>
> Your dad is awake. Please call your grandmother ASAP.
>
> Laurel

I had thought about adding "It's amazing" or "Let me know what happens," but it felt like none of my business anymore. I had been asked to relay a message, so I did that. I had no rights to anything else.

After I sent the email, I stayed near the computer. Maybe he was still online somewhere and would get it right away, then write back. I refreshed my in-box every minute or so, but there was nothing. Finally, Nana came up behind me and put her hands on my shoulders.

"It's a miracle," she said. "Isn't it?"

"Yeah. A Christmas miracle. Too bad he's Jewish."

"I know it's hard, sweetie, but all we can do is wait to hear more."

David was getting his father back. Who knew what version of that father it would be, but still. He was *alive*. It made my stomach churn.

"Maybe he'll remember what happened," I said.

"Maybe. But I'm not sure that information is going to help anyone."

I closed out my email, promising myself not to check it again until the next day. I was going to be busy until then, and maybe busy beyond that, if I planned carefully. I didn't have to think about David traveling toward us. I didn't have to think about Mr. Kaufman being awake and David having his father back, and I didn't have to think about how that made me feel.

I found my phone and sent a text to Joe.

city 2mrw? goin stir craZ alrdy.

His reply—**yes! call l8r to talk**—came back within seconds.

"You've got to be frigging kidding me," said Meg when I called her in Philadelphia. "Was that supposed to happen?"

"Who knows," I said. "But it did." I was at work, walking three of the six dogs who were boarding for the holidays. It was frigidly cold but we were moving fast, and I could feel my body warming up.

"You think he's going to be pissed that they sold his house?" asked Meg.

I laughed a little. "Probably. But he was in pretty bad shape. I don't think he's going to be hitting the golf course anytime soon."

I sent a mental thank-you to Meg for forcing me to be shallow again, for bringing me up out of the deep, deep seriousness of it all.

"Keep me posted," she said. "I'm stuck here until tomorrow, then we drive back."

"How's your mom?"

"Would you believe me if I said she actually seems happier? I mean, of course it's Christmas and she's been dipping into the spiced rum, but I think the whole thing is a relief. It's been coming for so long."

I didn't know what to say to that. All I could think was, *And you couldn't tell me, even before the accident. Why couldn't you tell me?* But I didn't feel like going further with it. It only took me backward, and today I was all about forward motion.

"I'm glad, Meg. I'm so totally glad." I paused. "I'm going to the city with Joe tomorrow."

I could almost hear her smile. "Car or train?"

"Train."

"*Niiiiice.* Romantic."

"Does this mean we're officially dating now?"

"Uh-huh," she said.

364

"I'll hold you to that. Will call you for a debriefing tomorrow night."

Joe called me early the next morning. We were supposed to meet at the station for the 10:46 train to Grand Central.

"Laurel, I think we're going to have to reschedule our trip. I have the flu. I'm so pissed."

His voice was froggy, and it didn't sound like he was faking. I believed the pissed part.

"That's a huge bummer," I said.

"It is. I was really looking forward to it."

"Me too."

"But there's another week of break, and the decorations will be up until then. I'll call you as soon as I'm better. It shouldn't be more than a few days."

"Okay. I'll be around." Another of our awkward pauses. "Get well soon."

"Thanks, Hallmark."

After we hung up, I went back to bed, staring at the City with Joe outfit I'd picked and laid out the night before: jeans, boots, black turtleneck sweater. And all I could think was, should I check my email now or wait until the clock hits nine?

Screw it, I thought. *I'll go check email now.*

I tiptoed into the den, not wanting Nana to hear me and know what I was doing.

But there was nothing in my in-box.

The next two days passed slowly. I finished the rest of my applications—to NYU, Columbia, Cornell, and Smith—and submitted them with time to spare. Meg came back. We made one giant ice cream sundae at her house to celebrate her telling her dad that she thought he was an emotional shut-in with no idea how to love somebody, and she was glad she didn't have to see him anymore.

"It was the best silence on the other end of a phone call I've ever heard," said Meg, licking chocolate syrup off her spoon.

I let my spoon clink against hers in quiet solidarity as we dug for ice cream, and I knew she thought the fact that we were both dad-less, me for good and her for all intents and purposes for the time being, would bring us closer. I wasn't planning to correct her. There would always be a difference in our losses.

"I think I'm going to go back to the Palisades Oaks," I said.

"Why?" Meg frowned.

"Nobody's calling us, and I feel like I need to be there. If David doesn't go see him, somebody else besides Etta should go."

"Laurel, you're just the neighbors' daughter. . . ."

"Whose family he may have killed," I added, and that shut her down. I reached out and put my hand on her spooning elbow. "I just want to talk to him."

Now if only I could convince Nana.

When I got home, I was all prepared for the big talk, the arguments and the pleading. I was so focused on it that I almost didn't notice the thing in the hallway until I tripped on it.

A gigantic backpack.

The kitchen smelled of spaghetti sauce cooking, but instead of following that smell, I tracked the sound of the TV from the den. It wasn't like anything I'd heard in a long time.

I stood in the doorway and saw the video game on the screen, listened to the *whoop*s and *blip*s and *ding*s of it. The gaming chair rocked a bit, with Masher lying along one side.

I actually gulped, and then said, "Hi, David."

He swiveled Toby's chair toward me and smiled a crooked smile. He'd gotten a haircut.

"Hey, stranger."

THIRTY-SIX

Halfway across the Tappan Zee Bridge, I looked out onto the Hudson River and saw a single boat, putt-putting away from a dock with a trail of frothy water behind it. A fishing boat, maybe. And I thought about how I'd love to be on that boat, even if it was wickedly cold and my eyes watered from the wind. To be on that boat, instead of here in the Volvo with Nana driving two miles an hour and David in the backseat, quiet and grumpy.

"It's such a clear day," said Nana, her eyes locked onto the curve of the bridge as it unrolled ahead of us. She was saying these kinds of things ("Traffic is nice and light," and "This is my favorite radio station") to fill the silence. She didn't seem to understand that silence was the only normal thing about our drive to the Palisades Oaks. I needed all the normal I could get at the moment.

"Yeah, you can almost see down to Manhattan," I said anyway, then glanced in the side-view mirror, where I could see David's face pressed against the window behind me. His eyes were closed and he was wearing earphones, and I thought of how I'd woken up early that morning and tiptoed into the den to check on him. To make sure he was still there. And then to watch him sleep for a minute, wondering where he'd been and how he'd gotten to us. He hadn't said and we hadn't asked.

David didn't seem excited to see his father. He appeared mostly confused, and a little nervous. And just really, really tired, like he hadn't gotten a good night's rest in weeks. Although he clearly had no trouble on our couch, or now, in the backseat of our car. I got the sense that if we hadn't decided to drive him to New Jersey ourselves, he would have stayed in the den, sleeping and playing video games and wrestling with Masher, and never going to see his dad.

My phone beeped with a text from Joe:

feelN btr, city 2mrw?

It would have been impossible to communicate to Joe the complicated scenario of our trip. No words could do it, especially not in the form of a text message. I didn't reply.

"Did you see how Masher wanted to come with us this morning?" I asked Nana, loudly enough so that David, if he was actually awake and not faking sleep like I suspected, could hear. "He thought David was leaving again."

Nana just nodded, then said, "We should go out for an early lunch while David's with his dad. What are you in the mood for?"

I glanced in the rearview mirror and saw David open his eyes for just a moment.

Etta was waiting for us in the lobby of the Palisades Oaks, a paperback romance in one hand. She burst into tears when David lumbered through the automatic sliding glass doors, then stumbled toward him and wrapped her arms tight around his bony, tense shoulders. I noticed how those shoulders stayed hard and unyielding even after she finally let him go.

"Thank you," she said to Nana and me. "Gabe's really anxious to see him."

A pained look flashed across David's face.

"Laurel and I are going to have some lunch," said Nana. "We'll be back in an hour or so."

The grandmothers nodded to each other, and Nana put her hand on my back to usher me outside. On our way out, I turned and glanced back at David, who was watching me. I couldn't fight the feeling that we were delivering him to an unhappy fate.

"What happens next?" I asked Nana once we were seated at a Denny's a half mile down the road. My cell phone had beeped again with another message from Joe, but I didn't open it. It didn't seem right to bring Joe into this day.

"I don't know, sweetie. That's not up to us. And it doesn't really affect us either." She put on her glasses to look at the menu. "Unless, of course, David keeps dropping by like he did last night. Then I'll have to make a lot more spaghetti." She glanced sideways at me and winked, and I had to laugh a little.

After we ordered, Nana took a sip of her tea, then put it down and looked at me.

"Laurel, have you decided what to do about Yale?"

She'd had this approach planned. We were in a situation where I couldn't easily avoid the question.

"No," I answered, which was the simple truth.

"When do you need to make up your mind?"

"Not until May first. I'm going to wait until I hear from the other schools."

Nana nodded, and took another sip of tea. "I'm not going to push you, honey. I just want to know you're thinking about it. It's a big decision."

I looked at her, at the makeup that was already caking in the creases of her face even though it was only lunchtime. She seemed tired. Not physically so much as mentally, like she'd been doing way more thinking than she wanted to. I could relate to that.

"I'll make a deal with you," I found myself saying, and she raised her eyebrows for me to continue. "I'll think harder about Yale if you go on your trip back home in the next few weeks."

Now Nana frowned, but playfully. "That doesn't seem fair. You know I was planning on going anyway."

"Yeah, but you would have found some excuse to postpone it again."

She looked hurt and exposed for a moment, her eyes wide and unblinking. But then she said, "You're probably right."

"Nana, I'm okay to stay on my own. I want you to do what you need to do. Because you need to do it."

She just nodded, tearing up.

"Besides, Meg can always stay over if I need her to. Or who knows, maybe David will still be our houseguest."

I said that part as casually as I could. I didn't want her to think I wanted that, because I didn't even know if I wanted that.

Nana dabbed at her eyes with her napkin and said, "You like having him around."

I shrugged. "We have a lot in common. And he's nice."

She looked like she was going to say something else, something horrifying along the lines of *I hope there's no hanky-panky going on!* Or *But what about your*

Joe? I silently pleaded with my grandmother not to go there.

Fortunately, she didn't. Instead she said, "Suzie called me before she went on vacation and said you don't seem to be enjoying your sessions anymore."

Nana must have come to Denny's with a list.

"That implies I ever enjoyed them in the first place," I said, stirring my diet soda with a straw so the ice clinked.

"Don't be a smarty-pants," said Nana. "Suzie may not have been a barrel of laughs, but you often came home looking a little happier. Maybe not happier. More . . . comfortable. At peace. Has she helped you?"

I thought of the moments in Suzie's office when she'd say something, and I'd repeat it in my head, and stash it away in a mental file cabinet where I could find it easily in the future. I pictured her staring at the window and thinking of what to ask me next, and never looking bored with my answers. Thanks to her I was now on Volume Two of my journal, filled with long ramblings and short random thoughts, with sketches and doodles, with collages made from magazines. When a notion got stuck half-formed in my head, I knew how to coax it all the way out so I could get a good look.

"Yes, she's helped me," I said, realizing for the first time that it was true. "But lately, it feels like we're going in circles. We keep rehashing the same things over and over. Maybe I just need a break."

Nana nodded. "Perhaps you could just call her when you need her."

"I can do that?"

"Laurel, of course you can do that. You can do anything you want."

"Thank you," I said, my nose tickling and my eyes burning. I was not afraid to let a few tears come.

"You don't need to thank me, sweetie."

"I mean . . . thank you. For everything, Nana. Thank you for everything."

And then Nana looked at me with such love. The kind of look that feels embarrassing, and unnecessary, and maybe like it would be better spent on someone else because how could I possibly deserve it? I'd gotten this look from my grandmother occasionally before the accident, and a lot more since. I'd always glanced away and let it hit the side of my face, to avoid looking back at her.

But this time I didn't do that. This time I did look back at her, with my own version of it.

Almost two hours later, we went back to the Palisades Oaks. I honestly think we set the record for the slowest eating of a Denny's meal in history.

Etta came down when they called up to Mr. Kaufman's floor. She had been crying more—I could tell from the dried mascara streaks—but she smiled a bit as she walked off the elevator.

"David's out in the garden," she said, then added, "it went well."

"So how is he? Gabriel, I mean," asked Nana.

Etta shrugged. "He's alert. His mind is a little foggy, and he can't remember much. Everything's in bits and pieces, but the doctors say that's normal. Hopefully as time goes on the pieces will get bigger and, you know, come together."

"And physically?" Nana wasn't shy about this stuff. It was not unfamiliar territory to her.

Etta's face darkened a bit. "They're still doing tests, but they don't think he'll ever walk again. Right now he has some use of his arms and hands; they say that's a good sign." The sun hit her in the face, and maybe it inspired her, because she said, "But you never know with Gabe. He's a tough nut. He could surprise them all."

We just nodded. Etta smiled a bit at me and said, "They tell me you came to see him back in October." I nodded again. "Do you want to see him now?"

Nana looked at me sideways, her lips pressed tightly shut like she had to make a real effort not to speak for me. Several long moments passed.

Finally, I asked, "You said David's in the garden?"

"Yes, he started going on about the smell and he needed some air."

"I'll go find him," I said, and walked away from Etta and Nana. The situation was bizarre enough so that it was a valid answer to the Seeing Mr. Kaufman question. It all fit somehow, in its weird, peach-colored way. The truth was, it didn't feel right to go upstairs without going through David first. I'd bristled at his permission before, but now I wanted it.

I went down a long hallway, following a sign marked THE OAKS GARDEN, and pushed open the door at the end of it. I found myself stepping out onto a big patio, surrounded by bare bushes and leafless potted trees, the dusty flagstones edged with pockmarked slush piles.

In the middle of the patio was a fountain, all angels and urns, and sitting on the edge of it was David, smoking a cigarette.

He saw me and lowered his cigarette hand to the ground like he was trying to hide it. "Hey," he said.

"Hi," I answered, and went to sit next to him. We hadn't talked much since he'd arrived at my house with his enormous backpack. It was like email and real speaking were two different languages, and we were both fluent in one and sucky at the other. But I had already figured out how I was going to break the ice.

"It smells totally gross in there," I said.

David exhaled, smoky. "Yeah, right? What is that?"

"I think it's a combination of a bunch of really disgusting things you don't want to think about."

He snorted a bit, then raised the cigarette to his lips.

"Can I have a puff?" I asked.

"Of this?" He looked genuinely surprised, and I was glad. "You don't smoke."

"I've done it before. With Meg and Mary Dill one night last year." The three of us had shared one, and we'd all been completely lame at it, but suddenly it seemed like the thing to do.

"Sure," said David, handing me the cigarette. "But just for the record, you don't have a *puff*, you have a *drag*. If you're going to pick up bad habits, you should get the lingo right."

"Drag. Got it." I took it from him and put my mouth on it, and said a silent prayer that I wouldn't cough my guts out. But I breathed the smoke into my lungs and held it for a second, then blew it out. It tasted horrible but felt funny, in a good way. Like I was someone else for a second. I handed the cigarette back to him and asked, "How was it?"

"Unbelievably weird."

"I bet."

"My dad and I . . . we were never—"

"I know."

"It was easier before he woke up. Not necessarily better. Just easier."

"Right."

David took a final puff—I mean drag—and threw the cigarette butt in the fountain. We both looked at it for a moment, floating on the water. He sighed and fished it out, then walked it over to a nearby garbage can.

"So, what happens next?" It was my chicken question. I didn't have to bring up details like whether he was going to stay. He could fill in the blanks he wanted to, and I was sure I'd be happy with that.

"I guess I have to stick around for a bit. The doc said it's good for him to see me."

"But you'd rather not," I pressed.

David looked hard at me, and seemed to make a decision. *It's okay, it's her. She knows.* After a few seconds, he said, "I don't know what I want. I just want to get on with my life. I thought I had that figured out, but now . . . I mean, am I going to have to take care of him? If he's in a wheelchair? Is that what I'm going to be about?"

I just shrugged. I had been waiting for my window of opportunity.

"Does he remember what happened the night of the accident?" I tried to make my curiosity sound casual instead of raging.

A shadow flickered across David's face. "No. At least, not yet." He looked sadly at me. "No answers for you there, Laurel. If that's what you're waiting for."

Was it? Maybe not, after all. Because I still wanted to go upstairs.

"Do you mind if I see him anyway?"

David paused, and his features tensed for a moment. "My grandmother says you already did . . . right after I told you I didn't want you to."

"He's awake now," I said firmly but gently, resisting the urge to apologize.

"Yeah, but he's really out of it. He barely knows who people are."

"I'll just stay for a minute. It's just that . . . I'm here. I don't think I'll be back." Then I took a deep breath, inhaling the strength to fight for what I knew I deserved. "Don't you think I have a right?"

David stared at the fountain for a moment and then, without looking at me, said, "Go. Just promise me you won't ask him about the accident."

I nodded and slipped silently away from him, out of the garden.

The room hadn't changed since the last time I'd been there, except for the quiet.

Mr. Kaufman lay in the same bed, wearing the same navy pajamas, but he was breathing on his own. I realized how comforting the sound of the respirator had been, the steady rhythm something known and predictable in a totally messed-up scenario.

His eyes were closed, and I felt a combination of relief and disappointment. In theory, I'd wanted to see him awake. I'd wanted to talk to him and have him talk back. But the thought of that had also terrified me.

What would he think when he saw me? What would he say? Would he apologize? I'd tried to come up with something for me to say but couldn't.

If he's sleeping, I shouldn't wake him. . . . Maybe I can come back.

But as I'd said to David, I knew I wouldn't be back. It was now or never. I moved the armchair slowly, so it squeaked loudly against the floor.

Mr. Kaufman's eyelids fluttered open and locked onto the ceiling. I froze for a moment, watching them. His gaze traveled to the window and downward, finally landing on me.

We locked eyes for a long moment. I tried to make my face mirror his, expressionless and calm. But my heart pounded.

"Know . . . you," he said, his voice raspy but with a trace of his old strength behind it.

"Yes," was all I said.

"Dina?"

I slowly shook my head.

"Not. Dina. D . . . D . . ."

My mother. He was trying to remember my mother's name.

"Deborah," I said.

"How . . . are you?"

He thinks I'm her. The thought of it almost knocked me off balance. *Keep it together.*

"It's Laurel, Deborah's daughter."

His eyes scanned me up and down, then flickered with recognition.

"Look . . . like her," he said. There was something in the

way he said it that made me wonder what Mr. Kaufman thought of my mother. Did he think she was beautiful? Did he have a little crush?

Seeing him struggle with speech, with reality, I knew I shouldn't be there. Like David had said, he wasn't going to give me any answers. But I couldn't move from where I stood.

And then he frowned, a familiar frown I'd seen him make so often in the past.

"Who . . . why . . ."

I leaned in like I was offering to help him find his words.

"Why . . . you . . . here?"

The question came out weak and shaky but landed with a booming thud in the space between us.

Why am *I here?*

Why isn't it my mother? Why is it me, alive, and the others dead?

It was a gigantic question, a question I'd been hoping to find the answer to since April.

I looked at Mr. Kaufman and now, the casually puzzled expression on his face gave the question an entirely new meaning.

He wanted to know why I was here, visiting him.

Without thinking, I said, "I'm here because of my parents and Toby."

Another puzzled frown from Mr. Kaufman. Then I

remembered David's vague request. *Don't ask him about the accident.*

What *did* he remember? Or more to the point, what had they told him?

"Do you know what happened?" I asked, my voice rising into a high octave. I knew I was breaking the rules but couldn't stop.

He swallowed hard and said, using extra syllables, "A–cc–i–den–t."

"Do you remember who was in the car with you?"

His face crumpled, like someone balling up a brown paper bag.

"Bet–sy."

I took a quick breath, which felt hot as fire. My whole body was shaking. "Do you remember who else?"

Mr. Kaufman looked at me with surprise and a little bit of hurt, like I'd slapped him. He moved his head slightly from one side to another in his version of *no*, not breaking our gaze.

All movement in the room froze, the blinking lights on the IV machine and the soft billowing of curtains from the heating vent.

He doesn't know.

To him, my family was alive. He existed in that world, still. A world that I would have given anything to have back. Why should he get to stay there, when he was the one who tossed the rest of us out?

When I opened my mouth again, it felt like slow motion.

"My parents and my brother. Deborah and Michael, and Toby." I had to push the names into the stalled air. "They were there too. And they're dead now. Too."

There was a pause where nothing happened. Mr. Kaufman's face did not change, and I wondered if he'd heard me.

Then, his mouth opened into a wide, hollow O.

Out of it came a sigh filled with pure agony. A dusty, terrible gush that reminded me of Pandora's box.

He started to cough, almost gagging on his own breath, before the other sound came. Sobbing. Like a child's sobbing. Soft and utterly broken.

I backed up against the wall in horror. *Oh my God, Laurel. What have you done?*

Footsteps down the hallway, fast with the little squeak of rubber-soled shoes.

"What's going on?" barked a nurse as she exploded into the room.

I stammered in denial. "We were just talking . . . he got upset."

The nurse rushed to Mr. Kaufman's bedside, and I turned and ran.

In the hallway I saw the door marked STAIRWAY and crashed through it, taking the steps quickly as if someone were chasing me. Putting as much distance as possible between myself and the sound that came

384

out of Mr. Kaufman's mouth.

I'm so sorry, I'm so sorry, I kept saying to myself. That wasn't supposed to happen. A gust of regret and cringing shame pushed me faster down the stairs.

When I reached the ground floor, I pushed open the stairway door and tried to figure out where I was. I looked right and saw the peach glow of the lobby at the end of the hall. I looked left, and saw a big wooden door, different from all the other doors in the building.

A small sign on it said CHAPEL.

In seconds I was through it, and shut it behind me. It took a few moments for my eyes to adjust to the dark.

The room was only large enough to hold two wooden benches and a stone pedestal with some flowers on it, set in front of a stained-glass window. In the glass, a woman dressed in white knelt on a patchwork bed of grass and roses before a large black cross.

I collapsed onto the rear bench, pushing the heels of my hands into my eye sockets, and screamed silently. Maybe that would be enough to make me feel human again before anyone came to find me.

But I needed the sound that wanted to come out. In the past, this kind of thing always took me over, breaking free of some holding pen down in my gut and raging wild until I could tame it again.

Here, now, I called it up. Let it loose, almost begging for the damage I knew it could do.

I put my hands on the back of the bench in front of me and gripped hard, let my head drop as if my neck was finally tired of holding me up. Then, the low, guttural wails burst and the tears rushed. My right hand crunched into a fist and started banging on the wood.

I want. I want. I want. It stuck in a single stubborn loop, like a toddler throwing a wicked temper tantrum.

There was so much I wanted, but could never have. It came tumbling out of me, the smallest things first. My mom smiling at me, my dad putting his arm around my shoulders. My brother laughing at one of our inside jokes, like how he always let me know I had food on my chin by saying, "Hey, Laurel. Keepin' it real!"

Then the bigger ones. Like having three people in the world who would always know me and love me.

I also wanted there to be a reason why I was here. If there couldn't be a reason why my family died, maybe I could at least have that much.

Or perhaps just a future that wasn't so complicated, filled with holes and what–ifs, everything colored a few shades darker than normal.

And then, finally, I just wanted to be Laurel. Not a tragedy. Not a survivor. Just me. Who would ever let me be that?

Someone knocked on the chapel door, and I sucked in a sob.

"Laurel?" David's voice. Worried.

"Yeah."

He opened the door and saw my face, covered in tears and snot, and the set of his mouth changed. Without a word, he let the door close and slid onto the bench, circling his arms around me in such a smooth motion I didn't even see it happen. I just felt them, warm and sturdy and confident.

David said nothing. He didn't ask what was wrong or even say *shhhhh* the way some people do by instinct. He just tucked his chin over the top of my head as I curled into him. I was crying softly now, but easily. It was like a language that only he understood, because we were the same species.

David saw me, my house, my life, as a refuge somehow. Here, in his arms, I realized he could offer the same to me.

Finally, when my crying had disintegrated into just sniffles, I raised my face to his.

"Is he okay? Your dad?"

David looked at me tenderly, protectively. An expression I'd never seen on him before.

"Yes. My grandma's up there with him now." He paused, and the expression faded. I knew what was coming. "What happened?"

I didn't want this to end yet, so in place of the truth I just said, "I'm sorry."

But it ruined the moment anyway. David leaned away

from me to get a better look at my face, his brow furrowing.

"For *what?*"

I bit my lip hard. "I told him . . . about my parents and Toby."

Now he stood up, sliding out of my arms so that they fell, limp, against the wood of the bench.

"WHAT?"

"When I realized that he didn't know yet, I lost it. . . ."

David took a deep breath, steadying himself.

"I asked you not to mention the accident."

"He wanted to know why I was there. . . ." I knew it was a weak excuse.

"The doctors told us not to talk to him about the accident yet. They wanted to wait until he was more stable. . . ." His voice rose with every word.

"I was wrong, I know. I'm sorry."

"You should be!"

His scolding, indignant tone made me instantly furious. What was I thinking? He would never completely understand.

"You would have done the same thing," I said, trying to make my voice match the pitch of his. "Think about it, David. Just think about someone besides yourself for a change and imagine what it's like for me."

David opened his mouth to say something in response, but froze.

We were caught like that, staring each other down in a

minuscule chapel, when Nana found us. The look on her face told me she had an idea of what had happened.

"Laurel and David," she said sternly. "I'd like to leave now before traffic picks up."

David forced a smile at her and nodded, then followed her out. I took one more look at the stained glass and then turned, trailing behind them.

THIRTY-SEVEN

eedless to say, the car ride home was more awful than the one that morning. This time, even Nana was too beaten down by the strain of the day to make small talk. It was a very long forty-five minutes of quiet, quiet, quiet with just the hum of the car and static-laced news radio.

I felt a dull pain behind my eyes from all the crying, but it was a good hurt. Like someone had swept something away back there and suddenly, I could see again. As we crossed back over the Tappan Zee, the water looked clearer than it had that morning.

My cell phone beeped one more time, now with a voice

mail. Desperate for something to do, I listened to it.

"Laurel, it's Joe. I'm kind of worried about you, you haven't answered my texts. Can you please just call me and let me know everything's okay?"

But there was no way I could call him back, even if I'd wanted to. I couldn't even think about why I didn't want to.

Finally, we pulled into our driveway to find a red truck squatting in front of the house.

Joe's truck. I gasped, then shut myself up.

And Joe, sitting on our doorstep with a takeout cup of coffee in his hands. Wearing a ski hat topped with a pompom, and fingerless gloves. He looked up when he saw our car and squinted.

"You have a visitor," said Nana as she turned off the car. My eyes darted to the rearview mirror to see David glance up and register Joe. He looked confused for a second, then lifted one side of his mouth into a half smile.

Then he quickly got out of the car and said, "I'm taking Masher over to the dog park."

He walked toward the house, and Joe stood up. I watched Joe watch David warily, like they were crossing paths in a dark alley. Then, a few feet before David reached the front door, Joe started walking over to our car. Where I sat, unable to move.

"Hey, man," said David, nodding quickly as they passed each other.

"David," said Joe flatly. Joe opened Nana's door for her, helped her out.

We heard Masher barking, then David fiddling with his key in the front door, finally getting it open and stepping inside. Nana watched Joe move around to my side of the car, then she turned quickly and went into the house too. It was starting to get dark now, and the temperature had dropped sharply since we'd left the Palisades Oaks.

Joe opened my door, but I climbed out before he could help me. He glanced at the house and back at me, quizzically. "David Kaufman has a key to your house?" was all he asked, his breath visible in the twilight.

"Uh-huh," I said casually, then closed the car door and glanced up at Joe. He looked cold. And still sick. "What are you doing here?"

"Meg told me about David's dad, and that you were going out there today." He paused. "I left you a bunch of messages. . . . I thought you might need someone to talk to after."

Now the front door opened again. David and Masher. Neither of them looked at me as they climbed into the Jaguar. Joe and I stepped aside as David backed up past us and then, once out of the driveway, sped down the hill.

I felt something catch in my throat, and my eyes get wet. If Joe hadn't been standing there, I was pretty sure I would have started chasing after the car.

But now that it was gone, I looked back at Joe, at his

runny nose and bloodshot eyes, waiting for me to say something.

Someone to talk to.

But I couldn't think of anything. Where would I even start?

I thought back to that night in the truck outside Yogurtland, and how happy I'd been for those moments Joe had had his skin on mine. Things were best between us when we weren't talking. At least, not about anything that mattered.

My hesitation must have been obvious, because Joe said, "Or we don't have to talk. You just look like you could use a distraction. If your grandmother says it's okay, can we go have dinner? I brought you a Christmas present."

There was suddenly nothing I wanted more than to get distracted somewhere public and normal with Joe. We could eat and maybe do more sketches together and make jokes about the other diners, then make out somewhere in his truck.

But then I looked down the driveway, and I could almost still hear the Jaguar's tires screeching.

The only thing I knew for sure at that moment was that David would be back.

If I was gone when that happened, would he leave again? For good?

David, do you know that's a chance I can't take?

Now Joe reached out tentatively, slowly, and took my hand. His glove scratchy, his fingertips icy as they laced through mine.

"Let me take you out," he said, trying to sound confident.

I felt my ears burning and my throat closing and the tears coming.

"Joe," I sputtered. "Why are you being so nice to me? I completely blew you off today. You sent me all those sweet, concerned messages and I didn't answer."

I thought he would let go of my hand, but I felt his grip tighten instead. "It's okay. I understand."

"You're not mad at me?"

"No."

Now I was the one to pull my hand from his.

"But you should. You should get mad at me, even just a little. You'd get mad at anyone else."

"You're not anyone else," he said.

"Yeah, you told me. I'm amazing in spite of everything I've been through." The bitterness was rising now; I could almost taste the bile, and it was all I could do to keep it down.

"Uh-huh," said Joe, an almost-question.

"Joe, I shouldn't be anything in spite of anything. I want to be someone you can get pissed off at when I do something that's not cool."

His eyes changed shape as he started to get it, and he

dropped his head. It reminded me a bit of what Masher did when he knew he'd done something wrong.

"I'm sorry, Laurel. You're right. Let's just go somewhere and talk about it."

"I can't," I said weakly, forcing it out before my throat clapped shut again.

I looked toward the road again, and this time Joe followed my gaze. And I could see him get this other thing. David. His face scanned the house and the driveway uncomfortably, like a stranger in a foreign country, hopelessly lost.

"Joe, you—you are—" What? Wonderful. Delicious. Something that was doomed before it even began.

"Stop," he said. Then he took off his hat, pulling it by the pom-pom, and shook his hair out a bit. "It's all good." Now he caught my eyes and held them. "I'll see you."

He pulled his keys out of his jacket pocket and loped toward the truck. I walked parallel to him, aiming for the front door, and stood there long enough to watch him drive away. Unlike David's Jaguar, Joe's truck moved slowly, but quietly. Maybe he was hoping I'd stop him.

When he was gone, I took a step and felt my foot knock something over. I looked down. It was a wrapped gift that had been leaning against the house, shaped like something framed. I picked it up and slowly tore it open.

On a sheet of notebook paper, in pencil, Joe had drawn a figure in jeans and a plain T-shirt, wearing sneakers.

Her hair down and her arms hanging simply, confidently, by her sides. Me.

There was no cape or helmet or anything on my shirt. But Joe had written a name on a slant in the corner:

SURVIVORGIRL

Was that what made me so amazing to Joe? I never wanted him to see me as someone with superpowers. Even Superman wanted Lois Lane to love him as Clark Kent, not as the Man of Steel.

I stared at the drawing until my hands were too numb to hold it. Finally, I went inside where Nana waited for me, knowing better than to ask any questions.

An hour went by. No David. Two more hours. Then Nana and I ate frozen lasagna on TV trays while watching an old movie. The final credits rolled and still, no David. I saw Nana checking her watch, and I got even more pissed at him, for making her worry, this grandmother he had no official claims on.

Finally, Nana said, "It's late. Go to bed. He'll come when he comes."

So I did as she told me, not wanting to cause her another ounce of stress. I changed and brushed my teeth, trying to shake off the pain of Joe's *Oh, I get it* expression. Then I got into bed with Elliot and Selina and tried to read *Persuasion* for AP English like we were supposed to over break.

When in doubt, Laurel, do what you're supposed to.

And somewhere in there I managed to fall asleep.

The first thing I felt was a hand on my cheek. Not really a full hand, just a good part of four fingers, pressing lightly.

"What?" I said, startled out of a dream where Joe and Meg and I were fishing off a boat on a river.

"Shhh. It's me. Sorry, I didn't mean to freak you out."

I felt something settle on my bed, and I propped myself up to see David's silhouette, growing more and more 3-D as my eyes adjusted to the dark.

"David. Where have you been?"

"At the park. And then, driving around."

I smelled something weird on his breath. "Have you been drinking?"

"Uh, yeah . . . coffee?"

"Oh."

"I'm about as sober as I've ever been right now."

"Okay." I was still trying to shake the sleep from my head, to be sure that this wasn't a dream.

"I talked to my grandmother. She said my dad's fine." His voice sounded gentle, airy, but I still felt overcome with shame as he mentioned his father.

"I'm so sorry, David. I really messed up there."

"It's okay. I'm sure I would have done the same thing, if it were me. Plus, you kind of did us a favor, because I think me and Etta were both too chicken to tell him."

We were silent, but I could feel something different in the shadows between us, the tension gone.

"I needed to see what it might be like, to be back here," said David after a few seconds. "Every inch of every road has some kind of memory for me." He paused. "Not all of them are good. . . . Although it's the good ones that hurt the most now. You probably know that too."

I had to be able to see his face as he said these things, so I reached out and turned on my bedside lamp. We both flinched from the light, and then David scanned my nightshirt. It was a new one for Christmas, with frogs and candy canes all over it. Extremely dorky.

"Nice outfit," he said.

"Thanks." I smiled, and then he smiled. I sat up and then, as an invitation, offered one of my pillows to him. He propped it against the wall and took off his shoes and scooted back to lean on it, sitting cross-legged on my bed. His getting all comfy made me a little brave. "What if you got a place near your dad?" I asked.

David nodded thoughtfully. "I've considered that. I'm not sure a strange town where I don't know anyone would help. For months I've been in nothing but strange towns where I don't know anyone, and it's not making me feel better." He looked at me. "You would stay. You would do the right thing."

I started to protest, but knew it was true. "Yeah, I

probably would. What I'm confused about is who decides what the right thing is."

"I think it's a panel of hundred-year-old white guys in a room in a tall building somewhere."

"Eating pork rinds and smoking cigars."

"And getting lap dances, because that would be the perfect kind of hypocritical."

I chuckled, and then stopped, and blurted out, "I still haven't decided whether or not I want to go to Yale."

"Why not?" he asked flatly. There was no reaction there, no judgment. He was the only person in the world who could do it like that.

"I feel like I need to be here. For *them*. This was their life, and now I'm the only one living it anymore. If I'm not, then am I betraying them?"

"And anyone else would tell you, oh, but your parents would want you to move on and get an education and fulfill all the dreams they had for you."

"Yeah," I said.

"I don't know, Laurel," said David, and I loved how he said my name, like he enjoyed it. He looked up at the ceiling. "Maybe instead, your folks would have wanted you to dedicate your days to remembering them. Maybe it makes them feel better, wherever they are, to see you give up your life so you can be closer to them, since they don't have one anymore."

"I wouldn't be giving up my life," I whispered.

"Of course you would be. What the hell else are you going to do here?"

"A lot. My work at the animal hospital, for instance."

He tilted his head into a *Come on!* slant. "There are animal hospitals in New Haven, if it's that important to you."

"Nana wants me to go. She wants to spend the winters in Hilton Head. So I feel like for *them*, I should stay but for *her*, I should go."

David paused, then said, "Aren't you talking to your therapist about all this?" like it had just occurred to him.

"I'm sorry. Am I boring you?"

"I'm just thinking maybe I'm not the best source of advice here. Look at me. You said it yourself. Everything I'm doing is completely and totally all about myself and what I want."

"You've given me good advice before," I said, prodding him.

He paused, then looked at me squarely and said, "Just forget about the *for* thing. Don't do anything *for* anyone else but you. You can be a little selfish." Then he smiled crookedly. "Come on. You know you want to."

I remembered all the things I'd silently screamed to myself back in the chapel at the Palisades Oaks. He was right.

"Thanks, David," I said, trying to make his name sound like I, too, enjoyed saying it. But the end curled up into a strange ball of sound, high and tight. And before I knew it, I was crying again.

Within a few seconds I heard the short, sharp breaths coming from David that meant he was crying too. And then I felt his hands on my shoulders, and a shifting of weight on the bed, and now he had me in his arms.

I wiped my face with the palm of my hand and raised it up, and kissed him. I don't think he was expecting it, because he jerked his face away for a half second. But then he kissed me back. Fast, with energy. He moved his hands to either side of my face and I felt like I was falling, not into a place or a hole, but into colors. Red and orange and purple. Deep and rich.

David took one hand off my face and pressed it against my chest, pushing me down into the bed. Then one of his legs was on one of mine and the feeling of weight there, of being covered, was suddenly the best thing in the world.

You slut! said a teasing Meg in my head, as we kept kissing. David ventured away from my mouth and onto my neck, my ear. I giggled.

"Is this okay?" he whispered, and I just nodded, not sure what he meant. Was anything okay? Did it matter?

And now David's hand was slipping under my nightshirt collar, reaching for what passed for my right breast. Practiced, experienced. I wondered for a second how much sex he'd had when he was out in the David Zone, and whether it was with anyone really pretty.

Is this it? Is this going to be where I actually do it for the first time?

It was an intellectual question, like I was sitting at my vanity table a few feet away, watching myself on the bed. Then David's other hand slipped down to the bottom of my frogs-with-candy-canes nightshirt, and started to push it up.

I felt my body get tense, like it was fighting him off, but forced my mind to override that. Now both of David's hands slid smoothly from my waist to my head, taking my nightshirt with them. Before I knew it, it was off, and all that was left was my underwear. I couldn't remember which pair I was wearing and could only hope it was one of the new ones.

David stopped and looked me up and down, his face full of wonder, as if seeing a sculpture unveiled. I looked back at him, this boy so beautiful all of a sudden—or maybe always—and knew I should be doing something. *It's my turn, right?* I wanted to but was still frightened to make that first reach.

With a deep breath I did it anyway, reaching my hands under his T-shirt and laying them on his stomach, which still felt cool from being outside. I ran my fingers across it, the soft hair, what felt like an exceptionally deep belly button. David sighed, and I felt brave enough to keep going, lifting his shirt and kissing him where his skin met the top of his jeans.

In another quick, expert motion, David pulled his shirt over his head and pressed his chest to mine. I was falling into colors again, but this time a little too steeply. It made me dizzy, and the beginning of terrified.

David reached one hand down toward my underwear, lifting the elastic away from my skin.

That's when I stopped him and said, "No."

As David pulled his head away from mine, I noticed we had matching sweaty patches of hair where they'd been connected. "Please don't tell me to stop," he said breathlessly.

"I have to tell you to stop," I said.

"Laurel . . . please."

"David . . ." The dizziness ebbed. It was like stepping off a merry-go-round.

He rolled over onto his back, still panting. "I thought you wanted this."

"I don't know," I said, then after a horrible silent moment, "I'm the girl who's not sure what she wants for herself, remember?" I tried to make my voice sound normal again, and not like I'd just been teetering on the edge of losing my virginity.

David threw his arm over his face now. Was he embarrassed to look at me, or for me to look at him?

"Can I want some of it, just not all of it?" I asked.

He nodded from behind his own arm. "Yes," he said softly. "Of course you can." He pulled his arm away and looked at me now with regret. "I'm sorry if I pushed you too far."

"I pushed too. It's been a weird day."

"A very weird day." He paused. "I should go, and leave you alone."

David climbed over me out of the bed, grabbed his shirt, and walked slowly out of the room, leaving the door open. I listened to his padded footsteps travel downstairs, the jingle of Masher's collar as the dog jumped off the couch to greet him. I got up and found my nightshirt, slipped it on along with a pair of sweats and slippers, and then followed. Not because I didn't want David to be upset, or because I wanted to explain some more, but because I really just needed to be with him.

Downstairs, David stood in the living room, staring at the Christmas tree all lit up. Nana and I had forgotten to unplug it before we went to bed. Now I was glad we had, because it was lovely.

David didn't turn around, but I could tell from the hunch of his shoulders that he knew I was there. "Your Christmas tree is very small," he said.

"That's because it's alive," I said, and stepped up beside him. I fought the urge to touch his arm. "I don't want you to leave me alone."

We were silent for a moment, and then David asked, "Have you ever been there? You know . . . the place, where it happened?"

405

The spot right before the second light on Route 12. Which I hadn't driven on since April. "No," I said. I'd wanted to. Nana had gone twice, but I couldn't scare up the courage to go with her. The guilt of that tugged at me sometimes, like a debt I had yet to pay back.

"Neither have I."

We watched the tree for a moment, blinking red, green, and white across the wall. Then David turned to me, the hair around his ears still a little sweaty, which made me feel like in some way, we were still connected there.

He asked, "Feel like taking a ride?"

THIRTY-EIGHT

Somehow she managed to look good in this, I thought, looking at the zigzag stitches of my mother's long, wine-colored down coat—one that Nana had inexplicably decided to keep. I'd grabbed it out of the closet because it seemed like it would keep me warm over my nightshirt and sweats, and pulled on a pair of my father's old duck boots. It was one of those outfits where normally you'd think, I hope I don't get into an accident looking like this. But I didn't, because there wasn't much room for me to think about anything else but where we were going, and besides, the whole topic of accidents was complicated at that particular moment.

The brakes on the Jaguar screeched a bit as David turned onto Route 12, and he grimaced. "I'm going to have to get those looked at," he said. It was the first time he'd spoken since we rushed down the frigid driveway and into the car. "It's a good thing I kept this baby in nice shape. I had no idea my dad would ever see it again."

I smiled at him and turned to look out the window, trying hard to stop myself from shivering, even with the heat turned way up. I was finally doing this, and I was petrified.

Route 12 had always been one of my favorite roads. It was lined with woods on either side, and often, we'd spy deer wandering just yards from the pavement. *This is what my family saw*, I reminded myself, even though it was all stark and spindly now; back in the spring this landscape was thick, lush. Maybe Toby was looking out the window at these exact trees in the last few minutes he was alive. What were my parents talking about and thinking about as they passed that spot, and that spot, and that one?

We drove for another minute or so. Just enough time for a car to pick up too much momentum, for someone to get lost in conversation or his own thoughts and not watch the speedometer.

"I think it's right up around this bend," said David, and he began to slow down. I could see, now, that this was where a person could forget about the sharpness of the curve, and the traffic light not too far beyond it, and slam on the brakes. I looked at the northbound lane, and thought of how another person might lose control and let their car go over the double yellow line and make someone swerve off the road to avoid them.

"What if we can't find it?" I asked.

"We'll get close enough," he said confidently, determined. When we saw the traffic light up in the distance, I scanned the road but wasn't sure what I was looking for. I guess I just expected to *know*.

David pulled the car into the breakdown lane and we sat there, listening to the gusty breath of the dashboard heater. It was almost midnight, and there weren't many cars on the road.

I peered out the window but it all looked unremarkable, until David said, "There. Look."

I followed his gaze to a speed limit sign about twenty yards ahead of us. It had a thick purple ribbon wrapped around it, which even in the dark looked faded and old. Then I remembered Nana telling me that there'd been a little makeshift memorial at the accident scene for several weeks after, with people bringing candles and flowers. Toby's classmates left notes, which the police eventually collected and gave to Nana. Who then put them in his dresser, unread.

"You think that's it?" I asked.

"Yes," he said. He got out of the car, so I did too. And

the first thing I saw was how the side of the road sloped down steeply here, several hundred feet, before leveling out into woods.

The ditch where my family had actually died. I had to catch my breath when I saw it, and realized it wasn't at all what I'd pictured. I wasn't sure what I'd been afraid of for so long, and just being there made me feel stronger.

David walked to the edge of the slope and looked down, his face blank. He pulled an object out of his front jeans pocket, kissed it, and threw it as far as he could. I couldn't see what it was.

Was there something I was supposed to do or say, standing here above this place? All I could think was, *Now I've seen it, and I owed them that.* It was like a favor I'd just returned.

And then, unexpectedly, I started to feel glad I was there.

I hadn't visited my family's graves since the funeral. There wouldn't be anything there until April, the one-year anniversary, because Nana was sticking to Jewish tradition in the headstone department. And it didn't feel like I needed to go anywhere to be with them. They were still in every inch of space at our house, around our house, and every other place I went.

But this was where they had gone away. It was where it had all changed. A place where I could say everything, or nothing at all.

It suddenly seemed enough for me to say, silently in my head, *I just love you all so much.*

David came over to where I stood, and kicked at a pebble. "That's done."

"I'm freezing," I said.

Everything else was too big for words.

We got back into the car, which thankfully he'd kept running, so the warmth was a sweet relief. David put his hands on the wheel but did nothing else. We sat there, looking out at the charcoal gray sky through the windshield.

"When we told my dad that Mom's gone . . . ," he said. "Seeing him deal with that, so new and everything . . . it was like the past eight months never happened for me. It was like losing her all over again."

I reached out, unafraid, and touched his hair. He didn't look at me, but he didn't stop me as I started to stroke it. "Your mom was cool," I said.

David nodded. "You wouldn't know it from looking at her, but she was. I only see that now, of course. She got me. She put up with a lot of stuff that most moms wouldn't, to make up for what Dad was doing."

I pulled my hand away involuntarily. "What was he doing?"

I must have sounded really nervous because David laughed. "Nothing like that, nothing you'd see in a TV movie or something. He just didn't like me, and he wasn't afraid to show it. Although he did hit me once and I got a big bruise, right here." He touched the corner of one eye, and I remembered David showing up at school with a shiner, telling people he'd gotten into a fight at a party.

"I deserved it," he continued. "We were both drunk and I totally provoked him. Nice, huh? Real sweet suburban family. I guess he got an involuntary rehab with this whole thing."

We were quiet for a moment and then I asked him, "So you think you'll stay?"

It wasn't about Mr. Kaufman. It was about me. I was ready to admit that I wanted David near me. It was one thing I now knew I wanted for myself; maybe I should tell him that.

He turned and smiled at me, and took the hand that had just been petting his hair. "I don't know, Laurel. It felt really good to go." Then his smile disappeared, and he looked very serious. "I think you should try it."

I didn't get it at first, but then I did. "You mean Yale."

"Yale, or anywhere else that's not here. Which equals your life. Versus not Yale or anywhere else that's not here, which equals sitting here in this car at this place, in, you know, a metaphorical sense, indefinitely."

I did get that one. I could see that.

I watched a pickup truck speed by us. Then a few seconds later, a minivan. It was amazing how fast it seemed they were going, with us standing so still.

"Can you make this car move again, like, quickly?" I asked.

David's smile came back. "I sure can."

He put the car in gear and pulled slowly back onto the road, where up ahead of us the light had just turned green. It seemed strange yet perfect to me that within a second—less than a second—we were farther down the route to Freezy's than our families had gotten that night back in April.

We were continuing on.

EPILOGUE

It wasn't quite noon yet, but the bench had already grown warm in the late August sun. I looked over at Meg, who was leaning back with her eyes closed, soaking in the rays as they splashed down on us.

"Pretty soon this will be gone," she said. I knew she was talking about the heat, but I also took it to mean her and me, sitting together on the main street of our hometown, surrounded by things we'd known forever.

Although the bench officially fit three people, we had scooted to either end so that neither of us was leaning on the plaque on the back of the bench. It read:

IN LOVING MEMORY OF OUR FRIENDS AND NEIGHBORS

MICHAEL MEISNER

DEBORAH MEISNER

TOBY MEISNER

I had to hand it to Andie Stokes and Hannah Lindstrom; it was simple and tasteful and I was glad, so very glad, that they'd done it. We'd had an unveiling ceremony for the bench in April, just a few days after the anniversary of the accident. Almost a hundred people showed up, and I stood with Nana and Meg, listening as Andie gave a lovely speech thanking everyone for their donations.

She had asked me to say something, but all I could do was step up to the microphone and say, "Thank you," in a shaky voice.

I'd hugged Andie tight afterward, even though our friendship—if that's what it ever was—had faded. I didn't even mind that the newspaper was taking pictures of us.

Mr. Churchwell had been there and I'd hugged him, too; it was a quick, barely touching one. I still thought he was a huge dork, but now that I knew all he'd ever tried to do was his job, I didn't mind giving him something back.

Suzie had also come. She stood far away and looked sadly out of place, wearing black among all the spring colors. I hadn't had a session with her in more than a month, although we left it that I would call as soon as I needed to talk. But I hadn't needed to. At one point during Andie's speech, my eyes met Suzie's and we smiled at each other. I knew I had a lot to thank her for.

And Joe. Who stood with a couple of his friends near the front, where I could see him. After that day in the driveway, we'd gone back to a quick, painful nod-and-hi greeting whenever we passed each other at school. There was something about the way Joe's shoulders hunched when this happened, the way his bangs swept over his eyes as he looked away first, that still pierced me.

At the ceremony, I'd glimpsed Eve showing up late and moving her way into the middle of the crowd, blending in perfectly.

So to me, the bench was not just about my mom and dad and Toby, but also about that day, when I was able to measure how far I'd come by looking at the people who had helped me get there.

And it was in front of the Village Deli, as I'd suggested. Which was convenient, because Meg and I had come today to buy sandwiches for my trip.

I was leaving at one o'clock sharp for the drive to Ithaca. Freshman orientation at Cornell started the next day. Cornell, where I could take pre-veterinary courses and art courses, and see what further down the road looked like. Cornell, which was a place I could picture myself when I visited the campus with Nana, which was close enough to come home if I needed to but far enough to make me think twice about it. Cornell, which in the end was *my* choice, and not my father's.

"So, how soon can I come visit?" Meg asked now, her eyes still closed to the sun. "I hear Cornell guys are much hotter than Wesleyan guys." She and Gavin had come to what we thought was a very wise "Let's stay close but officially break up because we want to fool around with college people" decision.

"Any time, you know that. You don't even have to call first. Just show up at my dorm with a sleeping bag."

Meg smiled and then opened her eyes to look at me. She had to shield her face in a strange salute to do it. "I'll take you up on that. I don't want us to become one of those friendships that fizzles out after high school."

I lowered my sunglasses to look at her. "I don't think that could possibly be possible even in the strangest depths of possibility. You know that, right?"

"Yes," said Meg, smiling. "I do know that."

We reached toward each other at the same exact moment—how often does that happen?—and hugged. I smelled her shampoo and the chocolate that still lingered on her breath. Or maybe it was mine. We'd just shared a Hershey bar as our good-bye feast.

Meg's parents' divorce was happening, and everyone seemed okay with it now. Mrs. Dill was dating someone; Meg pretended it grossed her out, but I knew she was proud of her mother for getting out there. She'd started speaking to her dad again too—at my urging. They went out for dinner every week, and Meg would call me after-ward and say something like, "I understand a little more about what happened there."

We didn't compare the way we each had to mourn our families' pasts. It wasn't about one being better or worse than the other. We would always be different, but some-how we'd silently agreed to just be there for each other.

"We should get going," Meg said now, while we were still hugging. "Nana will be pacing around the house."

I nodded but didn't let her go right away—just one more second—and then we headed back to her car with our sandwiches.

To say the Volvo was packed would not be doing the situ-ation justice. It was so jammed with stuff, with each box and bag and item fitted carefully together like a jigsaw puzzle, that I wasn't convinced we'd be able to get any-thing out. It surprised me how many things I needed to start college with, and how many things from home I just had to have with me at school.

I'd gotten good at sorting through all the stuff. On New Year's Day, Nana had proposed that every weekend, we fill two boxes with items that belonged to my parents or Toby. Some boxes would go in the attic—things we wanted to keep or couldn't make a decision about yet—and some would get donated to a charity that needed them. With each piece of clothing, each book, each souvenir pen or rain boot or tube of mascara, we tried to call up a memory to wrap it in. Every time I sealed up a box with clear plastic tape, I felt more free.

Then it was my turn. Packing my life into boxes and labeling them, I realized that even though as a family we'd take yearly vacations, most of my stuff had never gone anywhere before. I was almost excited for the twenty pairs of shoes I was taking on their first real adventure.

Meg pulled her car into my driveway, behind the Volvo, and looked at the wall of crap visible through the rear window.

"Wow," she just said. "You beat me."

We watched Nana open the front door and wave to us, then point to her watch.

"Looks like your flight attendant is ready for takeoff," said Meg.

"Tray tables up and seat backs in the upright position," I said, opening the car door. I waved my Village Deli bag at Nana. "All set!"

All set. Like it was that simple. But then again, why couldn't it be?

I leaned back into the car. "Are you getting out?" I asked Meg.

She shook her head. "I can't stand long good-byes, you know that. We already had our paws all over each other. Consider yourself sent off."

"Fair enough," I said.

"So, *adios*," said Meg, biting her lip.

"*Hasta la vista.*" I started to close the door, then stopped. "And oh, by the way. I love you."

Meg sniffled now, unable to hide her tears anymore. "I love you, too. Now get out of town."

She backed down the driveway and I watched her, not waving. When she was gone, Nana came out of the house and put her arm around me. "Everything's in the car?" she asked.

"It is now," I said, opening the front door of the Volvo and putting the sandwich bag inside.

"Then how about one last bathroom trip and we're on the road?"

I looked at her, with her gigantic, round sunglasses and her "driving clothes," a velour tracksuit and white sneakers. It was one of many outfits she'd bought for Hilton Head. She'd be leaving for the fall and winter in just a few weeks.

"Yeah, good idea," I said. I didn't have to go, but I was glad for a few minutes in the house before we left.

I walked through the living room, did a lap around the kitchen, a dip into the den. Was I supposed to be feeling something specific here? I'd lived in this house my whole life. I was coming back, of course. Then I realized, it wasn't the house I needed to say good-bye to. It was just this time, this state of being.

I went upstairs and did a quick search of my room to

make sure I hadn't forgotten anything. Nana had made my bed, and I thought, *It could be months before I lift back these covers again.*

A quick peek into Toby's old room. It was empty of cats now; I'd found good homes for all of them and sometimes got emails from their people, with pictures.

I opened the door to my parents' room and looked at the bed, and had a flashback to a morning many years earlier, when we were leaving to go camping, and Toby and I were so fired up we had to wake our parents. "Let's hit the road before it hits us first!" we yelled, jumping on the bed, throwing one of my dad's favorite expressions at him.

I went back downstairs and looked out the window.

There was David.

He sat on the patio, Masher's head in his lap, talking on his cell phone. I opened the sliding glass door and he turned around to look at me.

"Hey," I whispered, "we have to leave in a few minutes."

He nodded and said, "Okay, thank you," into the phone, then flipped it shut. "Sorry about that, it was Dr. Ireland."

"Is your dad all right?"

David stood up and came toward me. "Better than all right. He wrote a few sentences by hand yesterday."

"That's great," I said, as David put his arms around me and rested his chin on my shoulder.

"And he says that having my dad help me study for the GED is making a big difference."

"I knew it would," I said, burying my face in his hair.

One week after the memorial bench ceremony, we'd had the headstone unveiling at the cemetery. It was just Nana and David and me, by choice. The three of us sharing two umbrellas in the rain, as the rabbi spoke. We didn't say a thing until after we'd placed three rocks on each stone. One for each of them, one for each of us. Nobody spoke until after we got back in the car, and Nana took off her hat and said, "Let's go have wine with lunch."

By that time, David and Masher were living in an apartment two towns over, where David had a job specializing in sound equipment at a music store. He drove to the Palisades Oaks twice a week. Which was maybe half as much as he was coming to our house.

Once Nana figured things out about us, she forbade David from sleeping here at night, even on the couch. He wasn't allowed over if she wasn't home, and if we were in my room the door had to remain open. But she loved having him stay for dinner or asking him to do odd jobs. She accidentally called him by my father's name once.

David was going to be looking in on the house while Nana and I were gone, stopping by, hanging out. I had a feeling the couch was going to get a lot of use at night. And once I was settled in at school, outside of my grandmother's jurisdiction, he would be visiting me there.

Overnight. The possibilities of it were too scary and wonderful to think about at that moment.

Now David pulled away and looked at me, a hand on either side of my face. "So are you ready?"

"Will everyone please stop asking me that?"

"Okay. Are you not unready?"

I laughed. "Yes. Yes, I am not unready."

"Then let's go. We have a long drive ahead of us."

He took my hand and led me through the house to the front door. Masher followed us, and when we got to the foyer I turned and squatted down in front of him, burying my hands in the ruff around his neck.

"See you later, boy. Be good. David and Nana will be back tomorrow night, but Meg will come to feed you. Make sure David doesn't forget to feed the cats once Nana's out of town."

Masher licked my face once, neatly, then turned and headed into the den, as if to say, *Yeah, yeah, get the hell out of here already.*

Fortunately, I'd already said good-bye to Selina and Elliot that morning, because I knew they'd be hiding when it was time to leave. "Bye, kitties!" I yelled into the house, loud enough so they could hear me from whatever corner they were holed up in. "I love you!"

I put my sunglasses back on as I stepped out the front door. David closed it and locked it with his key.

We climbed into the car, David at the wheel and Nana

in the front, me in the back next to my new laptop.

As we pulled out of the driveway and pointed the car down the hill, I looked at the house one more time. A wide, swallowing look, like I could take one more gulp and I'd have everything I needed to take with me.

Then I closed my eyes.

That was it. That was *Before*. Now here we go into *After*.

ᎧᏒ ACKNOWLEDGMENTS ᎧᏒ

I'VE RECEIVED SO MUCH from so many people on this long, strange, marvelous trip.

My agent, the supersmart, generally spectacular Jamie Weiss Chilton, gifted me with her special brand of insight and passion. I thank higher powers every day that she fell in love with this book, and believe me, it loves her right back. My wonderful editor, Rosemary Brosnan, pushed me in her gracious yet fierce and brilliant way to make Laurel's story better and better. Rosemary and the talented team at HarperCollins Children's Books have made the whole publishing-a-first-novel thing a truly joyous and educational process.

My experience at the Big Sur Writing Workshop was instrumental in shaping the manuscript at an early stage, slapping me gently upside the brain and sending me back down the Pacific Coast Highway with fresh focus. I'm grateful to Susan Merson and the members of the Los Angeles Writers Bloc, as well as the literary ladies of the Write On, Mama critique group, for their intelligent reading and comments. My dear friends Cindy Frigard, Kim Purcell, and Robyn Castellani were also early readers and key feedback-givers. Josephine Schiff and Elizabeth C. contributed their expertise on school counseling and grief therapy, respectively. And I have to say thank you to Peggy Sweeney, for all of her Meg-ness.

I'm lucky to have the family I do—the Castles, Locascios, Springs, and Minardis—who gave me so much enthusiasm, support, and childcare even though they had no idea what my book was about or whether it was any good. My parents, Jay and Sue, have always provided a constant, unquestioning faith that's helped me be a writer in one way or another my entire life.

And finally, thank you to Bill, for sharing his creative and generous spirit with me every day, and to Sadie and Clea . . . my two favorite Afters.